Rober   **ain**
'Inno
not go
over nake
men. What do
would say?'

'I'm no innocent. And I don't care what Uncle Mortimer thinks.' Frederica had tried for years to make him think well of her, to no avail. And now he was going to marry her off.

'Not innocent?' he scoffed.

With a mother like hers, how could she be innocent? She certainly wasn't ignorant.

'W-would you like to find out?' Her words came out in a breathy rush, too eager, too desperate.

'No,' he said.

'Because you don't find me attractive?'

He half groaned, half laughed. 'Not that. Definitely not that. I don't want to lose my job.'

'I would never tell anyone.'

'You are a naughty little puss. Do you know that? A temptress.' His lips brushed her ear, her throat, her collarbone, sending shivers down her spine. 'Leave now, before I take you at your word.'

...ory of THE GAMEKEEPER'S ... and I were doing a lot of driving ...to my daughter's university. I would use the long journeys to write. One evening, we were coming home quite late and I suggested that I would read what I had written earlier that day. My husband, who is game for anything, agreed. So by the dim reading light I read out the beginning of the story. After quite a while of me reading and him driving, we stopped at a light and I paused to look up. He stared at me and said, 'I have no idea where we are.' He'd become so absorbed in the opening scenes he'd missed his turn-off. It took us quite a while to find the right road. Needless to say I never did that again! I do hope you find Robert and Frederica's story just as absorbing as he did that night.

THE GAMEKEEPER'S LADY

Ann Lethbridge

All Rights Reserved including the right of reproduction in whole or
in part in any form. This edition is published by arrangement with
Harlequin Enterprises II BV/S.à.r.l. The text of this publication or
any part thereof may not be reproduced or transmitted in any form
or by any means, electronic or mechanical, including photocopying,
recording, storage in an information retrieval system, or otherwise,
without the written permission of the publisher.

This book is sold subject to the condition that it shall not, by way of
trade or otherwise, be lent, resold, hired out or otherwise circulated
without the prior consent of the publisher in any form of binding or
cover other than that in which it is published and without a similar
condition including this condition being imposed on the subsequent
purchaser.

® and TM are trademarks owned and used by the trademark owner
and/or its licensee. Trademarks marked with ® are registered with the
United Kingdom Patent Office and/or the Office for Harmonisation in
the Internal Market and in other countries.

First published in Great Britain 2010
Harlequin Mills & Boon Limited,
Eton House, 18-24 Paradise Road, Richmond, Surrey TW9 1SR

© Michèle Ann Young 2010

ISBN: 978 0 263 87618 5

Harlequin Mills & Boon policy is to use papers that are natural,
renewable and recyclable products and made from wood grown in
sustainable forests. The logging and manufacturing process conform
to the legal environmental regulations of the country of origin.

Printed and bound in Spain
by Litografia Rosés, S.A., Barcelona

Ann Lethbridge has been reading Regency novels for as long as she can remember. She always imagined herself as Lizzie Bennet, or one of Georgette Heyer's heroines, and would often recreate the stories in her head with different outcomes or scenes. When she sat down to write her own novel, it was no wonder that she returned to her first love: the Regency.

Ann grew up roaming England with her military father. Her family lived in many towns and villages across the country, from the Outer Hebrides to Hampshire. She spent memorable family holidays in the West Country and in Dover, where her father was born. She now lives in Canada, with her husband, two beautiful daughters, and a Maltese terrier named Teaser, who spends his days on a chair beside the computer, making sure she doesn't slack off.

Ann visits Britain every year, to undertake research and also to visit family members who are very understanding about her need to poke around old buildings and visit every antiquity within a hundred miles. If you would like to know more about Ann and her research, or to contact her, visit her website at www.annlethbridge.com. She loves to hear from readers.

Previous novels by this author:

THE RAKE'S INHERITED COURTESAN
WICKED RAKE, DEFIANT MISTRESS
CAPTURED FOR THE CAPTAIN'S PLEASURE
THE GOVERNESS AND THE EARL
  (part of *Mills & Boon New Voices…* anthology)

and in Mills & Boon® Historical Undone eBooks:

THE RAKE'S INTIMATE ENCOUNTER

This book is dedicated to my husband,
and my hero, Keith.

Chapter One

London—1816

Lord Robert Deveril Mountford propped himself up on his elbow in his bed. He brushed aside Maggie, Lady Caldwell's waterfall of chestnut curls and kissed her creamy shoulder. 'Two weeks from now?'

Dark eyes sparkling, she cast him a dazzling smile. 'Evil one. Can't you fit me in any sooner?'

'Sorry. I'm going out of town for a few days. Hunting.'

'Furred, feathered or female?' She stood up, slipped her chemise over her head and reached for her stays.

He slapped her plump little bottom. 'Whatever comes along, naturally.' Pleasantly sated, he yawned and stretched.

Maggie sighed. 'It is time you settled down, you know.'

Robert tensed. 'Not you, too.' He leaned across to

lace her stays, then pulled the silky stockings off the blue canopy over the bed and tossed them at her.

She sat to pull them over her shapely legs. 'Why not? There are all kinds of nice young things available. Take my niece. She has a reasonable dowry and her family is good quality.'

A sense of foreboding gathered like a snowball rolling downhill, larger and colder with each passing moment. It wasn't the first time one of his women had tried to inveigle herself or a member of her family into the ducal tribe, but he hadn't expected it from this one. He had thought he and Maggie were having too much fun to let familial obligations intrude.

He didn't want a wife cramping his lifestyle, even if the ducal allowance provided enough for two, which it didn't.

Dress on, Maggie went to the mirror and patted her unruly curls. 'Just look at this mess. Caldwell will never believe I was at Lady Jeffries's for tea.' She gathered the scattered pins from the floor and tried to bring some order to her tresses.

Naked, he rose to his feet and stood behind her. Her eyes widened in the glass, the heat of desire returning.

He picked up the hairbrush, all at once disturbingly anxious for her to be gone. 'Let me.' With a few firm strokes, he tamed the luxuriant brown mane, twisted it into a neat knot at the back of her head, pinned it and teased out a few curls around her face. 'Will that do?'

A lovely lush woman still in her prime and wasted on her old husband, she turned and laughed up at him. 'My maid doesn't arrange it half as well. If you ever need a position as a lady's maid, I will be pleased to provide a recommendation.'

He gazed at her beautiful face, then brushed her lips with his mouth. 'Thank you. For everything.'

He liked Maggie. Too bad she had to bring up the subject of marriage. He bent to retrieve her shoes and she sat on the stool. As he put them on her small feet, he caressed her calf one last time. A faint sense of regret washed through him. Too faint.

She sighed and ran her fingers through his hair.

The clock in the hall struck four.

'Oh, botheration,' she said, jumping to her feet. She took another quick peek in the glass. 'I think I will pass muster.' Her trill of laughter rang around the room.

He stood up with a wry smile. Maggie always maintained such good spirits. She never indulged in tantrums or fits of jealousy about his other women. She'd been the perfect liaison. Until now.

He'd send a token tomorrow, a discreet little diamond pin with a carefully worded message. No fool, Maggie. She'd understand.

She reached up and cupped his cheek with her palm. 'One of these days some beautiful young thing is going to capture that wicked heart of yours and you'll be lost to me and all the other naughty ladies of the *ton*, mark my words.'

Too bad she couldn't leave well enough alone. He caught her fingers and pressed them to his lips. 'What? Be tied to just one woman when there are so many to enjoy?'

'You are a bad man,' she said. 'And I adore you.'

She whirled around in a rustle of skirts, a cloud of rose perfume and sex. She opened the door and dashed down the stairs to her waiting carriage.

Yes, Robert thought, he would miss her a great deal. Now whom did he have waiting in the wings to fill his

Tuesday afternoons? A knotty, but interesting problem. The new opera dancer at Covent Garden had thrown him a lure last week. A curvy little armful with come-hither eyes. And yet, somehow, the thought of the chase didn't stir his blood.

It wouldn't be much of a chase. Perhaps he should look around a little more. Looking was half the fun.

He whistled under his breath as he readied himself for an evening at White's.

Kent—1816

It was almost perfect. Wasn't it? She just wished she could be sure. In the library's rapidly fading daylight, Frederica Bracewell narrowed her eyes and compared her second drawing of a sparrow to the one in the book. The first one she'd attempted was awful. A five-year-old would have done better. Drawn with her right hand. She sighed. It didn't matter how hard she tried, right-handed she was hopeless.

Devil's spawn. An echo of Cook's harsh voice hissed in her ear. Good-for-naught bastard. She rubbed her chilled hands together and held the second drawing up to the light. It was the best thing she'd done. But was it good enough?

The door opened behind her. She jumped to her feet. Heat rushed to her hairline. Heart beating hard, she turned, hiding the drawings with her body.

'Only me, miss,' Snively, the Wynchwood butler, said. A big man, with a shock of white hair and a fierce bulldog face, but his brown eyes twinkled as he carried a taper carefully across the room and lit the wall sconces.

Her heart settled back into a comfortable rhythm.

'I didn't realise you were working in here this afternoon or I would have had William light the fire,' the butler said.

'I'm not c-c-cold,' she said, smiling at one of her few allies at Wynchwood. She didn't want him losing his position by lighting unnecessary fires.

She picked up her rag with a wince. She'd completed very little of her assigned task: dusting the books. Uncle Mortimer would not be pleased.

In passing, Snively glanced at the pictures on the table. 'This one is good,' he said, pointing at the second one. 'It looks ready to fly away. People pay for pictures like that.'

'Do you think so?'

'I do.' Snively's face hardened. 'You ought to have proper lessons instead of copying from books. You've a talent.'

Always so supportive. Sometimes she imagined the starchy butler was her father. It might have been better if he was. Who knew what kind of low man the Wynchwood Whore had bedded.

'It is not s-seemly for a woman to d-draw for money,' she said quietly, 'but I would love to go to Italy and see the great art of Europe. Perhaps even s-study with a drawing teacher.'

His mouth became a thin straight line. 'So you should.'

'Lord Wynchwood would never hear of it. It would be far too expensive.'

Snively frowned. 'If you'll excuse me saying so, the wages you've saved his lordship by serving as housekeeper these past many years would pay for a dozen trips to Italy.'

'Only my uncle's generosity keeps me here, Mr

Snively. He could just as easily have left me at the workhouse.'

He glowered. 'Your turn will come, miss. You mark my words. It will.'

She'd never heard the butler so vehement. She glanced over her shoulder at the door. 'I beg you not to say anything to my uncle about these.' She gestured at the drawings.

'I wouldn't dream of it, miss. You keep it up. One day your talent will be recognised. I can promise it.'

She smiled. 'You are such a d-dear man.'

The library door slammed back.

Frederica jumped. Her heart leaped into her throat. 'Uncle M-M-Mortimer.' The words came out in a horrible rush.

The imperturbable Snively slid the book over her drawings and turned around with his usual hauteur. 'Good evening, Lord Wynchwood.'

Uncle Mortimer, his wig awry on his head, his cheeks puce, marched in. 'Nothing better to do than pass the time with servants, Frederica? Next you'll be hobnobbing with the stable boy, the way your mother did.'

Beside her Snively drew himself up straighter.

She trembled. She hated arguments. 'N-n-n—'

'No?' the old man snapped. 'Then Snively is a figment of my imagination, is he?'

'My lord,' Snively said in outraged accents, 'I was lighting the candles, as I always do at this time. I found Miss Bracewell dusting the books and stopped to help.'

'I'm not chastising you, Snively. My niece is the one I need to keep in check.' Frederica wasn't surprised at her uncle's about face. A butler of Snively's calibre was hard to come by these days.

'S-s-s—' she started.

'Sorry? You are always sorry. It is not good enough.' He frowned. 'Didn't you hear me ringing?'

She took a quick breath. 'N-no, Uncle. You asked me to d-d-dust the books in here. I d-d-did not hear your bell.'

'Well, listen better, gel. I've some receipts to be copied into the account book. I want them all finished by supper time.'

Frederica hid her shudder. Hours of copying numbers into columns and rows. Trying to make them neat and tidy while not permitted to use anything but her right hand. Her shoulders slumped. 'Yes, Uncle.'

'Come along. Come along, don't dilly dally. It is cold in here. My lungs cannot stand the chill. Snively, send word to Cook to send tea to my study.'

Snively bowed. 'Don't worry, miss, I'll return everything to its proper place.

He meant he'd put her drawings in her room. If Mortimer found she'd been wasting her time drawing, he'd probably lock her in her chamber for a week. Which might not be so bad, she reflected as she hurried out of the room. She threw the butler a conspiratorial smile.

Without Snively and her impossible dream of travelling to Italy and learning from a real artist, her life would be truly unbearable.

Refreshed and relaxed after his afternoon with Maggie, Robert strolled through the front door of White's and handed his coat and hat to the porter. 'Lord Radthorn here yet, O'Malley?'

The beefy red-haired man blinked owlishly. 'No, Lord Tonbridge.'

Robert didn't bother to correct the fool. It never did

any good. Only close family, friends and the odd woman could ever tell him and Charlie apart.

He took the stairs up to the great subscription room two at a time. The dark-panelled room buzzed with conversation and laughter despite the youth of the evening.

A group of gentlemen crowded around a faro table, the game in full swing. Guineas and vowels were heaped at the banker's elbow—Viscount Lullington, a fair-haired Englishman with thin aristocratic features whom many of the ladies adored. He had a Midas touch with gambling and women. Only Robert had ever bested him on either count—something that did not please the dandified viscount. But that wasn't the reason for the bad blood between them. It went a whole lot deeper. As deep as a sword blade.

The one Robert had put through his arm dueling for the favours of a woman. Robert glanced around the panelled room. No sign of Radthorn amongst the crowd, but a glance at his fob watch revealed he'd arrived a few minutes earlier than their appointed time. He drifted towards the faro table.

'Who is in the soup?' he asked Colonel Whittaker as he took in the play.

'Some protégé of Lullington's,' Wittaker muttered without turning. 'The young fool just bet his curricle and team.'

Lullington smoothed his dark blond hair back from his high forehead, his intense blue gaze sweeping the players at the table. A clever man, Lullington, his fashionable air a draw for unwary young men with too much money in their pockets.

Too bad the man had chosen tonight to play here.

As if sensing Robert's scrutiny, Lullington glanced

up and their gazes locked. His lip curled. Slowly, he laid his cards face down on the green baize table.

'Mountford?' Lullington never confused him with his twin. 'How did you get into a gentleman's club?' he lisped.

Robert recoiled. 'What did you say?'

The viscount's lids lowered a fraction. He shook his head. 'You never did have a scrap of honour.'

All conversation ceased.

The hairs on the back of Robert's neck rose. Fury coursed through his veins. He lunged forwards. 'You'll meet me on Primrose Hill in the morning for that slur. Name your seconds.'

The young sprig to Lullington's right stared opened mouthed.

'Gad, the cur speaks. Does it think because it is sired by a duke, it can mix with gentlemen?'

An odd rumble of agreement ran around the room.

Robert felt as if he'd been kicked in the chest. 'What the deuce are you talking about?'

Lullington's lip lifted in a sneer. 'Unlike you, I would never sully a lady's reputation in public.'

Robert felt heat travel up the back of his neck. So that's what this was all about. Lullington's cousin, the little bitch. He should have guessed the clever viscount would use the incident to his advantage. 'The woman you speak of is no lady,' he said scornfully. 'As you well know.'

'Dishonourable bastard,' Wittaker said, turning his back.

'No,' Lullington said softly, triumph filling his voice. 'Mountford is right not to bandy the lady's name around in this club. Mountford, I find the colour of your waistcoat objectionable. Please remove it from our presence at once. None of us wants to see it here again.'

One by one each man near Robert turned, until Robert stood alone, an island in a sea of stiff backs. Some of these men were his friends. He'd gone to school with them, drunk and gambled with them, whored with them, and not a single one of them would meet his eye.

One or two of them were the husbands of unfaithful wives. The triumph in their eyes as they turned away told its own story.

Good God! They'd decided to send him to Coventry, because he'd refused to marry a scheming little bitch.

The only man who remained looking his way was Lullington, who lifted his quizzing glass as if he had spotted a fly on rotten meat.

'It is a lie and you know it,' Robert said.

'Cheeky bastard,' Pettigrew said.

'Oh, it's cheeky all right.' Lullington's lisp seemed more pronounced than usual. He gave a mocking laugh like splintering glass. 'It remains. Pettigrew, will you have O'Malley throw this rubbish out, or shall I?'

One of the men—Pettigrew, Robert assumed—left the room, no doubt to do the viscount's bidding. Robert stood his ground, forced reason into his tone. 'I didn't touch the girl.' Damn. If he said any more, he'd be playing right into Lullington's hands.

Ambleforth, round and red about the gills, a man Robert had known at Eton, shuffled closer. He caught sight of Lullington's glass swivelling towards him and stopped, shaking his head. ''Fore God, Mountford,' he uttered in hoarse tones. 'Go, before you make it any worse.'

Worse. Heat flooded his body, sweat trickled down

his back. How could this nightmare be worse? Lullington had turned every man in the room against him for a crime he hadn't committed. The girl had brought it on herself.

'If you'll just step outside, my lord?' O'Malley grasped his elbow. 'We don't want no unpleasantness, now does we?'

Robert yanked his arm away. 'Take your greasy paws off me.' He swung around to leave.

'Thank God,' Lullington said into the heavy silence. 'The air in here was becoming quite foul. Did you hear gall of the fellow? Actually had the nerve to challenge me. I wouldn't let him lick my boots.'

A ripple of uncomfortable laughter followed Robert down the stairs. He clamped his jaw shut hard. He wanted to ram his fist through Lullington's sneering mouth, or bury his sword, hilt deep, in the man's chest.

He certainly wasn't going to marry Lullington's scheming little cousin to please them. Charlie was the only one with the power to get him out of this predicament.

He snatched his hat from O'Malley and stormed out onto the street, almost colliding with someone on the way in. He opened his mouth to apologise, then realized it was Radthorn. He reached out and pressed a hand on his friend's shoulder. 'John, thank God.'

'Mountford?' Embarrassment flashed across John's handsome face. 'You're here?'

What the devil? 'We had an appointment, remember?' Robert dropped his hand. Had John joined the rest of them in sending him to Coventry? It certainly seemed so.

'Damn you,' he said. The curse made him feel only marginally better as he barrelled up St James's Street.

Charlie was his only hope, because the duke had long ago washed his hands of his dissolute second son.

Mountford House was no different from all the other narrowly sedate houses on Grosvenor Square. A spinster on a picnic couldn't be more externally discreet and so seething with internal passions. These days Robert only visited the Mountford London abode in Father's absence. He might not have visited then, if it weren't for Mother. He certainly didn't visit Charlie who grew more like Father every day, only interested in his estates and the title and the name.

The door swung open. Robert ignored the butler's hand outstretched for his hat and coat. 'Is Tonbridge home?'

'Yes, Lord Robert. In his room.'

'Thank you, Grimshaw.'

He took the stairs two at a time and barged into Charlie's chamber. A room with all the pomp and circumstance required for the heir to a dukedom, it was large enough to hold a small ball. The ducal coat of arms emblazoned the scarlet drapery and every piece of furniture. It always struck Robert as regally oppressive. Charlie took it as his due.

Charlie, Charles Henry Beltane Mountford, named for Kings and Princes, the Marquis of Tonbridge and the next Duke of Stantford, neatly dressed, his cravat pristine, his jacket without a crease, sat at his desk, writing.

He looked up when Robert closed the door. 'I've been expecting you,' he said coolly.

Robert rocked back on his heels. 'You knew?

You bastard. Why the hell didn't you give me some warning?'

Charlie's mouth flattened. 'I sent word to your lodging. My man missed you.'

Robert ran a glance over his older brother. It was like looking into a distorted mirror. He saw his own brown eyes and dark brown hair, his square-jawed face and the cleft in the chin that made shaving a chore. He saw his own body, tall and lean, with long legs and large hands and feet, but he hated the rest of what he saw. The weary eyes. The lines around his mouth. He looked like their father.

He looked like a man who had given up the joy of life for duty and honour.

'I need a loan so I can pay the girl off. With enough of a dowry, she'll soon find a husband willing to hold his nose and that will be an end to it.'

Charlie tipped his head back and squeezed his eyes shut for a second. 'I'm sorry, Robin. I don't have that kind of money.'

'Ask Father for a loan. He never refuses you anything.'

'It's all over town. Do you think he won't know why I'm asking for such a large sum?'

'Tell him it's a gambling debt.'

Charlie shook his head. 'You play, you pay. You know the rules. It's time you settled down, anyway. Take some responsibility. Father will think the better of you for it.'

Robert clenched his fists at his side in an effort not to smash his fist in Charlie's face. He took a deep breath. 'What the hell, Charlie—do you think I'm going to marry a girl who was prepared to sacrifice her reputation for the chance of becoming a duchess? I did you a favour.'

Charlie's gaze hardened. 'Don't bother. I don't need your kind of favours.'

'What if it had been you she'd lured into the library? Would you have married her, knowing she trapped you?'

Charlie curled his lip. 'Come on, Robin, we both know there isn't a female alive who can lure you if you don't want to go. But if it had been me, I would have offered for her immediately. It would be my duty to the family name.'

Robert swallowed the bile rising in his throat. 'I won't be blackmailed into wedding a scheming little baggage.'

'Marriage wouldn't hurt you one bit.'

A sick feeling roiled around in Robert's gut. 'I'm not getting married to a woman who wanted my brother.'

Charlie looked at him coldly over the rim of his brandy glass. 'Then you shouldn't have kissed her.'

'Damn it.' Robert felt like howling. 'She kissed me.'

'You've been going to hell for years. Marriage will do you good. It will please Father.'

Robert's gaze narrowed. He suddenly saw it all. The glimmer of regret in Charlie's eyes gave him away. 'You have already discussed this with Father. This is a common front, isn't it?' He balled his fists. 'I ought to beat you to a pulp. How dare you and Father play with my life?'

Charlie's mouth tightened. 'No, Robert. You did this all by yourself. Even though I agree with you, it was her bloody fault, you ought to offer for the girl or you'll leave great blot on the family name.'

'That's all you bloody well care about these days.'

'It's my job.'

They used to be friends. Now they were worse than strangers. Because Charlie disapproved of everything Robert did.

Robert stared at his older brother. Older by five minutes. Three hundred seconds that gave Charlie everything and left Robert with a small monthly allowance courtesy of his father. And because he'd thought to do his brother a favour, thought it might restore their old easy fun-loving companionship, he'd been cast adrift on a sea of the last thing he wanted: matrimony.

Hot fury roiled in his gut, spurted through his veins, ran in molten rivers until his vision blazed red. 'No. I won't do it. Not for Father and not for you. She made her bed, let her lie on it.'

'Don't be a fool. Lullington won't forget this. You'll never be able to show your face in town again.'

'I'm a Mountford. With Father's support…'

Charlie shook his head. 'He's furious.'

Bloody hell. Cast out from society, perhaps for all time? It wouldn't be the first time the *ton* had discarded one of their own. Robert felt sick. 'He'll come around. He has to. Mother will make him see reason.'

'Never at a loss, are you, Robin?' Charlie frowned. 'But I won't have you upsetting our mother. I'll talk to Father. Convince him somehow. It's going to cost a lot of money and if I do this you have to swear to mend your ways.'

Ice filled Robert's veins. He wanted to smack the disapproving look off his brother's face. 'What makes you a saint?'

Charlie gave him a pained look. 'I'm not.'

'I don't suppose you could lend me a pony until

quarter day. I've some debts pressing.' Inwardly, he groaned. At least one of which was Lullington's. Not to mention a diamond pin to present to Maggie.

'Damn it, Robert.' He got up and went to a chest in the corner. He unlocked it and pulled out a leather purse. 'Fifty guineas. If that's not enough I can give you a draft for up to a thousand. But that's all.'

'A thousand?' Robert whistled. 'You really are dibs in tune.'

'I don't have time to spend it.' He looked weary, weighed down. Robert didn't envy him his position of heir one little bit.

Sure his problems were solved, Robert grinned. 'You need a holiday from all this.' He waved a hand at the cluttered desk. 'Want to exchange places again?'

'You will not,' a voice thundered. 'And nor will you give him any money.'

Father. Robert whipped his head around. The brown-eyed silver-haired gentleman framed in the doorway in sartorial splendour glared as Robert rose to his feet. Rigid with anger and pride, Alfred, his Grace the Duke of Stantford, locked his gaze on Charlie. 'He has brought dishonour to our name. He is no longer welcome in my house.'

Robert felt the blood drain from his face, from his whole body. He couldn't draw breath as the words echoed in his head. While he and Father didn't always see eye to eye, he'd never expected this.

Charlie's eyes widened. 'Father, it is not entirely Robert's fault.'

Mealy-mouthed support at best, but then that was Charlie these days. 'The woman—'

'Enough,' Father roared. 'I heard you. You are not satisfied with being a parasite on this family, a dissolute wastrel and a libertine. No. It's not enough that you drag our name through the mud. You want your brother's title.'

The taste of ashes filled Robert's mouth. 'Your Grace, no,' he choked out, 'it was a jest.'

Stantford's lip curled, but beneath the bluster he seemed to age from sixty to a hundred in the space a heartbeat. In his eyes, Robert saw fear.

'You think I don't know what you are about?' the old man whispered. 'An identical brother? I always knew you'd be trouble. You almost succeeded in getting him killed once, but I won't let it happen again.'

Nausea rolled in Robert's gut. The room spun as pain seared his heart. 'I would never harm my brother.'

'Father,' Charlie said. 'I wanted to join the army. I convinced Robert to take my place.'

The duke's lip curled. 'I expected he needed a lot of convincing.'

'No, I didn't,' Robert said. 'I thought it was a great lark. How would I know what a mess Waterloo would be? Napoleon was a defeated general.'

They'd all thought that and Charlie, desperate to join the army from the time he could talk, saw it as a chance to fulfil his dream despite Father's refusal.

Robert had avoided the family while he played at being Charlie for weeks before Waterloo. Had a grand old time. Until he'd felt Charlie's physical pain in his own body. He'd known something was wrong. But when the lists came out announcing Robert Mountford's death and the family started to grieve, they thought he'd gone mad. He'd insisted on going to the site of the battle. When he finally found Charlie, one of the many robbed of his clothes and out of his head in a fever, the truth had to come out. After that, Father had refused to have anything to do with Robert. Until today.

'You are not my son,' the duke said.

Charlie stared at Father. 'No,' he whispered. 'You are going too far. I won't let you do this. Robert will marry the girl. Won't you?'

Reeling, Robert almost said yes. His spine stiffened. He would not be blackmailed, forced into a mould by his father or anyone else, especially not Miss Penelope Frisken. 'No. I did not seduce her and I won't accept the blame.'

'You idiot,' Charlie hissed.

'I want that cur out of my house,' the duke commanded. 'I won't see the name of Mountford blackened any further by this wastrel. He'll sponge on me no longer.'

Sponge. Was that how he saw it? Without his allowance, he wouldn't be able to pay his debts. Any of them. He had debts of honour due on quarter day, as well as several tradesmen expecting their due. He'd gone a little deeper than he should have this month, but then he'd expected to come about. And there was always his allowance.

'You can't do this.'

His father glared. 'Watch me.'

A horrid suspicion crept into his mind. Was this Lullington's plan all along? He was clever enough. Devious enough.

How else had the information about what had happened at White's reached the duke so quickly? Now Father had the perfect opportunity to be rid of the cuckoo in his nest.

He'd always been inclined to laugh off matters others thought important, but when Charlie had almost died on the battlefield at Waterloo, he knew he should have thought it out a bit more carefully. He never expected this as the end result, though, and he wasn't going to beg forgiveness for something he hadn't done.

His stomach churned. He gulped down his bile and drew himself up straight. His face impassive, he stared at his rigid father. 'As you wish, your Grace. You will never have to set eyes on me again, but first I would like a few minutes alone with Lord Tonbridge.'

The duke didn't glance in Robert's direction, addressing himself only to Charlie. 'There's nothing for him here. No one is giving him money. I mean that, Tonbridge. Tell him to be out of my house in five minutes or I will have him horsewhipped.' He wheeled around and shut the door behind him.

Charlie fixed his tortured gaze on Robert's face. 'I'll talk to him. I had no idea his anger went so deep.'

Robert tried to smile. 'If you try to defend me, it will only make things worse. He's suspicious enough. He'll think I have some hold on you. Don't worry about me. I'll manage.'

'How?'

'I'll find work.'

At that Charlie cracked a painful laugh. 'What will you do? Find a woman to employ your services in bed?'

Robert's hand curled into a fist. He smiled, though it made his cheeks ache. 'Well now, there is an idea. Any thoughts of who? Your betrothed, perhaps?'

Colour stained Charlie's cheekbones. 'Damn it, Robert, I was joking.'

'Not funny.' Because it came too close to the truth. He'd prided himself on those skills. Bragged of them. He stared down at the monogrammed carpet and then back up into his brother's face. 'You don't think I planned to take the title?'

'Of course not,' Charlie said, his voice thick, 'but damn it. I should never have gone.'

'I'd better be off.' Robert straightened his shoulders.

Charlie held out the bag of guineas. 'Take this, you'll need it.'

Pride stiffened his shoulders. 'No. I'll do this without any help. And when the creditors come to call, tell them they'll have their money in due course.'

Charlie gave him a diffident smile. 'Stay in touch. I'll let you know when it is safe to return. I'll pay off the girl. Find her a husband.'

Even as Charlie spoke Robert realized the truth. 'Nothing you can do will satisfy Lullington and his cronies. I'm done for here. Father is right. My leaving is the only way to save the family honour.' A lump formed in his throat, making his voice stupidly husky. 'Take care of yourself, brother. And take care of Mama and the children.'

An expression of panic entered Charlie's eyes, gone before Robert could be sure. 'I don't want you to go.'

Puzzled, Robert stared at him. Charlie had always been the confident one. Never wanting any help from Robert. In fact, since Waterloo, he'd grown ever more distant.

Wishful thinking. It was the sort of pro-forma thing family members said on parting. He grinned. 'I'd better go before the grooms arrived with the whips.' Just saying it made his skin crawl.

Charlie looked sick. 'He wouldn't. He's angry, but I'm sure he will change his mind after reflection.'

They both knew their father well enough to know he was incapable of mind-changing.

Robert clapped his brother on the shoulder. The lump seemed to swell. He swallowed hard. 'Charlie, try to have a bit more fun. You don't want to end up like Father.'

Charlie looked at him blankly.

Robert let go a shaky breath. He'd tried. 'When I'm settled, I'll drop you a note,' he said thickly, his chest full, his eyes ridiculously misted.

He strode for the door and hurtled down the stairs, before he cried like a baby.

Out on the street, he looked back at a house now closed to him for ever. Father had always acted as if he wished Robert had never been born. Now he'd found a way to make it true.

He turned away. One foot planted in front of the other on the flagstones he barely saw, heading for the Albany. Each indrawn breath burned the back of his throat. He felt like a boy again pushed aside in favour of his brother. Well, he was a boy no longer. He was his own man, with nothing but the clothes on his back. Without an income from the estate, he couldn't even afford his lodgings.

All these years, he'd taken his position for granted, never saved, never invested. He'd simply lived life to the full. Now it seemed the piper had to be paid or the birds had come home to roost, whichever appropriate homily applied. What the hell was he to do? How would he pay his debts?

Ask Maggie for help? Charlie's question roared in his ear. No. He would not be a kept man. The thought of servicing any woman for money made him shudder. If he did that he might just as well marry Penelope. And he might have, if she hadn't been so horrified when she realised he wasn't Charlie.

Father would scratch his name out of the family annals altogether if he turned into a cicisbeo. A kept man.

It would be like dying, only worse because it would be as if he never existed. The thought brought him close to shattering in a thousand pieces on the pavement. The green iron railings at his side became a lifeline in a world pitching like a dinghy in a storm. He clutched at it blindly. The metal bit cold into his palm. He stared at his bare hand. Where the hell had he left his gloves?

Gloves? Who the hell cared about gloves? He started to laugh, throwing back his head and letting tears of mirth run down his face.

An old gentleman with a cane walking towards him swerved aside and crossed the street at a run.

Hilarity subsided and despair washed over him at the speed of a tidal bore. He'd never felt so alone in his life.

God damn it. He would not lie down meekly.

He didn't need a dukedom to make a success of his life.

Chapter Two

Kent—1819

She wouldn't. She couldn't.

The words beat time to Frederica's heartbeat. Pippin's hooves picked up the rhythm and pounded it into hard-packed earth. The trees at the edge of her vision flung it back.

The damp earthy smell of leaf mould filled her nostrils. Usually, she loved the dark scent. It spoke of winter and frost and warm fires. Today it smelled of decay.

She couldn't. She wouldn't.

She would not wed Simon the slug. Not if her uncle begged her for the next ten years.

The ground softened as they rode through a clearing. Pippin's flying hooves threw clods of mud against the walls of a dilapidated cottage hunched in the lee of the trees until a tunnel of low-hanging hazels on the other side seemed to swallow them whole. Frederica slowed Pippin to a walk, fearful of tree roots.

At the river bank, she drew the horse up. Her secret place. The one spot on the Wynchwood estate where she could be assured of peace and quiet and the freedom to think. A narrow stretch of soft green moss curled over the bank where the River Wynch carved a perfect arc in black loam. The trees on both sides of the water hugged close.

Barely ankle deep in summer, the winter flood rushed angrily a few inches below the bank, swirling and twisting around the deep pool in the crook of its elbow. Downstream, beyond Wynchwood Place's ornamental lake, the river widened and turned listless, but here it ran fast, its tempo matching her mood.

Breathless, cheeks stinging from the wind, she dismounted. Pippin dipped his head to slake his thirst. Satisfied he was content to nibble on the sedges at the water's edge, she let his reins dangle and strolled a short way upstream. She stared into the ripples and swoops of impatient water, seeking answers.

No one could force her to wed Simon. Could they?

The casual mention of the plan by her uncle at breakfast had left her dumbfounded. And dumb. And by the time she had regained the use of her tongue, Uncle Mortimer had locked himself in his study.

Did Simon know of this new turn of events? He'd never liked her. Barely could bring himself to speak to her when they did meet. It had to be a hum. Some bee in Uncle's bonnet. Didn't it?

If it wasn't, they'd have to tie her in chains, hand and foot, blindfold her, gag her and even then she would never agree to marry her bacon-brained cousin.

A small green frog, its froggy legs scissor-kicking against the current, aimed for the overhanging bank beneath her feet. She leaned over to watch it land.

'What the devil do you think you are doing?'

The deep voice jolted through her. Her foot slipped. She was going—

Large hands caught her arms, lifted her, swung her around and set her on her feet.

Heart racing, mouth dry, she spun about, coming face to face with a broad, naked chest, the bronzed skin covered in dark crisp curls and banded by sculpted muscle.

The breath rushed from her lungs. Swallowing hard, she backed up a couple of steps and took in the dark savage gipsy of a man with hands on lean hips watching her from dark narrowed eyes. Hair the colour of burnt umber, shaded with streaks of ochre, fell to a pair of brawny shoulders. His hard slash of a mouth in his angular square-jawed face looked as if it had tasted of the world and found it bitter.

Fierce. Wild. Masculine. Intimidating. All these words shot through her mind.

And frighteningly handsome.

A tall rough-looking man, with the body of a Greek god and the face of a fallen angel.

Heat spread out from her belly. Desire.

A shiver ran down her spine. Her heart hammered. Her tongue felt huge and unwieldy. 'Wh-who are you?' Damn her stutter.

Arrogant, controlled and powerful, he folded strong bare forearms over his lovely wide chest. He looked her up and down, assessing, without a flicker of a muscle in his impassive face. A dark questioning eyebrow went up. 'I might ask the same of you,' he said, his voice a deep low growl she felt low in her stomach.

She clutched at the skirts of her old brown gown to hide the tremble in her hands and inhaled a deep breath. Every fibre of her being concentrated on speaking her next words without hesitation, without showing weakness. 'I am Lord Wynchwood's niece. I have every right to be here.' Panting with effort, she released the remainder of her breath.

He took a step towards her. Instinctively, she shrank back. He halted, palms held out. 'For God's sake, you'll end up in the river.'

The exasperation in his tone and expression did more to ease her fears than soft words would have done. She glared at him. 'Of c-course I w-won't.'

He backed up several paces. 'Then move clear of the edge.'

Since he had ruined the solitude, shattered any hope for quiet contemplation, she might as well leave. Head high, she strode past him, carefully keeping beyond his arm's length, and caught up Pippin's reins. Prickles ran hot and painful down her back as if his dark gaze still grazed her skin. She couldn't resist glancing over her shoulder.

He'd remained statue-still like some ancient Celtic warrior, bold and hard and simmering like a storm about to rage. A terrifyingly handsome man and thoroughly annoyed, though what he had to be annoyed about she couldn't think.

How would he look if he smiled?

The thought surprised her utterly. 'Wh-who are you, s-sir? W-what are you doing in these woods?'

'Robert Deveril, milady. Assistant gamekeeper. I live in the cottage yonder.' He hesitated, pressed his lips together as if holding back something on the tip of his tongue. She knew the feeling only too well. Except for her, it was because it was easier to say nothing.

And yet after a moment, he continued, 'I thought

your horse had bolted the way you tore past my house, but I see I was mistaken. Forgive me, milady.'

Suntanned fingers touched his forelock in a reluctant gesture of servility. If anything, he looked more arrogant than before. He pivoted and strode towards the path with long lithe strides.

'Y-your h-house?' A recollection of flying dirt striking something hollow filled her mind. No wonder he'd been surprised and come to see what was happening. Heat flashed upwards from her chest to the roots of her hair. 'P-p-p—' *Oh, tongue, don't fail me now.* She forced in a breath. 'Mr D-Deveril,' she called out.

He halted, then turned to face her, looking less than happy. 'Milady?'

'I apologise.'

He frowned.

'It w-w-will not h-happen again.' Mortified at her inability to express even the simplest of sentences when off-kilter, she turned to her mount. It wasn't until the cinches on Pippin's saddle disappeared in a blur that she realised she was close to crying and wasn't sure why, unless it was frustration and the realisation of just how inconsiderate she'd been.

'Let me help you, milady.'

At the sound of his deep, rich, oh-so-easy words, she almost swallowed her tongue. 'G-g-go away,' she managed.

Clinging to Pippin's saddle, she turned her head. A good two feet away, he waited, calmly watching her, the anger still there, but contained, like that of the panther she'd once seen in a cage. Beautiful. And dangerous.

Yet she wasn't afraid. She just didn't want to look like a fool in front of this man.

'Look,' he said reasonably, 'I'm sorry I scared you. I

thought you were in trouble when I saw you teetering on the brink. The rains have made the bank treacherous.'

'I'm a g-good s-s-swimmer.' She tried a smile.

'It's no jesting matter. No doubt you'd expect me to pull you out.'

Simon's face swam before her eyes like a pudgy Banquo's ghost. 'I'd prefer you didn't bother.'

His eyes gleamed. Amusement? 'My, you are in high ropes.'

He was laughing at her. He saw her as a joke. A wordless fool. He was so perfect and she couldn't string two words together. A spurt of resentment shot through her veins. 'This was m-my p-place. You have s-spoiled it.' She gulped in a supply of air. Her stutter was out of control. At any moment she'd been speechless. A dummy. For the second time today. 'G-good d-day, sir.'

His face blanched beneath his tan as if somehow she'd stabbed him and the blood had drained away. His hands fell to his sides, large hands that bunched into fists, knuckles gleaming white. 'I beg your pardon, my lady.'

An apology he scorned. She could see that in his expression.

She grabbed for Pippin's reins. Tried to pull herself up. The horse sidled. *No, Pippin. Don't do this now.* 'Shhh,' she whispered.

A strong calloused hand grabbed the bridle beside her cheek. Her heart leapt into her throat at the size of it. Afraid her heart might jump right out of her mouth, she drew back.

'You'll scare him,' she warned.

He murmured something. Pippin, the traitor, stilled. Deveril lifted the saddle flap and adjusted the cinch. He cocked a superior brow. 'You were saying?'

There it was, the arrogance of man. She breathed in slowly. 'F-for an assistant gamekeeper you are very haughty.'

'Once more I find the need to apologise.' A rueful grin curved his finely moulded lips.

Breathtaking. Heartstopping. A smile so dangerous ought to be against the law. Her anger whisked away as if borne aloft by the breeze tossing the branches above their heads. All she could do was stare at his lovely mouth. She inhaled a shaky breath. 'N-no. I was n-n...' She swallowed, then closed her eyes, surprised when he didn't finish the word. 'I was not very polite. I am sorry.'

He bowed his head in gentlemanly acknowledgement. 'Can I help you mount, my lady?'

Since when did assistant gamekeepers have elegant manners and glorious bodies? Every time he spoke, her knees felt strangely weak and she just wanted to stand and look at him. He made her want things young ladies were not supposed to think about. She wanted to touch him. Trace the curve of muscle and the cords of sinew. Feel their warmth.

And he wanted to help her onto her horse. 'Thank you, Mr R-Robert Deveril.'

His eyes widened. 'I must apologise for my earlier abruptness. I thought you an interloper.'

'I had not heard the cottage was let.' She frowned. She'd barely stumbled on her words. 'We d-d-don't have an assistant gamekeeper.'

'I started on Monday.'

No one ever told her anything. 'This is a lovely spot.' She glanced around, drinking it in with a sense of sadness. She wouldn't be able to come here any more.

'Aye, it is. Even at this time of year.' Slivers of amber

danced in his dark eyes like unspent laughter. He really was outstandingly beautiful, despite the day's growth of beard. Or maybe because of it.

'You are not from this part of the country, are you?' she asked.

An eyebrow flicked up. He smiled again, another swift curve of his mouth, instantly repressed, but still her skin went all hot and prickly. 'I'm from the west. Dorset way.'

His accent had changed, broadened. He thought to trick her, but she always noticed every word, every inflection, in other people's voices. How could she not? This man hailed from London, and had been educated well, of that she was certain. She mentally shrugged. It mattered little to her where he came from. She prepared to mount.

'Allow me,' he said.

He bent and linked his hands, then cast her a frowning look. 'Don't let me keep you from this place, milady. I shan't disturb you again.'

A furnace seemed to engulf her face. 'Th-thank you. And it is not my lady, just plain Miss Bracewell.' She caught herself lifting her chin and tucked it back in.

His head tilted to one side as if considering her words, then his gaze slid away. 'Yes, miss.'

She placed one booted foot in his cupped hands and he tossed her up without effort.

Tall and broad, straight and grand beside the horse, he planted his feet in the soft earth like a solid English oak. A man she would love to draw.

Naked.

The wicked thought trickled heaviness to the dark, secret place she tried never to notice. Little flutters made her shift in the saddle. Wanton urges. The kind that led

a woman into trouble. Her gaze drank him in. Her heart
sank. Was it any wonder she felt this way, when Slimy
Simon loomed in her future? 'Good day, Mr Deveril.'

She wheeled Pippin around.

She couldn't help looking back one last time. He
raised a hand in farewell. Her heart gave a sweet little
lurch, which once more set her stomach dancing.

The horse broke into a trot and plunged into the trees.
Robert could hear the sound of twigs snapping even as,
utterly bemused, he followed in its wake. By the time he
reached the clearing, the spirited gelding and its rider
had disappeared.

A strange little thing, this Miss Wynchwood. In her
drab brown clothing, she reminded him of some wild
woodland creature ready to run at a sound. Certainly no
beauty—her eyes were too large, the colour changing
with her thoughts from the bluish-grey of clouds to the
grey-green of a wind-swept ocean. Her tragic mouth
took up far too much of her pixie face.

He'd wanted to kiss that mouth and make it tremble
with desire instead of fear. He'd longed to release the
tightly coiled hair at her nape and see it fall around her
face. Pulled back, it did nothing to improve her looks.
And yet she was oddly alluring.

Her style of conversation left much to be desired,
though. Short and sharp and rude. Clearly a spoiled
rich miss who needed a lesson in manners. Her Grace
would not have tolerated such abruptness from one of
Robert's sisters.

A dull stab of pain caught him off guard. Hades.
Even now thoughts of home sneaked unwanted into his
mind. He stared at the mud splattering the door of his
cottage. What a reckless little cross-patch to ride at

such speed through the woods. He groaned. And quite likely to report him to Lord Wynchwood for taking her to task.

Damnation. What the hell had he said?

He'd been terrified she'd fall in the river, furious at her carelessness. He'd spoken harshly. He'd made her angry.

Angry and woman did not mix well.

He shouldered his way into the hut he called home and kicked the door shut. Damn, it was cold, but at least he had a roof over his head. He sorted through his bed-clothes on the cot against the wall, found his jacket and shrugged into the coarse fabric. He stirred the embers to get the fire going and hung the kettle on the crane. He'd been making tea moments before running outside because he thought the walls were collapsing. Moments before he'd ripped into the girl whose family owned these woods like a duke's son instead of a servant. He'd been scathing when he should have thanked her for the honour her horse's hooves had paid to his dwelling, or at least kept his tongue behind his teeth.

Such a small, fragile thing making all that rumpus. A good wind and she'd blow away. And when he boosted her on to her horse, she'd weighed no more than a child. Her eyes, though, had looked at him in the way of a woman. And his body had responded with interest. He cursed.

This was the best position he'd found in over two years and he'd be a fool to lose it because of a slip of a girl.

He stabbed the fire. Sparks flew. His nostrils filled with the scent of ashes. If he wasn't mistaken, once he'd cooled down, he'd treated her the way he treated his sisters, with amused tolerance. No wonder she'd been annoyed. No doubt he'd be apologising tomorrow. Unless she had him turned off.

Blast. For the first time he'd found a place with a chance for advancement and enough wages to start paying off some of his debts and he'd scolded his employer's niece.

Would he never come to terms with his new position in life?

He poured boiling water into the teapot and took it to the table set with a supper of bread and cheese. He cut a hunk of bread and skewered it with his knife. He took a bite and munched it slowly.

If there was a next time, he'd be more careful. He'd remember his place.

Chapter Three

'There you are, Miss Frederica.' The butler, Mr Snively, emerged from the shadows at the bottom of the staircase. He gave her a small smile. 'I thought I better warn you, Lord Wynchwood is asking for you. He is in his study.'

Frederica winced. 'Thank you, S-Snively. What is his current m-mood?'

Snively's muddy eyes twinkled, but there was sadness in them too. 'He's seems a little irritated, miss. Not his normal sunny self.' He winked.

She almost laughed. 'It's probably his g-gout.'

'Yes, miss.'

'And the w-weather. And the state of the Funds.'

'Yes, miss. And I gather he's lost his glasses.'

She grinned. 'Again. I'll go to him the moment I am changed.'

Snively shook his head and the wrinkles in his bull-dog face seemed to deepen. 'No point, miss, he knows you took Pippin.'

Dash it all. One of the grooms must have reported her hasty departure. She sighed. 'I'll go right away. Thank you, Snively.'

He looked inclined to speak, then pressed his lips together.

'Is there s-something else?'

'His lordship received a letter from a London lawyer yesterday. It seems to have put him in a bit of a fuss. Made him fidgety.' Snively sounded worried. 'I wondered if he said anything about it?'

Uncle Mortimer was always fidgety. She stripped off her gloves and bonnet and handed them to him. 'Perhaps Mr Simon Bracewell is in need of funds again. Or perhaps it is merely excitement over my p-pending nuptials.'

Snively's dropping jaw was more than satisfying. He looked as horrified as she felt. He recovered quickly, smoothing his face into its customary bland butler's mask. But his flinty eyes told a different story. 'Is it appropriate to offer my congratulations?'

'N-not really.' All the frustration she'd felt when Uncle Mortimer made the announcement swept over her. 'I'm to m-marry my cousin S-Simon.' After years of him indicating he wished she wasn't part of his family at all.

His eyes widened. His mouth grew grim. 'Oh, no.'

She took a huge breath. 'Precisely.' Unable to bring herself to attempt another word, she headed for the study to see what Great-Uncle Mortimer wanted. Steps dragging, she traversed the brown runner covering a strip of ancient flagstones. This part of Wynchwood Hall always struck a chill on her skin as if damp clung to the walls like slime on a stagnant pond.

A quick breath, a light knock on the study door and she strode in.

Great-Uncle Mortimer sat in a wing chair beside the fire, a shawl around his shoulders, his feet immersed in a white china bowl full of steaming water and a mustard plaster on his chest.

In his old-fashioned wig, his nose pink from a cold and his short-sighted eyes peering over his spectacles at the letter in his hand, he looked more like a mole than usual.

He glanced up and shoved the paper down the side of the chair. Was that the lawyer's letter to which Snively referred? Or another letter from Simon begging for funds?

'Shut the door, girl. Do you want me to perish of the ague?'

She whisked the door shut and winced as the curtains at the windows rippled.

'The draught,' he moaned.

'Sorry, Uncle.'

'I don't know what it is about you, girl. Dashing about the countryside, leaving doors open on ailing relatives. You are supposed to make yourself useful, not overset my nerves. Have you learned nothing?'

He put a hand up to forestall her defence. 'What sort of start sent you racing off this morning? I needed you here.'

Of all her so-called relatives, she liked her uncle the best since he rarely had enough energy to notice her existence.

'I d-don't—'

'Don't know? You must know.'

She gulped in a deep breath. 'I don't want to marry S-S—'

'Simon. And that's the reason you dashed off on Pippin?'

She nodded.

'Ridiculous.' He leaned his head against the chair back and closed his eyes as if gathering strength. 'I am old. I need to know that my affairs are in order. Simon has kindly offered to alleviate me of one of my worries. It is the perfect solution. You do not have to get along, you just have to do your duty and give him a son. Surely you would like a house and children of your own, would you not?'

A dream for most normal women, the image sent a chill down her spine. 'No.'

'There is no alternative.'

'I can s-support myself.'

His bushy eyebrows shot up and he opened his eyes. 'How? Good God, you can scarcely string two words together.'

Heat rushed up to her hairline. Anger. 'I d-draw. Art.' Even as she said the words, she knew her mistake.

His face darkened. He sat up straight. 'What respectable woman earns money from daubing?' He made it sound like she had proposed selling her body.

'I'm not r-respectable.'

He narrowed his eyes. 'You have been brought up to be respectable. You will not bring shame on this family.'

Like your mother. Like the Wynchwood Whore. He didn't say it, but she could see he was thinking it by the tight set to his mouth and the jut of his jaw.

Dare she tell him about the drawings she'd already sold? Prove she could manage by herself? The money she earned would give her an independence. Barely. What if he prevented her from completing the last pictures of the series? It would void her contract, a contract she'd signed pretending to be a man. She sealed the words behind her firmly closed lips. Not that he ever let her finish a sentence.

'And another thing,' he said. 'No more excursions on Pippin. There is too much to do around this house.'

She stared at him. 'W-what things?'

'Simon is bringing guests for the ball. There will be hunting, entertainments, things like that to arrange. I will need your help.'

Horror rose up like a lump in her throat. 'G-guests?'

'Yes. The ball will also serve as your come out.'

A rush of blood to her head made her feel dizzy. 'A come out?'

Mortimer tugged his shawl closer about his shoulders. 'Don't look surprised. Anyone would think this family treated you badly. It is high time you entered society if you are going to be Simon's wife. We can hope no one remembers your mother any more.'

'I d-d-d—'

Mortimer thumped the arm of his chair with a clenched fist. 'Enough,' he yelled. He lowered his voice. 'Damn it. Any other girl your age would be in alt at so generous an offer. Make an effort, girl. Why, you are practically on the shelf.'

'I w-w-w—'

'Will.'

Breathe in. Breathe out. 'Won't. I don't want a husband.' A husband would ruin all her hopes for the future.

The red in Mortimer's face darkened to puce and his ears flushed vermilion. He reminded her of an angry sunset, the kind that heralded a storm. His bushy grey brows drew together over his pitted nose. 'I am the head of this family and I say you will obey me or face the consequences.'

Did he think she feared a diet of bread and water or isolation in her room? 'I—'

'No more arguments, Frederica. It is decided. I have only your best interests in mind. I have clearly allowed you far too much liberty if your head is full of such nonsense. Art, indeed. Where did you ever get such a notion?'

'I…' Oh, what was the point? She didn't really know where the notion came from anyway.

'What you need to do, girl, is learn to make yourself useful. Find my glasses. I know I had them here earlier.' He poked around in the folds of his robe.

Frederica stifled a sigh. 'Uncle.'

He looked up. She pointed to her nose and he put a hand up to his face. 'Ah. There they are. Now run along and prepare for our guests. Hurry up before you add a headache to my ills.'

Mortimer pressed one gnarled hand against his poultice and closed his eyes. 'Ask Snively for more hot water on your way out.'

Dismissed, Frederica lowered her gaze and dropped a respectful curtsy. 'Yes, Uncle.'

She turned and left swiftly, before he found some other task for her to do. It was no good fighting the stubborn man head on. And Snively was right, he was unusually crotchety. And this idea of his to marry her to Simon was strange to say the least. He'd never expressed a jot of interest in her future before. Perhaps age was catching up to him.

As she headed for the butler's pantry to deliver her message, her mind twisted and turned, seeking an escape. She would not marry a man she despised as much as he scorned her.

Simon was the key, she realised. He would never agree to this scheme.

And to top it all off, she was to attend a ball? With strangers, people who might know of her mother. People who would expect her to make conversation. And dance. Never once had she danced in public. She'd probably fall flat on her face.

For a moment, she wasn't sure which was worse: the thought of marriage or the thought of a room full of strangers.

A shudder ran down her spine. Of the two, it had to be Simon. Simon didn't have a soul. He'd crush hers with his inanity.

Robert shouldered his shotgun, the brace of hares dangling from its muzzle. Fresh meat for dinner. His mouth watered.

He strode down Gallows Hill, mud heavy on his boots, the countryside unfolding in mist-draped valleys and leafless tree-crested hills. The late-afternoon air chilled the back of his throat and reached frigid fingers smelling of decayed vegetation into his lungs.

On the hill behind him, the rooks were settling back among the treetops with harsh cries. He whistled blithely, unusually content at the prospect of stew instead of bread and cheese, or the rations of salt beef provided by his employer.

Perhaps he'd request a recipe for dumplings from Wynchwood's cook next time he arrived in her kitchen with a plump pheasant for his lordship's dinner. A wry smile twisted his lips. How the mighty were fallen.

A sudden sense of loss made his stomach fall away.

The whistle died on his lips. Damn it. He would not sink into self-pity. Live for the moment and plan for the future must be his motto or he would go mad.

He slogged on down the hill, unable to recapture his lighter mood. At the bottom, he took the overgrown track alongside the river, pushing aside brambles and scuffing through damp leaves. Without vegetables his stew would be a sorry affair. Perhaps instead of going up to the house in the morning for a list of the cook's requirements from the local village, he'd go now. She might have some vegetables to spare.

The trees thinned at the edge of the clearing. Stew. He could almost smell it.

Robert stopped short at the sight of a hunched figure perched on an old stump a little way from his cottage, her brown bonnet and brown wool cloak blending into the carpet of withered beech leaves. He knew her at once, even though she had her back to him and her head bowed over something on her lap. Miss Bracewell.

Hades. It seemed she'd taken him up on his invitation to return whenever she liked.

He inhaled a slow breath. This time he would not scare her. This time he would be polite. Polite and, damn it, suitably humble, since no word had come back to him about yesterday's disastrous encounter.

He'd not had the courage to ask Weatherby about her either. If something had been said, he didn't want to remind the old curmudgeon.

He circled around, thinking to come at her head on. A twig cracked under his boot. He cursed under his breath.

She leaped to her feet and whirled around. Sheets of paper fluttered around her, landing like snowflakes amid the dry leaves.

Large and grey-green, her eyes mirrored shock. Another emotion flickered away before he could guess its import. Strange when he rarely had trouble reading a woman's thoughts. It left him feeling on edge. Out of his element.

He touched his hat. 'Good day, Miss Bracewell.'

An expression of revulsion crossed her face.

It took him aback. Women usually looked at him with favour. Had he upset her so much? And if so, why was she back?

The focus of her horrified gaze remained fixed above his right shoulder. On his dinner, not on him. Not that he wasn't the stuff of nightmares, with his worn jacket and fustian trousers mired with the blood of his catch. He'd gutted them up on the hill, preferring leaving the offal for scavengers rather than bury it near his hut. He put the gun and its grisly pennant on the ground at his feet with an apologetic shrug.

Her breast rose and fell in a deep breath. 'Mr Deveril.'

Recalling his mistakes of the day before, he snatched his cap off his head and lowered his gaze. 'Yes, miss. I am sorry if I disturbed you.' One of her fallen papers had landed near his foot. He retrieved it. His jaw slackened at a glimpse of a drawing of his own likeness, jacketless, shabby, unkempt, disreputable.

Shock held him transfixed.

She leaped forwards and snatched it from his hand. At a crouching run, she scuttled about picking up the rest of the sheets. Each time he reached for one, she plucked it from beneath his hand, allowing only fractured glimpses of squirrels in their natural setting.

All the sheets picked up, she stood with the untidy bundle of papers clutched against her chest as if fearing he might make a grab for them, staring at him as if he had two heads and four eyes. Obviously she found his presence disturbing.

Her wariness gnawed at his gut like a rat feeding on bone. He quelled the urge to deny meaning her harm. She should be afraid out here alone in the woods without a chaperon.

Glancing down for his rifle, he saw scattered charcoal and the upturned wooden box beside the stump. He crouched, righted the box and scooped up the charcoals. He dropped them into the box. A glint caught his eye—a fine gold chain snaking amongst the leaves. He picked it up, dangled it from his fingers.

'It's mine,' she said in her strangled breathy voice.

Without looking at her, he felt heat rise from his neck to the roots of his hair. Did she think he would steal it? He let it fall into the box amongst the dusty broken black sticks.

'I b-broke it,' she said in the same forced rush of words.

He glanced at her.

She tucked the messy pile of paper between two board covers and tied the string. 'I caught it on a branch on my way here.' She offered him a conciliatory smile.

He blinked, startled by the sudden change in her expression. She looked witchy, oddly alluring, almost beautiful in a vulnerable way. He pulled himself together. 'What are you doing here?' He sounded sullen, ungracious, when he'd meant to sound jocular. He half-expected her to take to her heels in terror.

This woman had him all at sea.

But she didn't run, she merely tilted her head to one side as if thinking about what to say.

'L-looking for squirrels.' She tapped her portfolio.

And she'd picked this clearing when hundreds of other places would do. What was she up to? He gestured to the stump. 'Don't let me disturb you.'

'N-no. I was finished. The light is fading. Too many shadows.'

A true artist would care about the quality of the light. And the drawings he'd seen were excellent. Most ladies liked to draw, but her pictures seemed different. The squirrels had life.

Perhaps her artistic bent was what made her seem different. Awkward, with her utterance of short, sharp and direct sentences, yet likeable. A reason not to encourage her to return.

'May I help you mount your horse?' He glanced around for the gelding.

She bit her lip. A faint, rosy hue tinted her pale, high cheekbones. 'I w-walked.'

Robert frowned. Riding in the woods was risky enough, but a young female walking alone in the forest with the sun going down he could not like.

'I'll drop my dinner off inside and walk you back to Wynchwood.'

'P-please, don't trouble. I know the way.'

'It's no trouble, miss. It's my duty to my employer to see you home safe.'

In his past life, he would have insisted on his honour and charmed the girl. His mouth twisted. As far as his new world knew, he had neither honour nor charm.

A protest formed on her lips, but he continued as if he hadn't noticed. 'I have to go up to the house before supper to collect an order from Mrs Doncaster.'

Her glance flicked to the pile of fur. A shudder shook her delicate frame. It reminded him of shudders of pleasure. Heated his blood. Stirred his body.

Unwanted responses.

Furious at himself, he glowered at her. 'Do you not eat meat, Miss Wynchwood?' Damn, that was hardly conciliatory. Hardly servile. He wanted to curse. Instead, he bent, picked up his haul and strode for his front door.

'Y-yes,' she said.

He swung around. 'What?'

'I eat m-m-m—' she closed her eyes, a sweep of long brown lashes on fine cheekbones for a second '—eat meat—' her serious gaze rested on his face '—but I prefer it cooked.' She smiled. A curve of rosy lips and flash of small white teeth.

Devastatingly lovely.

What the deuce? Was he so pathetically lonely that a smile from a slip of a girl brought a ray of light to his dreary day? And she wasn't as young as he'd thought the first time he saw her. She was one of those females who retained an aura of youth, like Caro Lamb. It was something in the way they observed the world with a child-like joy, he'd always thought, as if everything was new and wonderful.

It made them seem terribly young. And vulnerable.

Another reason for her to stay away from a man jaded by life.

He glanced up at the pink-streaked sky between the black branches overhead. 'I'll be but a moment and we'll be on our way.' Shielding her view of the carcasses with his body, he dived inside his hut. He hung the hares from a nail by the hearth and stowed his shotgun under his cot out of sight. Swiftly, he stripped off his boots and soiled clothing, grabbing for his cleanest shirt and trousers. He had the sense that if he lingered a moment too long she'd be off like a startled fawn. Then he'd be forced to follow her home. She might not take kindly to being stalked.

To his relief when he got outside, she was still standing where he left her, staring into the distance as if lost in some distant world, the battered portfolio still clutched to her chest.

He picked up the box of charcoal from the stump. 'Are you ready?'

She jumped.

Damn it. What made her so nervous?

'Yes,' she said.

'After you, miss.'

Then suddenly she turned and walked in front of him. The hem of her brown cloak rustled the dry brown leaves alongside the track. For the niece of a nobleman, her clothes were sadly lacking. Perhaps she chose them to blend with her surroundings when drawing from nature.

She spun around to face him, walking backwards with cheeks pink and eyes bright. 'There was something I wanted to ask you.'

Of course there was. No female would arrive at his door without an ulterior motive. In the past it usually involved hot nights and cool sheets. But not this one. She was far too innocent for such games. He waited for her to speak.

'Do you hunt a great d-d—' Her colour deepened. 'A lot?' she finished.

She stumbled over a root. He reached out to catch her arm. She righted herself, flinching from his touch with a noise in her throat that sounded like a cross between a sob and a laugh. Her eyes weren't laughing. Unless he mistook her reaction, she looked thoroughly mortified.

He resisted the urge to offer comfort.

Damn it. Why did he even care? She was one of his employer's family members. Even walking with her could be misconstrued. But he didn't want her to trip again. He didn't want her hurt.

God help him.

He caught her up, and she turned to walk forwards at his side.

'Do you?' She peered at him from beneath the brim of her plain brown bonnet with the expression of a mischievous elf. His hackles went up. Instincts honed by years of pleasing women. She definitely wanted something. He felt it in his gut. Curiosity rose in his breast. He forced himself to tamp it down. 'It is all according to Mr Weatherby's orders and what Cook requests for his lordship's table. Most of my work relates to keeping down vermin.'

'You hunt foxes?'

'Gentlemen hunt foxes.' He couldn't prevent the bitter edge to his tone. 'I trap them and keep track of their dens so the hunt can have a good day of sport.' There, that last sounded more pragmatic.

'Is there a den nearby?'

They left the woods and followed the river bank, the same path he'd walked earlier. 'There are a couple. One up on Gallows Hill. Another in the five-acre field down yonder.' He pointed toward the village of Swanlea.

Her eyes glistened with excitement. An overwhelming urge to ask why stuck in his throat. He had no right questioning his betters.

'Badgers?'

Great God, this girl was a strange one. 'Stay away from them, miss. They're dangerous and mean. We hunt them with dogs.'

The light went out of her face a moment before she dropped her gaze. He felt as if he'd crushed a delicate plant beneath his boot heel. Good thing, too, if it kept her away from the sett not far from his dwelling.

'I've never seen one,' she murmured.

'They come out only in the evening. Usually after dark.'

Once more he had the sense he had disappointed her, but why the strange urge to make amends? If she disliked him, so much the better. He held his tongue.

The path joined the rutted lane that led to the village in one direction, and over the bridge to the back entrance of Wynchwood Place in the other. The way to the mansion used by such as he. The lower orders.

He scowled at the encroaching thought.

Off in the distance, on a natural rise in the land, the solid shape of the mansion looked over green lawns and formal gardens. A house of plain red brick with a red-tile roof adorned by tall chimneypots. Nothing like the grandeur of the ducal estates, but a pleasant enough English gentleman's country house.

Their footsteps clattered with hollow echoes on the slats of the wooden bridge. At the midpoint she halted and looked over the handrail into the murky depths of the River Wynch. 'When I was young, my cousin, Mr Bracewell, told me a troll lived under this bridge. I was terrified.'

She glanced over her shoulder at him, a tentative smile on her lips. A vision of his sister Lizzie, her eyes full of teasing, her dark curls clustered around her heart-shaped face, flowed into his mind. A river of memories, each one etched in the acid of bitterness. Mother. The children. And Charlie before he got too serious to make good company. The acid burned up from his gut and into his throat. He clenched his jaw against the wave of longing. He bunched his fists to hold it at bay.

Slowly he became aware of her shocked stare, of the fear lurking in the depths of strange turquoise eyes. 'L-listen to me ch-chattering. You want to get h-home to your d-d— meal.'

Fear of him had turned her speech into a nightmare of difficulty. He saw it in her face and in the tremble of her overlarge mouth. He was such a dolt.

Before he could utter a word, she snatched the box from his hand and fled like a rabbit seeking the safety of a burrow.

Hades. The past had a tendency to intrude at the most inopportune moments. He thought he had it under control and then the floodgates of regret for his dissolute past released a torrent emotion. Silently he cursed. Now he'd spend more hours wondering whether she'd report him to her uncle or Weatherby. The girl was a menace. Whatever else he did, he needed to avoid her as if she had a case of the measles.

For all his misgivings, he followed her discreetly, making sure she arrived at the door safely. As any right-thinking man would, he told himself. Especially with so fragile a creature wandering around as if no one cared what she did or where she went.

While she didn't look back, he knew she was aware of his presence from the way she maintained her awkward half-run, half-trot. Her ugly brown skirts caught at her ankles and her bonnet ribbons fluttered. A little brown sparrow with broken wings.

The thought hurt.

Perhaps she now thought him a rabid dog? A good thing, surely. Hopefully she thought him terrifying enough to keep away from his cottage. He ought to be glad instead of wanting to apologise. Again.

At the entrance to the courtyard, she cut across the lawn. He frowned. What the devil was she up to now? Instead of entering through the front door, she was creeping through the shrubbery toward a side door. Well, well, Miss Bracewell was apparently playing truant. The little minx was nothing but trouble.

She slipped inside the house and he continued around the back of the house to the kitchen door, passing through the neat rows of root vegetables and assorted herbs in the kitchen garden. Mrs Doncaster knew her stuff and Robert had been doing his best to pick her brains, with the idea of planting his own garden in the spring.

The scullery door stood open and, removing his cap, Robert entered and made his way down the narrow stone passage into the old-fashioned winter kitchen.

Mrs Doncaster, her face red beneath her mobcap and her black skirts as wide as she was high, looked up from the hearth at the sound of his footfall. A leg of mutton hung over the glowing embers, the juices collecting in a pan beneath and the scent of fresh bread filled the warm air. Robert's stomach growled.

'Young Rob,' she said with a frown. ''Tis too busy I am to be feeding you tonight.'

Robert smiled. 'No, indeed, mistress. Mr Weatherby is sending me to town tomorrow—is there anything you need?'

'Wait a bit and I'll make you up a list.'

Wincing inwardly, he forced himself to ask his question. 'I'm also in dire need of some carrots if you've any to spare, and a few herbs for my stew.'

'Oh, aye. Caught yerself some game, did you?'

She tucked a damp grey strand of hair under her cap. 'Maisie.' Her shriek echoed off the rafters. Robert stifled the urge to cover his ears.

The plump Maisie, a girl of about sixteen with knowing black eyes, emerged from the scullery. 'Yes, mum?' When she spied Robert, her round freckled face beamed. 'Good day to you, Mr Deveril.'

'Fetch Robert some sage and rosemary and put up a basket of carrots and parsnips, there's a good girl,' the cook said.

Maisie brushed against him on the way to the pantry. They both knew what her sideways smile offered, had been offering since the day he arrived. She wasn't his sort. Far too young and far too witless. And the warning from Weatherby that his lordship would insist on his servants marrying if there was a hint of goin's-on, as the old countryman put it, had ensured Robert wouldn't stray. He edged into a corner out of Cook's way.

'Saucy hussy, that one,' Mrs Doncaster said, swiping at her hot brow.

'Do you need more coal?' Robert asked, pointing at the empty scuttle beside the blackened hearth.

'You're a good lad, to be sure,' she said with a nod. 'You thinks about what's needed. You got a good head on your shoulders. I can see why Weatherby thinks so highly of you already. Take a candle.'

Praise from the cook? And Weatherby? His efforts seemed to be paying off. More reason to make sure he didn't put a foot wrong. Hefting the black iron bucket, Robert made his way through a low door and down the stairs. The coal cellar sat on one side of the narrow passage, the wine cellar on the other.

Helping the cook had paid off in spades, or rather in vegetables and the odd loaf of fresh bread, but he wanted far more than that. He needed the respect and trust of his new peers if he was going to get ahead.

He tied a neckerchief over the lower part of his face. Dust rose in choking clouds, settling on his shoulders and in his hair as he shovelled the coal up from the mountain beneath the trapdoor through which the coalman deposited the contents of his sacks. Removing the kerchief, Robert ducked out of the cellar and heaved the scuttle back up the wooden flight.

'Set it by the hearth,' the cook instructed. 'Wash up in the bowl by the door.'

Robert washed his hands and face in the chilly water and dried them off on a grubby towel hung nearby. He'd wash properly at home.

'Drat that girl,' Mrs. Dorset said. 'I need her to turn the spit while I finish this pastry.'

'I'll do it.' Robert made his way around the wooden table and grasped the iron handle. It took some effort to turn. How poor Maisie managed he couldn't imagine.

The aroma of the meat sent moisture flooding in his mouth. God. He hadn't tasted a roast for months.

'Slower, young Rob,' the cook said, her rolling pin flying over the floured pastry.

He grinned and complied. 'I met Miss Bracewell in the garden on my way in,' he said casually, hoping to glean a little more insight into the troublesome lass. 'Is she the only relative to the master?'

The cook's cheerful mouth pursed as if she'd eaten a quince. 'The devil's spawn, that one. You want to stay well clear of her.'

The venom in her voice rendered Robert speechless and...angry. He kept his tone non-committal. 'She seemed like a pleasant enough young lady. Not that she said much more than good day.'

'I likes her,' Maisie said, returning with basket in hand. 'She opened the door when I had me hands full once.'

'Goes to show she's not a proper lady,' the cook said and sent Robert a sharp stare. 'A blot on the good name of Bracewell, she is. Her and her mother. My poor Lord Wynchwood is a saint for taking her in. Mark my words, it'll do him no good.'

'What—?' Robert started to ask.

'Mrs Doncaster.' The butler's stern tones boomed through the kitchen.

Robert jumped guiltily. Old Snively was a tartar and no mistake. All the servants feared the gimlet-eyed old vulture. A smile never touched his lips and his sharp eyes missed not the smallest fault according to the house servants.

Snively's cold gaze rested on Robert's face. 'Gossiping with the outside staff, Mrs Doncaster?'

Robert felt heat scald his cheeks. Arrogant bugger. Who did the butler think he was? Robert gritted his teeth, held his body rigid and kept turning the spit, lowering his gaze from the piercing stare. This man had the power to have him dismissed on a word, and from the gleam in his eye the stiff-rumped bastard wasn't done.

'If you've no work to keep you occupied, Deveril,' Snively said, 'perhaps Mr Weatherby can do without an assistant after all.'

'I'm here to fetch a list for tomorrow, Mr Snively,' Robert said.

'Now see here, Snively,' Mrs Doncaster put in, clearly ruffled, 'if you kept that good-for-nothing footman William at his duty, I wouldn't need Rob's help, would I?

Fetched the coal up, he did. Without it, his lordship would be waiting for his dinner.'

Snively fixed her with a haughty stare. 'Planning, Mrs Doncaster. The key to good organisation. If you had William bring up enough coal for the entire day, you wouldn't need to call him from his other duties.'

'Ho,' Mrs Doncaster said, elbows akimbo. 'Planning, is it? Am I to turn my kitchen into a coal yard?'

It was like watching a boxing match threatening to spill over into the crowd, but Robert had no wish to become embroiled. It was more than his job was worth. It didn't help that the old bugger was right, he had no business coming here this evening.

Across the room, Maisie had her lips folded inside her teeth as if to stop any unruly words escaping. Robert knew just how she felt. The portly, stiff-necked Snively was terrifying. Mrs Doncaster's bravery left him in awe.

'Planning,' Snively repeated and swept out of the kitchen.

'Hmmph,' Cook grumbled. 'Johnny-come-lately. Thinks just because he worked in London, he can lord it over the rest of us who's been here all our lives. Hmmph. His back's up because he heard what we was saying. Always jumps to defend her, he does.'

The butler rose a notch in Robert's estimation. 'I'll be on my way now Maisie's back.'

'Yes. Go.' Mrs Doncaster, still in high dudgeon, waved him away.

Holding out the basket, Maisie lifted a corner of the cloth covering its contents. 'I've put a nice bit of ham in there for your breakfast,' she whispered with a wink, then trundled off to her spit.

A cold chill seemed to clutch his very soul with icy

fingers. They were all at it. Handing him food, putting him under an obligation. One day, by God, he would repay their charity. Somehow he'd find the means.

More debts to pay.

He pulled his cap on and made his way out into the growing dusk. 'Spawn of Satan'? What the hell had Mrs Doncaster meant? And why the hell had he bristled?

Chapter Four

'Bring the light closer, Frederica, for goodness' sake—how can I read in the dark?'

Frederica rose from her chair and moved the candlestick on the tea table two inches closer to her uncle.

Looking up from the most recent missive from Simon, Mortimer peered over his spectacles at her. 'That's better.' He coughed into his ever-ready handkerchief.

Frederica handed him his tea. She hated tea in the drawing room. A senseless torture for someone who had not the slightest chance of making polite conversation under the best of circumstances. Which made her almost easy conversations with Mr Deveril all the stranger.

'You s-said you needed to talk to me about something, Uncle?' She needed to get back her drawings of squirrels. She hadn't yet decided which ones to colour.

'Is everything prepared for Simon's visit?'

Inwardly she groaned. 'Yes, Uncle.' She took a deep slow breath. 'I've asked Snively to have the sheets for the guests' rooms aired and instructed him to hire help from the village for the day of the ball.'

He glanced down at the letter in his hand 'Radthorn is bringing guests, too, I gather. They will stay at the Grange with him. The ball is going to be far grander than usual. Simon has raised a concern.'

Hurry up and get to the point. She tried to look interested.

Uncle Mortimer lifted his glasses and rubbed at his eyes. 'He worries you have nothing appropriate to wear. That you won't be up to snuff. In short, he says you need dresses. Gowns and such. Kickshaws. He also says you need a chaperon, someone to keep an eye on you.'

Oh, no. Frederica's body stiffened bowstring tight. Vibrations ran up and down her spine as if at any moment she would snap in two. A chaperon would interfere with all her plans. 'I d-d-d—' Inhale.

'Do.' Uncle Mortimer shifted in his seat. 'Simon is right, you run around the estate like a veritable hoyden. Look at the way you ran off yesterday.' He shook his head. 'Do you even know how to dance?'

'Simon showed me some country dances.' Sort of. 'Mrs Felton in the village has my m-measurements and can make me up a gown or two, but I d-don't n-need someone watching over me. I'm almost five and twenty.'

Uncle Mortimer scratched at the papery skin on the back of his hand, a dry rasp in the quiet. A deep furrow formed between his brows. 'Simon said there must be waltzing.'

She gulped, panic robbing her of words. All of this sounded as if Simon had every intention of submitting to Mortimer's demands. Because he needed money, no doubt. She felt a constriction in her throat.

Breathe. 'I've n-never attended the T-Twelfth Night ball before—why this time?'

Uncle Mortimer stared at her for a long time. He seemed to be struggling with some inner emotion. 'Dear child. You cannot wed a man like Simon without at least learning some of the niceties. Given your…your impediment, I would have thought you would be eager to oblige. I am going to a great deal of expense and trouble, you know.'

He sounded kind when she'd never heard him sound anything but impatient. He was trying to make her feel guilty. 'I'd be h-happy s-single.'

'We are your family. You are our responsibility. Simon is generously shouldering the burden. You must do your part.'

'Simon must know I'll never be a fitting wife. After all, I'm m-my mother's daughter.'

A knobby hand pounded on the chair arm. Uncle Mortimer's tea slopped in the saucer. 'Enough. You will do as I say.' As if the burst of anger had used up all his energy, he sagged back in his chair and covered his face with one hand.

Frederica took the teacup from her uncle's limp grasp. 'Surely we can d-do without a chaperon.'

'No,' he whispered. 'Lady Radthorn has agreed. It will be done.'

Could this nightmare get any worse? 'Lady Radthorn?' Frederica had seen the old lady in the village. She looked very high in the instep. Not the kind of person who would take kindly to a noblewoman's by-blow sired by no one knew who, but everyone assumed the worst.

'No arguments. Lady Radthorn has arranged for the seamstress to attend you at her house tomorrow. You will need a costume for the ball. Several morning and evening gowns and a riding habit. The bills will be sent to me.'

Frederica felt her eyes widen as the list grew. 'It sounds d-dreadfully expensive.'

Uncle Mortimer's jaw worked for a moment. He swallowed. 'Nothing is too much to ensure that you have the bronze to make you worthy of Simon.' He closed his eyes and gave a weak wave. 'No more discussion. All these years I have paid for your keep, your education, the food in your stomach with never a word of thanks, ungrateful child. You will do as you are told.'

Selfish. Ungrateful. The words squeezed the breath from her chest like a press-yard stone placed on a prisoner's chest to extract a confession. Was someone like her wrong to want more than the promise of a roof over her head?

It all came back to her mother's shame. The Wynchwood Whore. She'd only ever heard it said once as a child, by Mrs Doncaster. Frederica had turned the words over in her mind with a child's morbid curiosity, and later with a degree of hatred, not because of what her mother was, she had realised, but because she'd left Frederica to reap the punishment.

The sins of the father will be visited upon their children. Who knew what her father's sins actually might be? For all she knew, her father could be a highwayman. Or worse, according to the servants' gossip.

Well, this child wasn't going to wait around for the visitation. She had her own plans. And they were about to bear fruit. In the meantime she'd do well not to arouse her uncle's suspicions. 'As you request, Uncle,' she murmured. 'If you d-don't n-need anything else, I w-would like to retire.'

He didn't open his eyes. Frederica didn't think she'd be closing hers for most of the night. She was going to finish her drawings and be up early to catch a fox on his way home. The quicker she got her drawings done, the sooner she could get paid. If she was going to escape this marriage, time was of the essence.

In the hour before dawn, normally quiet clocks marked time like drums. The ancient timbers on the stairs squawked a protest beneath Frederica's feet. She halted, listening. No one stirred. It only sounded loud because the rest of the house was so quiet.

Reaching the side door, she slid back the bolt and winced at the ear-splitting shriek of metal against metal. Eyes closed, ears straining, she waited. No cry of alarm. She let her breath go, pulled up her hood and slipped out into the crisp morning air.

To the east, a faint grey tinge on the horizon hinted at morning. Ankle deep in swirling mist, she stole along the verge at the edge of the drive. Her portfolio under her arm and her box of pencils clutched in her hand, she breathed in the damp scent of the country, grass, fallen leaves, smoke from banked fires. Somewhere in the distance a cockerel crowed.

Thank goodness there was no snow to reveal her excursion.

Once clear of Wynchwood's windows, she strode along the lane, her steps long and free. Gallows Hill rose up stark against the skyline. Its crown of four pines and the blasted oak, a twisted blackened wreck, could be seen for miles, she'd been told. She left the lane and cut across the meadow at the bottom of the hill, then followed a well-worn sheep track up the steep hillside.

By the time she reached the top her breath rasped in

her throat, her calves ached and the sky had lightened to the colour of pewter. Across the valley, the mist levelled the landscape into a grey ocean bristling with the spars of sunken trees.

She stopped to catch her breath and looked around. Bare rocks littered the plateau as if tossed there by some long-ago giant. Among the blanket of brown pine needles she found what she sought: a narrow tunnel dug in soft earth partially hidden by a fallen tree limb. Where should she sit for the best view?

She had read about the habits of the foxes in one of Uncle Mortimer's books on hunting. Her best chance of seeing one was at daybreak near the den. Hopefully she wasn't too late.

A spot off the animal's beaten track seemed the best idea for watching. A broom bush, one of the few patches of green at this time of year, offered what looked like the best cover. From there, the light wind would carry her scent away from the den.

She pushed into the greenery and sank down cross-legged. Carefully, she drew out a sheet of parchment and one of her precious lead pencils. Pencils were expensive and she eked them out the way a starving man rationed crusts of bread, but knowing this might be her only chance to observe the creature from life, she'd chosen it over charcoal, which tended to smudge.

As the minutes passed, she settled into perfect stillness, gradually absorbing the sounds of the awakening morning, cows lowing for the milkmaid on a nearby farm, the call of rooks above Bluebell Woods.

Someone whistling and stomping up the hill.

Oh, no! She looked over her shoulder…at Mr Deveril striding over the brow of the hill, a gun on his shoulder, traps dangling from one hand. He was making straight for the fox's den with long, lithe strides. Blast. He'd scare off the fox. She put down her paper and rose to her feet, gesturing to him to leave.

He stopped, stock still, and stared.

Go away, she mouthed.

He dropped the traps and started to run. Towards her. The idiot.

She shooed him back with her arms.

He ran faster, his boots scattering pine needles.

She felt like screaming. He'd ruined everything. Any self-respecting fox would be long gone by now and no doubt Mr Deveril would have him shot long before her next opportunity to come up here. Drat. She would need to find another den and right when she didn't need a delay.

She bent to pack up her stuff.

'Are you all right?' he asked, stopping short of the shrubbery. His massive shoulders in a brown fustian jacket blocked her view of the sky as his chest rose and fell from exertion. Lovely, beautiful man. She had the sudden desire to snatch up her pencil and draw. Him.

A dangerous notion. 'I would have been perfectly all right had you stayed away,' she muttered, pushing through the scratchy branches.

He frowned. 'You waved me over. I thought you must have had an accident. Fallen from your horse.'

'I walked.' As if it mattered how she got here.

'All the way up here?'

'An early morning stroll. For my health.'

His expression of disbelief said it all and his gaze dropped to the portfolio beneath her arm. 'You came up here to draw the fox?' He sounded disapproving, dismissive, just like everyone else.

'Not possible since you decided to gallop over here like a runaway carthorse.'

A muscle in his jaw flickered. His lips twitched. Amber danced in his eyes. Was he laughing? It certainly looked like it. She found herself wanting to smile, despite her disappointment.

'You looked as if you were trying to get my attention. I didn't realise you were here on a drawing expedition.'

'What else would I be doing up here? I had hoped to draw it, b-before you k-killed it.' She marched past him and headed downhill.

'Wait,' he commanded, deep and resonant.

How dare he order her about? She forged on.

'Miss Bracewell,' he called out. 'There is a better place from which to watch.'

She twisted to look back at him.

He stared at her silently, challenging her to return, looking like a dark angel with the grey sky behind and the dark pines above. A tempting dark angel. Her heart speeded up. She hunched deeper into her cloak. 'W-Where?' Now she sounded like a sulky child. What was it about this man that made her behave so badly? Apart from his physical beauty, that was, which would affect any warm-blooded woman.

'You would have missed him from there.'

'Oh?'

'I can show you, if you wish?'

'You said him? Is it a male?'

He smiled and her knees almost gave out as he transformed into a Greek god with a simple curve of his mouth. 'The dog fox. Aye. This tunnel is his escape route. The front door is yonder.' He nodded toward the blasted oak. 'I've seen him go in three times this week.'

The country accent missing from his earlier speech returned. She hesitated, her mind clamouring a warning even as her eyes worshipped the fierce beauty of his carved features. She longed to draw the character and darkness in his face and the athletic grace of his body. Not a clumsy attempt from memory, but from the flesh. Heat crawled up her face.

His smile disappeared. 'As you wish, miss,' he said, clearly taking her silence as refusal.

'I will.'

A brow winged up and he tilted his head. 'You mean, yes?'

She nodded, her head bobbing as if her neck had turned into a spring.

'This way, then, miss, if you please.'

She followed him to a knobby protrusion of rocks beside the blackened tree.

'There,' he murmured, pointing at the ground a few feet away.

Nothing. Then the darker black of a hole took shape among the shadows. 'I see it.' She tore off the portfolio's ribbon.

'Sit here,' he said, a large, warm hand catching her elbow, steering her to another pile of rocks. Sparks seemed to shoot up her arm, as if he'd touched a lightning bolt and transmitted its energy to her through his fingers.

Her mouth dried. A man of his ilk shouldn't be touching her at all.

Was this how her mother had felt with the lower orders? Entranced. Breathless. Hot all over. She could quite see why one might want to experience it again. And more.

Somehow she sank down in the place he suggested and saw with amazement that the rock on which she perched formed a comfortable backrest and screened her from the opening to the fox's den, except for a narrow slit between two rocks.

'Oh,' she said. 'This is perfect.'

'I aim to please,' he replied with a flash of a grin.

The breath in her chest left her mouth in a besotted rush. The man should not smile. It was fatal. And, from the broadening smile, he knew it.

He sank to his haunches beside her, his back against the rock on which she sat, his shoulder touching her skirts. He sat and stretched out legs which seemed to go on for ever and terminated in sturdy brown boots covered in mud. The rough fabric of his trousers clung to his thighs in a most revealing manner, suggestive of hard muscle and power.

In the confined space between the boulders, his shoulders hemmed her in. Trapped her. His steady, even breathing filled her ears, warmth radiated from him and the smell of bay drifted on the still air, instilling a strong desire to inhale his manly scent. From the corner of her eye she admired the black curl of hair on the bronzed skin of his strong column of a neck and the way it skimmed the collar of his coarse linen shirt. Once more her pulse galloped out of control.

Oh, yes, he would make an excellent subject. She had never drawn a man from life, but this one had an air of natural nobility for all his lowly station. Intangible to the eye, it radiated off him like an aura. No other man of her acquaintance had such elegant male beauty. Particularly not Simon.

But would she have the skill to do him justice? It would mean spending hours in his company—his naked company—if she was to work in the classical style she longed to emulate. Any decent art school in Italy would want to see more than drawings of birds and wildlife to accept her as a serious artist. If her portfolio presented a study of him, and if it was any good…

Would he even be willing? Perhaps if she offered to pay him? She didn't have much money, but she had some.

He glanced at her with a raised brow.

Heat suffused her face. What would he think of her, if she asked him to pose in the nude?

'Tired of waiting?' he asked.

She shook her head. 'Do you know why they call this Gallows Hill?' she choked out over the pounding of her heart.

'No.'

'They hung the last highwayman in the district here. Mad Jack Kilgrew. Apparently, he took to the roads when he wasn't allowed to marry the girl he loved.' She knew she was gabbling, but she couldn't stop. And since she didn't have the nerve to broach what was on her mind, she just kept going. 'They say all the local ladies were in love with him because he was so handsome and only ever stole kisses—the reason the menfolk hanged him out of hand.'

'Romantic claptrap,' he muttered.

She laughed. 'No. It is true. He stopped Mrs D-Dempster, the baker's wife, when she was a girl.'

'A man can't live on kisses,' he said.

'Well, he did. Along with the money he stole from their husbands.' She shivered. 'They say you can hear the rattle of the g-gibbet on the anniversary of his death.'

He grinned. 'You've been reading too much Mrs Radcliffe.'

The fatal grin again. She could not hold back an answering smile. For a long moment they said nothing. His gaze dropped to her lips and stayed there.

A heart-quickening tension gripped every nerve in her body. The small space between them seemed to shrink and she was certain his breath brushed her cheek. A shiver slid across her shoulders, something sweetly painful tugged at her heart. A longing to be held.

She'd felt nothing like it since childhood. She swallowed.

He jerked back as if he, too, resisted the strange pull. 'The fox will be along any moment now, if he's coming.' His voice sounded harsh, his breathing rushed, but his expression seemed quite blank as he stared ahead as if completely oblivious to what had just happened between them.

Nothing had happened.

She must have imagined the sense of connection. How could she feel such a thing for a man she'd met only a few times? But he was unlike anyone she had ever met. Handsome and arrogant, and occasionally humble. Well educated, too. He even knew about Mrs Radcliffe. Fascinating. And obviously very dangerous to her senses.

He touched her arm. 'Look,' he said in a soft whisper.

Pencil poised, she stared at the sleek red creature trotting into her field of vision. His bush hung straight to the ground, his shiny black nose tested the air and his ears pricked and twitched in every direction.

With held breath, she sketched his shape. Focused, imprinted the colours on her mind, even as her hand caught his outline, the shadow of muscle, lean flanks, the curve of his head. Attitude, intense and watchful— not fearful, though. Eyes bright, searching, body sleek, softened by reddish fur.

Apparently satisfied, the fox trotted the last few feet and, after one glance around his domain, disappeared into his lair.

Frederica didn't stop drawing. The image firmly in her mind's eye, she captured the narrow hips and deep chest, the tufted ears and pointy muzzle, the white flashes on chest and paws.

Finally, she stopped and rolled her shoulders.

'Did you see him for long enough?' he murmured.

She jumped. She'd forgotten his presence. 'Yes.'

'You draw with your left hand.'

The devil's spawn. She waited for him to cross his fingers to ward off evil spirits the way some of the other servants did. She should have used her right hand as she'd been taught by hours of rapped knuckles. But then the picture would be stilted. Useless. Tears welled unbidden to her eyes. How could she have let him see her shame? She never let anyone watch her draw. She transferred the pencil to her other hand. 'I-I—'

His hand, large and warm, strong and brown from hours outdoors, covered hers. 'My older brother is left-handed.'

She glanced up at his face and found his expression frighteningly bleak. 'Y-you h-have a b-b—' she swallowed and took a deep breath '—brother?'

'Yes. I have two brothers and three sisters.'

'How lucky you are. Do they live near?'

She winced at his short, hard laugh. 'I don't know about lucky. They live in London most of the time.' He shrugged. 'What about you? Do you have any siblings?'

How had she allowed the conversation to get on to the topic of families? Had he really not heard the gossip about her mother, or was he looking for more salacious details? 'I never knew my parents.'

The small breath of wind lifted a strand of dark hair at his crown in the most appealing way. 'An orphan, then. I'm sorry,' he said softly.

'You forgot your Somerset accent again, Mr Deveril.'

He pushed to his feet, unfolding his long lean body and stretched his back. 'So I did, Miss Bracewell. So I did.'

'Why pretend?'

'Weatherby wouldn't have hired a man educated above his station.'

The words rang true, but she sensed they hid more than they told. Clearly he was not about to reveal any secrets to her. With a feeling of disappointment, of an opportunity missed, she packed up her drawing materials. It really was time to go or she would be late for breakfast.

She held up her portfolio. 'Th-thank you for this. I presume it was my last opportunity to see him at all?'

His gaze followed hers to the tools of his trade, the fierce metal traps and the gun. He inclined his head. 'I expect so.'

She nodded. 'Good day, Mr Deveril.' Great way to

convince him to let him sit for her as a model: accuse him of murder.

She'd have to do better than that if she wanted to escape her fate with Simon. And she'd have to have a little more courage.

Chapter Five

The gamekeeper's office beside the stables smelled of old fur, manure and oil. A small lantern on a rickety table provided enough light for the task of cleaning his lordship's shotguns before daylight would send Weatherby and Robert out into the fields.

'Did ye catch the fox on Gallows Hill yesterday, young Rob?' the gamekeeper asked in his creaking voice.

Until yesterday, Robert had never balked at culling Reynard's population. Cunning and sly, their raiding of henhouses and other fowl made them unpopular vermin. Caught in its natural setting by an artist who seemed almost as wild as the creatures she brought alive on paper, the dog fox had looked magnificent.

The far-seeing hazel eyes on the other side of the table required an honest answer.

'No, sir. I don't think that'un's raiding Lord Wynchwood's chickens, after all. The only bones I saw were voles and rabbits.'

'Hmmph.' Weatherby stared down the barrel of the shotgun, then picked up his ramrod. 'Still, it's a fox.'

'The most likely culprit lives by the river,' Robert continued. 'I've set traps.'

'Make no mistake, Lord Wynchwood wants to see a brush, lad. It's results what counts with our master.'

And it was the creatures who counted with the young lady of the house. The thought of her knowing he'd killed the creature she'd drawn so lovingly made him feel sick. He was a soft-hearted fool. She'd got her drawing, made a damned fine job of it, too. She didn't need the animal as well. Yet the sadness in her eyes had caused him to forget his duty to his employer. He'd risked his position for gratitude in a pair of ocean-coloured eyes. He must have lost his mind.

'He'll have his brush,' Robert muttered. 'I'll check the traps later.' Robert placed the gleaming weapon in the rack on the wall. 'Do you have any instructions for today?'

'Hares, if you can get 'em, and trout, for his lordship's table.'

Robert nodded. 'By the way, I noticed a break in the hedge down by the river—might be the way our poacher is getting in. Shall I have it fixed?'

'I don't know how I managed before you came along,' Weatherby said.

Robert nodded his thanks and picked up his far-inferior shotgun to the one he'd cleaned for his lordship. 'Is there anything you'd like for your pot, Mr Weatherby?'

'Not today, lad. The missus exchanged a brace of pheasant for a nice bit of pork. I reckon it will do us for a couple of days.'

Roasted pork. Robert could almost taste it.

'What you need, lad, is a wife.' Weatherby groaned to his feet and shouldered his own gun. 'You'd get a proper dinner.'

Robert couldn't imagine anything worse. What woman would want to share this hard life of his? Not the kind of woman he'd want. But celibacy didn't appeal much either. Perhaps he'd snuggle up to the barmaid at the Bull and Mouth this evening. She seemed like a cheerful sort, and willing, from the gleam in her eye.

Weatherby gave him a dig with his elbow on the way to the door. 'How about our Maisie? She's taken quite a shine to ye.'

He repressed a shudder. As a kitchen wench, Maisie was a fine lass, but not one to whom he could bear to be shackled.

'I'm not looking for a wife until I'm better set up. I'd best be off, sir, if I'm to get all of this done before dark and catch his lordship's fox.'

Weatherby grunted. 'Right-ho. Talking of getting established, I heard of a position for a head gamekeeper opening up in Norfolk. Small place, mostly water birds. Might be a good start. I'd miss you here, but you've a talent for the work.'

Hard work did pay off. For the first time in his life Robert felt truly appreciated. He couldn't stop the grin spreading over his face. 'Thank you, Mr Weatherby. I'd appreciate your recommendation.'

'Ah. Time to thank me, if you get the job. We'll see, lad. We'll see.' He stomped out of the door. For Robert, hard on his heels, the chill winter day suddenly seemed a great deal brighter.

Out in the courtyard, he toyed with the idea of stopping by the kitchen and asking Maisie to deliver the book he'd dug out of his meagre store to Miss Bracewell.

Charlie had purchased it for him when he'd expressed an interest in helping with the ducal estates. It hadn't taken Father long to veto the idea. The estates were not his concern.

For some reason he'd kept the book.

Miss Bracewell would find it helpful in locating the animals she liked to draw—assuming she'd accept a gift from someone like him. The thought cut off his breath. Servants, particularly Maisie, loved gossip. He'd be giving them grist for their mills if he did something so stupid. He patted his pocket. He'd better keep it for when he could give it to her privately.

If the young lady stayed true to her habits, he'd see her somewhere on the Wynchwood estate in the next few days.

Later that evening, Robert strode back from the Bull and Mouth with a foul wind driving needle-sharp rain up under his hat into his face. Trickles of water ran down inside his collar. Not that he cared much. The glasses of heavy wet he'd sunk with a group of jolly companions prevented the cold from penetrating too deep. Hardworking men they were, who enjoyed a tall tale. And he'd told a few of his own to uproarious laughter. Especially those about some of his adventures with the ladies. Embellished a bit. And no names mentioned.

He'd enjoyed himself.

He frowned, not quite sure why he was heading home in the rain soaked through to the skin instead of being tucked up cosily in a warm bed with the saucy barmaid. Cheery though she was, he just hadn't fancied her. Too many images of Miss Bracewell swimming around in his head. Lascivious images brought on by too much beer.

He lifted his head to get his bearings. Rain ran down his face, but he was so wet already it didn't make a scrap of difference.

A little unsteadily, he plunged forwards. 'Steady, Robin, or you'll end on your backside.' He got back into his stride, sure he was going in the right direction.

The evening had reminded him of the first time he and Charlie had ventured to the tavern near one of the ducal estates. They'd got rollicking, barely able to hold each other up on the way home, singing and laughing fit to burst.

In those days, he and Charlie had been inseparable. He missed that closeness. He missed his family. He even missed Father. They'd be at Meadowbrook now for the Christmas season.

Oh, no. No thinking about that, Robin. Not tonight.

Keep it sweet and light. That was the trick. What *was* the song they learned from the barmaid? How had it gone?

He stopped. Thinking. No. Couldn't remember.

He started walking again, the mud sucking at his boots as he staggered forwards. A tree stepped out in front of him. He bowed. 'Beg your pardon.'

Careful, Robert. You aren't that bosky. Just a little warm.

He picked up his pace. Became aware of a tune hummed under his breath. That was it. He raised his voice.

Last night young Nancy laid sleeping,
And into her bedroom young Johnny went a-creeping,
With his long fol-the-riddle-i-do right down to his knee.

'Bloody rude.' He chuckled.

He knew one bedroom he'd like to creep into in the middle of the night with his fol-the-riddle-i-do, and it wasn't the barmaid's at the Bull.

And it wasn't going to happen.

A shame, though. He didn't know how he'd kept his hands off her up on the hill yesterday. A bit of a surprise, since he'd never been attracted to innocents. She was the kind of female men married, whereas he preferred high flyers or a merry widow. The lass was good at her drawings, though. Odd sort of occupation for a gently bred girl. It would all come to an end when she found herself married and raising a passel of children.

A husband with the right to caress her slender body, to palm her small breasts, to stroke those boyishly slim hips.

Desire jolted through him, hardening his body, quickening his blood.

What the hell was her family thinking, allowing her to roam the estate without an escort? A prime target for men like him. Or, worse yet, men without a shred of honour. They were out there. She would be an easy target.

What the hell. It wasn't his business what the wench did. He had his work and his prospects to worry about and that was enough for any man. He picked up the next verse.

He said: Lonely Nancy, may I come to bed you,
She smiled and replied, John you'll undo me,
With your long fol-the-riddle-i-do right down to
your knee.

That wasn't going to happen. He was likely going to be

spending a great many nights alone. He shivered at a sudden chill running down his spine.

He stopped dead, his mouth open at the sight of a shadow huddled against his front door.

The shadow rose like a wraith. 'Mr Deveril?'

'Miss Bracewell?' Well, how about that. He just had to think about her and she appeared—or was it a beer-induced vision?

He shook his head to clear his sight.

She lifted a hand. 'I need your help.'

He knew the kind of help he wanted to provide and it involved helping her between his sheets. He wrestled his evil thought to the ground and his body under control. 'At this time of night? Are you mad?'

Her eyes looked huge in the light of the lantern. 'I'm sorry. I'll go.'

'Good Lord, how long have you been waiting?'

'I d-didn't expect you to be out.'

If he had one scrap of sense, a smidgeon of honour, he would turn her around and send her straight home. And let her freeze to the bone? A few minutes while she warmed up wouldn't hurt. He might a libertine, but he wasn't a debaucher of innocents, no matter how badly they behaved.

'Come inside before you catch your death of cold.' He grabbed her elbow. Beneath his fingers, he felt a shudder rack her fragile body. He cursed under his breath and urged her through the door. It took only moments to coax the banked fire into a crackling blaze with a fresh log. A sudden gust down the chimney blew smoke into his face. He coughed.

She laughed, a low smoky chuckle, and his body tightened at the seductive sound.

He shook his head. 'Did no one ever tell you it's not

appropriate to visit a man in his house alone, late at night?' He tossed another log on the fire and poked at the embers. 'Why are you here?'

No answer. The door latch clicked. He leaped forwards and caught the door before she opened it enough to slip out. A blade of cold air cut through the room.

Rigid, she stared at the rough wood inches from her nose. 'I apologise for m-my intrusion. R-release the door.'

The raw hurt in her voice tore at his defences. He enfolded her fine-boned fingers in his. Ice cold. 'Come back to the fire. I'm sorry if I sounded harsh—my concern is for your reputation.'

She snatched her hand out of his.

'Is it not mine to r-r—' she took a ragged breath '—risk?' Despite the defiance in her gaze, she let him lead her back to the glow of the fire.

He shrugged. 'Then think about my position.'

Her shoulders slumped. She raised her lashes, eyes dark with regret and something else he couldn't make out. He could not read this woman. It was an odd feeling when most of them had been an open book.

Her soft mouth trembled. 'I am s-sorry. You are right. I should not have troubled you.'

Right now, looking into those fathomless eyes through the muzz of alcohol with heat from the fire warming his body, he didn't care about his job or her reputation. He desperately wanted to chase away the shadows in her face and see her smile.

'Apology accepted. Sit closer to the fire.' With hands that shook only slightly, he undid the strings of her oilskin cloak and tossed it aside. Beneath it she was as dry as a bone.

The grateful curve of her lips tempted him more than

he dared admit. He cupped her face in his hands, small
and chill and buttery soft to his work-roughened skin.
The muscles in her jaw flickered against his palms. All
he had to do was bend his head and claim those lushly
formed lips.

A brush of his mouth against hers, a taste of heaven,
one little sip.

Trust shone from her eyes.

The dregs of his conscience pierced his beer-soaked
mind. Inwardly he groaned and dropped his hands to
her shoulders and nudged her away.

Even the glow from the fire could not hide her blush.
So pretty. So innocently knowing. So arousing.

He forced himself to turn away. He stripped off his
coat and hung it behind the door.

'You are soaked through,' she said, sounding surprised. 'Did you not wear your oilskins?'

'It wasn't raining when I left.' He wasn't going to tell
her this coat was all he had. He retrieved a towel from
the dresser and rubbed at his hair.

She was frowning. 'You really ought to get out of
those wet clothes. You could catch an ague.'

He'd have been out of his clothes and under his
covers the moment he walked in the door if she'd not
been standing on his doorstep. He'd like to be under his
covers with her.

'Why did you come here, Miss Bracewell? You said
you wanted to ask me something.'

'I did. But I think perhaps I was mistaken.'

Women. Now he'd have to charm it out of her.

A shiver ran down his spine. Despite the fire, the
cold was creeping into his bones. She was right. He
did need to get out of these clothes. He couldn't afford
to get sick. And even if he was going to take her home

immediately, he should at least start out dry. 'Turn your back.'

Her little gasp reminded him that it was not his place to issue orders.

'Please,' he said. 'I am going to change and, short of going outside, there is nowhere to do it but here.'

'Oh,' she said. 'Come closer to the fire.' She moved away from the hearth and faced the corner near the dresser. She looked like a child being punished for some naughtiness.

He couldn't help smiling. She was naughty coming out here. He ought to smack her sweet little bottom. Damn. He did not need thoughts like that right now.

His glance fell on the brown-paper-wrapped parcel on the dresser top. He'd set it there before he went out.

He turned his back and set to work on the buttons of his vest with numbed fingers. 'That package is for you.'

'For me?' She sounded astonished. And pleased. Almost as if she'd never before received a gift. What did she think was in there, a diamond necklace?

He scowled. His days of giving gifts of jewellery were long past. 'Open it.'

Another shiver hit him. The effects of the ale were wearing off rapidly. He edged closer to the fire, stripped off the waistcoat, stripped off his neckerchief and shirt.

The sound of paper tearing was followed by a gasp. 'Oh. It's a book.' She sounded just as pleased as if it was diamonds.

'I thought you might find it useful. It has information about foxes and badgers. Their habits and habitats.'

'Won't you need the book? For your work?'

'Mr Weatherby is teaching me all I need to know.'

A feeling invaded his chest. A feeling he had not felt in a very long time. Happiness. Because she was pleased. And something more. Something he wouldn't acknowledge, not with this young woman who didn't have a subtle bone in her body. She was just too vulnerable for a man like him.

Damn. Between her and the beer he was so confused he didn't know what he was thinking. Then don't think. Get changed and get her home.

He shed his boots and stockings and peeled his trousers off. He scrubbed at his damp skin, focusing on nothing but getting dry.

Frederica listened to the sounds behind her. A man undressing. The rustle of cloth. The thump of boots. The sound of a towel plied vigorously. The urge to watch battled with modesty. Her mouth dried. Her heart fluttered in her chest. Warmth flooded her skin.

Just one little peek.

He'd asked her to turn her back, to respect his privacy. She wasn't going to betray his trust. But she did want to draw him and had promised herself she would pluck up the courage to ask.

She drew in a quick breath. 'Will you sit for me?'

'What?' His voice was deep and very dark and laced with danger.

She started to turn.

'Hold!' The word was harsh.

She heard him move across the room. Away from her. Away from the fire.

She huffed out a breath. 'I've always wanted to draw a person. In the flesh. I came to ask you if you would sit as a model.'

She heard a swoosh of fabric and turned to find him wrapped neck to toe in the quilt from the cot.

Disappointment washed through her. How wicked she was, to be longing to ogle a naked male.

It wasn't just about drawing. It was him. The desire to look at him made all the more tantalising because of the glimpses she'd already seen.

No wonder he wore a disgusted expression. He must think her completely wanton.

'Do you have any idea what people would say if they found you drawing me naked?' he asked.

Well, that wasn't a no, was it? 'I-I don't care what they say. I want to be an artist. One day I want to go to Italy. Take lessons from a master. Right now, I am using what I have to hand.'

'Using?'

Now he sounded angry.

She waved an impatient hand. 'Not you. I meant squirrels and foxes.' She hesitated. If she told him and he betrayed her, it would ruin all her plans. Like everyone else, he wasn't taking her art seriously. So galling. Why couldn't anyone respect what she wanted to do? She inhaled a shaky breath. 'I am being paid. For local animals. For a book about British fauna.'

He raised a quizzical brow and sat down on the bed. 'Are you now?'

Was he laughing at her? His face was perfectly serious, but there was that slight curl to his mouth. If she could see his eyes, she would know, but they were in shadow. She moved closer, clasping her hands. 'I know it sounds strange. I know women artists aren't thought well of here, but on the Continent there are several who are famous. I just want to know if I have talent. Drawing the human body from life is the greatest test. You have a beautiful body. You make a perfect male subject. I am willing to pay for your services.'

He stiffened. His brows lowered. His fists bunched the quilt.

He was going to refuse. Somehow he'd been insulted by her admiration. 'I cannot pay much,' she said quickly. 'Say a shilling an hour.' She was gabbling. She couldn't seem to stop. 'It would be enough buy an oilskin,' she added with a pointed glance at his sodden coat on the nail in the back of the door.

His expression as he gazed at her was unfathomable. 'You are a strange young woman.'

Did he see that as a good thing or as something bad? Somewhat encouraged, she let go the breath she'd been eking out in little gasps as she spoke. 'Will you? Please?'

He looked at her for a long moment. 'Does it mean so much to you that you'd risk your reputation?'

'Yes,' she said, nodding her head hard. 'Yes, it does.' And besides, she had no reputation worth worrying about. She was surprised he didn't know.

'When?' he asked.

A shudder gripped her chest. Her throat tightened. This would decide her fate. 'Now. Tonight.'

'Now?'

'You are already undressed.'

At that he laughed. A laugh from deep in his chest. It rolled over her like a summer's day breeze, promising good things to come. She grinned back.

His laughter slowly subsided, though his smile remained. 'A bird in the hand, is it, Miss Bracewell?'

'Frederica,' she said. 'Please, call me Frederica.'

'Frederica,' he murmured. 'An unusual name for an unusual girl. I'm all yours.'

Her wicked insides did a pleasurable little dance of excitement.

He meant for drawing, she pointed out crossly.

Chapter Six

~~~~~~~~~~~~~~~~~~~~~~~~~~~

She strode around the room, narrowing her eyes. She wanted to capture him as she saw him, glorious, beautiful, dangerous. A brooding Greek god.

'Move the cot closer to the fire, please,' she said.

He flung the end of the quilt over his shoulder, making him look rather like a Roman senator, and dragged the cot across the room. 'There?'

'More at an angle, so the light falls across its length.'

He shifted one end into the room.

'Yes. That's good.' She moved the table with the lantern closer. She frowned at the way the light fell and the shadows it created. 'The light isn't high enough.'

'Here.' Stretching to his full height, the curves of his biceps carved deeper by shadows, he hung the lantern from a nail on the beam above his head.

She swallowed and found her mouth dry. Anticipation. Anxiety. 'Thank you.' Heat rushed to her face. 'Now take the qu-quilt off and stretch out.'

He shrugged. 'Your wish is my command.' He planted his feet wide. The fabric fell to the ground. It was a bit like watching the unveiling of a masterpiece, only better, because he was warm flesh and blood.

Nothing she'd seen in pictures or sculptures had prepared her for such a sight as this, though. Firelight played across the curves of his muscled shoulders and arms. Shadows and light sculpted his broad chest in a way an artist would weep to emulate. His physique was a perfect triangle, far better than da Vinci's *Vitruvian Man* with wide shoulders tapering to narrow hips. Muscle rippled across his stomach with its line of dark hair drawing her eye to the nest of dark curls between his thighs and his magnificent male member, darker in colour than she'd expected, and larger.

He looked lovely.

Desire pooled in her loins. Breathless and hot, she glanced up at his face.

A sinew flickered in his tight jaw. 'Where do you want me?'

Clearly he'd seen her ogling as if she'd never seen a man before. She hadn't. Not in the flesh. Not alive and vital. She opened her mouth to apologise.

No. She was an artist, she needed to inspect her model. But she had better start behaving like an artist and get down to work, or he might change his mind.

She drew in a deep shaky breath. 'Reclining, I think. Raised on your elbow, one knee up.'

He moved to straighten the covers.

'No. Leave them tumbled. They will make a nice contrast to your clean lines.'

He raised a brow, but stretched out and posed as she had requested, one hand covering his private parts. Her vision did not include modesty. This male was meant for pride and arrogance. 'The other hand draped over your knee, please.'

He complied and glanced along his length. 'I'm not going to find myself in a caricature in Ackerman's shop window, am I?'

'Ackerman's?'

'In the Strand in London. They sell salacious prints as well as views of London.'

'You sound familiar with them.'

He stared at her; his eyes became unreadable, his expression blank. Not the expression she wanted on his face. 'I have heard of them.'

'Well, I am not drawing anything salacious, nor do I plan to sell this work. I simply want it for my portfolio.' And perhaps to treasure as a memory once she left.

The picture he presented was good, but not quite right. Too formal, too tense. Ignoring the pleasurable little clenches of her body when her fingers encountered warm skin and sinew, she adjusted his arm so his wrist rested on his knee and his hand fell relaxed. She pushed and pulled at his supporting arm, until he looked like a Roman at a feast. She raised his chin a fraction so the lantern fell full on the planes of his face and threw shadows on his neck. She stepped back. And lost her breath.

Oh, God. He was lovely.

'If you keep staring at me like that,' he said with a half-smile, 'you are going to have quite a different effect on some of my parts.'

Her face flamed. 'I'm not looking at you like anything. I'm simply posing you to get the best of the light. But keep that smile.'

'Can I ask you to hurry?' he said. 'We do not have all night.'

Brought back to reality in a flood of anxiety in case he changed his mind, she picked up her papers and pencils from the table and set to work. Her stomach clenched. What if she couldn't? What if her lines and curves showed nothing but the outer shell of the man?

Her wrist seized in a knot and her fingers trembled. She forced herself to begin with his head. Slowly the flow of lines across the paper settled her heartbeat and her fluttering stomach as she focused on form and shape and play of light and shadow across skin and bone and muscle.

'Where did you learn to draw?' he asked.

'From the books in my uncle's library. When he wasn't looking.'

He raised a brow at that. He probably thought her wicked. Mentally, she shrugged. He was probably right. With a mother like hers it wouldn't come as a surprise to anyone. And her father might have been a whole lot worse if the gossip she'd heard came anywhere close to the truth.

Or perhaps he was the one who'd bequeathed her a love of art? Hardly likely, given the low company her mother kept.

She focused on her flying fingers. 'Did you always want to be a gamekeeper?'

He spoke slowly as if picking his words. His expression reverted to blank and his accent to west country. 'I grew up on the estate of a great nobleman. I liked the work.'

He did not say which nobleman, clearly preferring to keep his origins a secret when most would be only too eager to speak of their high connections. Was that it? Was he, like her, the unwanted bastard of some noble house? The question was poised on the tip of her tongue, but something held it back. His guarded air. His frown. Already his attitude had changed from relaxed to tense.

Another skill needed by a portrait painter. The ability to set a subject at ease. *Find a less sensitive topic.* She jerked her chin towards the table, to the book he had given her. 'Where does your brother live?'

'I have no idea.' His face grew hard, his eyes shuttered. Were there no safe topics for this man?

She let some time elapse, worked on his shoulders, the line of his neck, before trying again. 'Where did you g-go this evening.'

'To the Bull.' The muscles in his face relaxed.

'Oh. What kind of drink do you prefer?'

'Brandy.' His answer came swiftly, then he shot her a sharp look. 'And ale.'

While he answered her questions, she sketched his hand in rough on a separate piece of paper. It would take too long to complete now. Fingers were hard. She moved on to his feet. Large feet at the end of long well-formed legs. 'Do you dance?'

'I do, when required.'

'What kind of dances?'

'Country dances, cotillions, waltzes.'

'Waltzes? You know how to waltz?' She stopped drawing and looked at him.

His mouth thinned as if he thought he had said too much. He took a breath and deliberately eased his jaw. 'Do you like to dance?'

She wrinkled her nose. 'I'm not sure.'

'All ladies love dancing,' he scoffed as if challenging her indecision. 'For me it was always a means to an end.' His expression darkened to that of a brooding angel staring into the depths of hell. An expression that brooked no further questions. And fired her artist's imagination.

Perfect. While he lost himself in his own thoughts her pencil flew.

A long time later she became aware of his gaze on her face.

'Almost done,' she said, looking down at her sketch. The lantern above his head flickered and died. 'Oh, we need more oil.'

'That was the last of it,' he said, his tone resigned. 'I have one or two candles in the dresser.'

Guilt washed through her. Absorbed in her work, she had forgotten all about him as a person. No, not true. She had never been so aware of any individual in her life; her senses were awash with his mood, his physical presence, and, while she worked, he became part of her, intrinsic to her being, as if they were one.

And as a result she had used up all his oil. She would beg some from Snively and bring it to him tomorrow.

Stretching her back and rolling her shoulders, she felt the pull of muscles. He must also be stiff from remaining still for so long. 'I am finished.'

'Good,' he said.

Her gaze flew to his face. No longer brooding, it exuded determination. And he had not asked to see the work. Afraid he might find it hopeless, perhaps, and not want to lie?

Frederica stared at the paper in the light from the candle on the table, at his face, his body, and saw the likeness and more. The drawing resonated with his dark persona, a simmer of anger beneath the outward calm. It was the best thing she'd ever done. At least she thought so. It still needed work. When she got back to her room and daylight she would touch it up from the memory branded on her brain.

Sadness sat like a rock in the pit of her stomach. She often felt that way when she completed a work. But this felt worse—a sort of emptiness, because he'd been kind and she would one day leave and never see him again. There weren't many kind people in her life.

'I suppose I should go,' she said in a hoarse breathless voice.

He looked at her sharply. 'I'll walk you.'

'Oh, no. I wouldn't like you to go out in the rain again. I'll be perfectly fine.' She got up and packed up her papers and pencils.

He got up, came around the table and grasped her shoulders in his big strong hands. Hands she would later draw, while she remembered their pressure on her skin and the flesh beneath. 'Don't be stubborn.'

She looked up at him. At the worry in his face. At the firm set to his lips. Earlier, she had thought he might kiss her. But he'd pushed her away. He didn't find her attractive. Of course he didn't. A man like him would have his choice of women. And he would not choose a plain, skinny female like her.

But he wasn't completely immune. Of that she was sure. There had been too much heat in his gaze when he'd stared at her earlier.

He must have thought she was awfully bold coming here at night. Wanton. Like her mother.

Prickles of shame ran across her shoulders. 'When we were children, S-Simon said my speech was enough to put any man off.'

'Whoever this Simon is, he's an idiot,' he said harshly.

He strode across the room, gloriously naked. She

watched him avariciously, like a miser might watch his pile of gold glint in the firelight. He moved with a grace and an economy of movement one didn't expect from such a large man. It was like watching a sonnet, muscle and sinew moving in perfect harmony.

She wanted to draw him crouched at the fire, the warm glow bronzing his skin and casting shadows over muscles and sharp angles. She wanted to draw him with the flicker of the candle making his dark axe-like features seem almost satanic as he set the candles on the rough-hewn table.

She wanted to touch him.

He opened the lid of a battered chest in the corner.

She came up behind him. "He is a sort of cousin."

He glanced over his shoulder. 'Sort of?'

'We are distant relations.' As in on the other side of the proverbial blanket. Didn't he know? She was sure the servants gossiped about it. She looked down into the chest. It held a couple of neatly folded shirts, trousers and some woollen stockings.

Unable to resist, she ran a fingertip over his shoulder blade and down the knobby protrusions of his spine as she visualised the skeleton beneath, the supporting ribs, the narrow hip bones...

He froze, mid-movement, the trousers in his hand.

She snatched her hand back as he whirled around. His eyes blazed anger, or some equally dangerous emotion that left her breathless and trembling like the aspens in Wynchwood churchyard.

He closed his eyes as if in pain. 'Innocent, gently bred females do not go around running their hands over naked men.' He pulled on the trousers, the fabric hiding his beautiful body from her hungry gaze.

He cursed. 'Any men. What do you think your family would say?'

'I'm no innocent. And I don't care what Uncle Mortimer thinks.' She had tried for years to make him think well of her, to no avail. And now he was going to marry her off to Simon.

'Not innocent?' he scoffed, but there was a glimmer of hope in his expression, like a small boy eying a biscuit barrel.

With a mother like hers, how could she be innocent? She certainly wasn't ignorant. A book by a woman of pleasure and caricatures by Thomas Rowlandson found hidden in her uncle's library, both deliciously explicit, had stirred illicit sensations in her body, just as his nearness induced the ache of arousal.

'W-would you like to find out?' Her words came out in a breathy rush, too eager, too desperate.

'No,' he said.

'Because you don't find me attractive.'

He half-groaned, half-laughed. 'Not that. Definitely not that. I've had too much to drink. You've got your drawing and I don't want to lose my job.'

'I would never tell anyone.'

'You are a naughty little puss. Do you know that? A temptress.' His lips brushed her ear, her throat, her collarbone, sending shivers down her spine, tightening her nipples. 'Leave now, before I take you at your word.'

Shivers turned to rivers of molten metal in her blood. Her heart beat so hard, she could not draw breath. She turned to face him, to look into his eyes, but his thoughts were hidden by shadows cast by the fire. 'I don't want to go. I want to kiss you.'

Heat flared in his eyes. 'One kiss, then,' he murmured seductively.

Weak with anticipation, she lifted her chin and closed her eyes. Nothing happened.

She opened her eyes.

He raised a brow. 'You said you wanted to kiss me.'

The raised brow and the glimmer of laughter in his eyes said he thought she wouldn't dare. Her breath stuck in her throat. Was he right? She had no experience kissing a man.

But she had seen the pictures. She leaned forwards and brushed her mouth against his firm lips. He didn't move. She placed her hands on his broad shoulders, feeling sinew and bone beneath her palms, along with growing heat. She touched her tongue to the seam of his lips.

He opened his mouth. Her insides clenched more powerfully than anything she had experienced during her imaginings. His hands slid up her back, drawing her closer. Lips, warm and soft, moved over hers with persuasive pressure. Her lips parted in response.

'Oh, yes, sweetheart,' he murmured against her mouth. He licked her lower lip. A delicious thrill trickled down her spine. See, she did know. It was in her blood. She slid her hands around his neck, ran her fingers through his hair.

He angled his head, his mouth moving and coaxing and teasing. Chills shivered through her body, leaving her weak. She parted her lips to his teasing tongue and she clung to him, panting against his wonderful mouth.

He pulled away. 'God, give me strength.'

Ragged breaths shaking her frame, she watched him rub his palms on his thighs and realised his breathing was equally fast. 'That is all you want?'

He half-laughed, half-groaned. 'What I want and what I can take are very different.'

While she didn't know exactly what she wanted, she knew they had been heading in the right direction during their kiss, and that it was just the beginning. When she worked on a sketch, each pencil stroke brought the design closer to completion. Heavenly perfection, if done well, a disaster if one misplaced a line. In the art of kissing, he was her master, and it seemed he was not prepared to complete this work.

'You find me lacking?'

'You little fool. I'm doing this for your sake. You are a lady. I'm…nothing. You will only ruin yourself.' The words seemed torn from him, regretful, as if he truly did not want to stop.

A sense of empowerment glowed within her, drove her to reckless abandon. She was, after all, the bastard daughter of the Wynchwood Whore. 'I am already ruined.'

Ruined? The word was a siren song to Robert's beleaguered senses. He'd meant to frighten her off. Scare her silly. Instead, he'd found himself battling the demon of self-control. Was this what the cook meant by devil's spawn? That this child-woman really was not the innocent she seemed? Was she his kind of woman after all? The kind who enjoyed casual, carefree encounters? The kind who had sampled others before him?

His brain, still hazy with drink and clouded by lust, was partly hopeful and partly angered at the thought of another man with his hands on her delicate body.

'Kiss me, R-Robert, please.'

Did she have any idea how alluring he found her little hesitation when she said his name? God, he hoped not, or he was lost.

He pulled her slight frame against him, cradled her in his arms, her hips against his groin, her small hands curled on his chest. It felt right. Too right. More than he deserved.

His heart sang when she lifted her face to him, her full lips begging to be kissed.

He couldn't look at her enough. It was as if he needed to absorb her into his skin, into the empty place in his chest that had been cold and hard and now felt soft and warm and full of longing.

She stroked his jaw. He hadn't shaved. He captured her fine-boned fingers, kissed the palm of her hand, her wrist, the inside of her elbow, felt her shiver of desire in the deepest fibre of his being.

Heaven could not be more blissful.

He caressed her back. Her neck above her woollen gown felt like silk. Exquisitely soft.

He slipped one hand under her knees and lifted her. Arms around his neck, she snuggled against his shoulder as if she belonged there. He buried his face in her hair, inhaled her unique scent. Intoxicated, he carried her to his cot where he lay her down. She gazed up at him, then raised her hands above her head, seemingly submissive, yet her sea-green and mysterious eyes held a glint of a dare.

Desire flamed in his body. Out of control, and yet control it he must. He swallowed a growl of frustration and knelt beside the bed. She captured his hand, kissed the knuckles one by one, her moist tongue lapping at his skin like a cat, tasting him.

'Lie down with me, R-Robert.' Her husky voice grazed the most sensitive parts of his body.

Desire, heat, lust, pooled in his loins. 'Are you sure?' He ground out the question from a throat so tight it hurt to speak. Even as the words left his mouth, in some deep part of him he dreaded her reply, whichever it was.

'Yes.'

His body demanded it, even as his brain advised caution. Damn caution. He'd given her every chance to leave. She understood exactly what she was doing. He dipped his head to taste of her mouth, to savour her honeyed sweetness with his tongue, and lost his senses.

Light, fluttering, teasing, her hands roamed his back, smoothed his shoulders, explored his chest and arms and set his skin on fire.

His tongue swept her mouth, his palm found her high, small breast beneath her bodice. The nipple pearled against his palm, begging for his mouth, his tongue.

She moaned when he squeezed her beautiful soft flesh. Her tongue flickered over his lips, then plunged into his mouth.

Hard as a rock, he wanted to ravage her, fill her with his essence, cover her with his scent, brand her as his own, possess her body and spirit. Dear God. No woman had ever brought him to such a state of mindless passion.

Where now was his legendary control? He hauled in a deep breath. She deserved more than a hurried engagement of the flesh, no matter how much he wanted to sheathe himself inside her heat.

Slow. Steady. Focus on her needs, her desires. He inhaled. With each deep breath, his heartbeat eased to a manageable level and control slid back into his grasp. He trailed kisses across her jaw, and soaked up her sigh of pleasure. He brushed his lips across the hollow of her throat and tasted the rapid pulse beat with his tongue.

Her thighs fell apart as if her limbs were now his to command. He licked the rise of flesh above her stays.

He grazed her nipple through her chemise, then blew on the damp fabric. She shuddered and her hips bucked beneath him.

'Slowly, love,' he whispered. He caressed her ribs. Front closing stays, thank God. He untied the bow at her bosom. Firelight gilded her elfin face and threw mystic shadows across her face. A woodland sprite, a magical being who filled him with tenderness.

Between kisses on her lips and cheek and chin, he unlaced her ties. Finally loose, he tossed the stays away and eased her chemise upwards over a beautifully turned knee, exposed her thigh, where he pressed little kisses all the way to her hip. He shuddered on an indrawn breath at the sight of her pale brown nest of curls.

Intending to reassure, he glanced at her with a smile and found her watching him, her eyes full of firelight, her chest rising and falling, her body tense as if she might flee.

'May I remove your chemise?' he asked.

She nodded and bit her lip.

Despite his body's protest, he paused. 'Are you sure?'

Again she nodded, her gaze drifting down his body. 'Are you?'

'Oh, yes, my sweet. Very sure.' He drew the filmy fabric over her head and gazed in awe at her loveliness. A tiny waist hollowed beneath ribs he could count, his gaze lingered on peach-sized breasts with skin so translucent the blue veins shone beneath. He swallowed and let his gaze wander her elegant length, springy curls at the juncture of her thighs, already bedewed with her moisture, just waiting for him, strong legs that would wrap his hips when finally he rode her to bliss.

The grey woollen stockings held up by sturdy garters

hid her calves and feet from view. He ran his forefinger under one stocking top and smiled at her. 'These too must go.'

The hiss of her indrawn breath tightened his balls. He almost lunged at her as desire clawed at his vitals. Not yet. Hand shaking, he rolled the garter down her leg and off, then tugged on the stocking until it slipped down her leg, inch by inch. He kissed each and every bit of beautiful skin thus exposed until he reached her toes.

Before he could say her nay, she stripped off the other stocking and tossed it aside.

Naked, she lay back. Her voracious gaze roved his body. The tip of her tongue moistened her lips. A shudder ran through him.

'Take off your trousers,' she said.

It was only fair. He stripped them off, grateful to be free of the confinement; his erection rose hard against his belly.

'Oh, my,' she whispered. 'It is lovely like this.' She reached out and touched the head of his shaft.

It jerked in response.

'Oh.'

He groaned. 'Any more of that and I will disgrace myself.'

'Then hurry up.'

'Demanding, aren't we?' In any other woman, he would have hated that demand. From her, it made his heart swell. 'Then I must obey, my lady.'

Careful not to crush her delicate form, he covered her with his body, took her lips in a kiss that demanded attention and heard her moans with deep satisfaction.

He caressed her, and kissed her breasts. She kissed him back, licked his ear, nibbled at his neck, her thighs open, her hips arching up begging for his attention. 'Soon, little one,' he crooned.

He stroked her hips, her swell of thigh, and suckled at her breast, until she became wild, her small fists beating at his shoulders, demanding what she wanted. Finally, he allowed himself to enter her body, to stroke the pulsing inner flesh with his shaft, to bring her to the height of passion, where he called on all of his skill with his hands and mouth to keep her trembling at the brink.

'Please, R-Robert,' she moaned.

Raging desire ran rivers through his blood. He could not hold back any longer. He drove deep into her warm depths, pounding into her in fierce possession. He couldn't hold back, couldn't stop. God, if she didn't reach her climax... He shifted his weight, found the little nubbin of her pleasure, circled his thumb.

She shuddered, moaned his name, shattered around his shaft.

He wanted to die inside her.

Some small scrap of sense exerted itself and he pulled free, shuddering to a finish on her belly while she lay boneless beneath him.

He cleaned her up with a corner of the quilt and pulled her into his arms.

What the hell had just happened? One second he'd been in control, the next he'd been a raging animal. He pulled the quilt over her sleeping form, glancing down into her pale face, still blissful.

This was what she'd come for, of course. Not the drawing. Like all the other women in his life, he'd seen it in her eyes. And he'd not been able to turn her away, despite his good intentions. He'd have been a lot less susceptible if he hadn't been celibate for nigh on two years. He'd never been without a woman for so long since he'd first discovered sex at the age of fifteen.

No excuses, Robert. Apparently, Father was right. He was nothing but a dissolute wastrel. He'd risked everything for a few moments of satiation and the warmth of woman's arms.

He felt like the worst kind of cur. He'd wanted to protect her, but he'd been unable to protect her from himself. This must not happen again.

On a slow, pulsing tide, Frederica's spirit returned to her body. For long moments she floated on the heat of passion, listening to her heart, hearing his breathing slow, his hand warm about her shoulders and hip. For the first time in her life, she felt as if she had drifted into a harbour, safe from all the storms of her existence. How much time had elapsed? Hours, minutes? She had no idea. She only knew she wanted to remain here, cradled in his arms for ever.

Yet it could not be. Following her destiny required leaving England.

The breathing at her side was not the deep measured rhythm of sleep, just a steady rise and fall. She glanced up to find him watching her, his expression unreadable.

'I thought you were awake,' he said, his voice rumbling in his wide chest against her ear. 'I must get you home before you are missed.'

Conscious of her nakedness beneath his steady gaze, she sat up and pulled on her shift. He helped her with her stays and began fastening her gown.

He looked at her with eyes so bleak she shivered.

'I'll see you to the bridge,' he said. 'I won't come any farther, in case we are seen from the house. And whatever you do, promise you won't let anyone see that drawing.'

'I won't. I'll bring you the money for the sitting as soon as—'

'No. I don't want your money. Consider it another gift.' He pressed the book into her hands, opened the door and looked at her coldly. 'Do not come here any more.'

The words sounded as chill to her ear as the sleet felt on her face.

Chapter Seven

The next morning, Frederica set the portrait on an easel. She'd risen early to draw in the hands, and changed the cot into a roman divan and the rough blanket into a dark velvet throw.

In her eyes, he looked gorgeous. She shifted the easel to catch the north light and squinted at the drawing, trying to view it with dispassion, when all she could think about was his hands on her body and the beautiful, terrible passion.

Had she captured the spirit of the man?

A scratch at the door. She jerked around, standing in front of the picture as Snively stepped in. 'Good morning, miss.' He raised a brow at the easel.

'G-good morning, Snively. W-what can I do for you?'

'A letter came from Dr Travis.'

'Oh, good.' She stepped forwards to take it, then stopped. 'Er...would you put it on the desk?'

'Certainly, miss. I hope it is good news.'

'So do I,' she said with an embarrassed smile, wishing he would go.

'Should be a nice little nest egg when all's said and done.' She'd told Snively about her contract with the doctor. She hadn't wanted the letters ending up on her uncle's desk to be opened without her knowledge. Snively, as usual, had been more than happy to help.

'As soon as I get the fox finished...' she nodded at the drawings on the desk '...he'll send the final payment.'

The butler set the letter down right next to the rough draft of Robert's hands. He leaned to his left, looking over her shoulder. 'Nice. Does him justice.'

Heat flooded her face. 'I drew it from imagination.'

'The kind of imagination that brings you home at three in the morning.'

She gasped.

'Don't worry. I won't tell anyone, but be careful of that young man, miss. He's not all he seems.'

Her heart sank. 'What do you mean?'

'It's just a feeling, miss. But you've trusted me before to put you right, so this is my advice. You've got through things pretty well up to now. Don't do anything rash. Your birthday is coming up. Your majority. Everything will seem much clearer then.'

'How?'

He tugged at his cravat. 'I can't say, miss. It's this feeling I have.'

'The same feeling you have about Mr Deveril.'

He glanced at the picture. 'No. That's a different feeling altogether.' His craggy face shifted into the small smile he sometimes gave her. 'It's very good, that picture, but you better not let anyone else see it.'

'On that I will take your advice, Mr Snively.'

'On the other too, I hope, miss.' He bowed and departed with his usual dignity.

Frederica pressed her hands to her hot cheeks. How could she have been so careless? She whisked the easel into the corner and turned it to face the wall. She covered it with an old shawl.

Dear old Snively, never one to get in a flap. And she could rely on him to keep quiet about what he'd seen, but if one of the other servants had walked in and seen the picture, there would have been a horrible fuss.

Could he have guessed just by looking at her that things had gone much further than her drawing Robert's picture? Did she look different?

She felt different. More like a woman. For a while, she'd felt desirable too. Their lovemaking had been so utterly wonderful. To her.

'Don't come here again.' He'd sounded weary.

Perhaps she'd disappointed him in some way. That must be it. Before they'd made love, they had been friends. Now, it seemed, they were nothing. He couldn't wait to be rid of her. When they walked home through the woods, he'd said not a word.

And he'd refused to accept any money. Did he consider she'd paid him with her favours? A rather horrid thought. It sounded like something her mother would do.

Or was it something much more mundane? Did he fear she'd betray him to her uncle? Well, she wouldn't. Never.

Frederica picked up the letter from the desk. Her hand shook as she read Dr Travis's words. He wrote first of his delight with the drawings received so far. He was happy to accept them for his book.

Her heart seemed to stop in her chest. He liked her

work. It was going to be published. In a book. Dreams did come true. Even if they could not be published in her own name.

He noted that the first instalment bank draft awaited her, or rather waited for a Mr Smith, at the publisher's office in London. The second instalment would be paid on publication.

Her excitement subsided. It might take months for publication. She'd understood the final and much larger payment would be due on delivery of the last of the pictures. Without all of the money right away she wouldn't have enough to leave Wynchwood.

She picked up a pen and dipped it in the ink. Slowly and carefully, she pointed out that this was not how she had understood his offer. If she provided everything he asked for on time, should he not be equally as timely?

Feeling rather bold, she sanded the letter and folded it. She'd have to await his answer, before making her own plans. Another delay.

And then there was the matter of her unwanted chaperon. The meeting with Lady Radthorn this morning. No doubt the dowager countess would find her a dreadful disappointment. Too thin. Too plain. The thought of trying on gowns in front of the elegant lady made her stomach churn.

Nothing too expensive, Uncle Mortimer had begged, even as Frederica had begged him to let her cry off from the ball. Not even her lack of knowledge of the waltz had changed his mind. Just sit it out, he'd advised. Tell anyone who asks that I do not approve of such scandalous cavorting.

Scandalous cavorting, like her mother. They'd be shocked if they knew she'd been doing a bit of scandalous cavorting of her own. After all, *a bad apple never falls far from the tree,* Uncle Mortimer always said. She glanced down at the letters, her key to leaving the tree far behind. Carefully, she tucked the doctor's letter into her clothes press and her reply in her pocket.

Until the doctor's answer came, she had a role to play. Uncle Mortimer must not suspect a thing, which meant facing Lady Radthorn.

There was one good thing, though. On her way through the village, she could post her reply to Dr Travis.

Stomach fluttering as if it might fly off by itself, Frederica followed the Radthorn butler's directions into an impressive drawing room full of family portraits and gilt furniture.

An elegantly gowned middle-aged woman with grey dusting her pale gold hair and a warm smile creasing her patrician face held out her hands. 'There you are, Miss Bracewell, and right on time, too. I like promptness in a young gel.'

Frederica didn't know she had an option but to be on time. She took a deep breath and made her curtsy. 'Good morning, my lady.' Good. No hesitations.

As she raised her gaze, she saw that Lady Radthorn was regarding her with narrowed eyes and slightly pursed lips.

'Curtsy is good,' the elderly lady murmured. 'Gown is dreadful.' She cocked her head to one side. 'Looks nothing like her mother.'

Frederica's jaw dropped. This woman knew her mother? 'I b-beg your pardon.'

'Oh, la, did I say that aloud? John, my grandson, is quite sure I have reached my dotage when I do that.' She laughed, a bright tinkling sound in the spacious room.

'Would you like tea? Of course you would. And besides, I want to take a look at your comportment. Nothing like serving tea to separate a lady from a hobbledehoy, I always say.'

Lady Radthorn glided to the bell pull and gave it a swift tug. 'Do sit down, my dear. My word, you look terrified. I assure you I have not sharpened my teeth this morning.'

Was that a joke? It was hard to tell with such a grandam. Sure her knees were knocking, Frederica crossed the room beneath the critical gaze and perched on the sofa indicated by the lady's imperious gesture.

The dowager countess took the chair opposite. 'Now I look at you more closely, I see you have your mother's lovely skin.' She touched her own lined face. 'Poets wrote odes to her complexion.'

Frederica's heart thudded uncomfortably in her chest, questions stuck in her throat, like a fishbone gone down the wrong way. She swallowed hard. 'You knew my mother?' She had a sick feeling in the pit of her stomach. It was all very well hearing vague rumours from servants and dire warnings from Uncle Mortimer, but the thought of someone actually knowing the person felt like opening Pandora's Box. She wished fervently she hadn't asked.

'Gloria came out the same year as my oldest son.' She smiled sadly. 'My poor John.' She gazed off into the distance, lost in the past. Everyone in the neighbourhood knew that the loss of her son and his wife to influenza had been a huge blow. The current Lord Radthorn had inherited the title as a minor. But that had been years ago.

Frederica shifted in her seat. 'I'm sorry.'

Lady Radthorn blinked as if clearing her sight. 'So foolish. What is past cannot be undone.'

Were all those of Lady Radthorn's generation prone to quote little homilies? Uncle Mortimer spouted them upon every occasion. She clasped her hands in her lap and tried to look calm. 'True. Some topics are better avoided.'

The dowager looked at her askance. 'What do you mean?'

Heat licked at Frederica's cheeks. Oh, why had she said anything at all? 'The topic of my mother. The Wynchwood Whore.'

Lady Radthorn clapped her hands to her ears. 'Child! Such language! Where did you hear such a thing?' She sounded horrified. And disgusted.

It might be one way to do away with an unwanted chaperon. Make her think she was utterly beyond the pale. 'It is the truth, is it not? The reason why no one in the family mentions her name?'

'I'm appalled.'

Good. Perhaps she'd send her home.

But Lady Radthorn clearly felt the need to say more. 'Oh, I'll admit it was all an embarrassment. But your mother was not…well, not what you said.'

Frederica stared at her open mouthed. Her heart gave a painful squeeze of longing. A yearning to know her mother and not feel ashamed.

It could not be true. The elderly lady was simply being kind, trying to make Frederica feel better. Her mother's wickedness had been drummed into her for too long for it to be sloughed off as a matter of degree. Her voice shook as she spoke. 'She had a child out of wedlock. I'm a b—'

'Lud, child, say not another word.'

Frederica snapped her mouth shut. Now she would be sent home in disgrace.

Lady Radthorn pulled out a lacy handkerchief and dabbed at the corners of her eyes. 'What is Wynchwood thinking, letting you believe this poison? Your mother married Viscount Endersley.'

The world seemed to spin as if she'd just stepped off a merry-go-round. 'My father is a viscount?'

Lady Radthorn coloured. Someone tapped at the door. Lady Radthorn pressed her finger to her lips.

Her mother was married? The stories she'd heard told of a young woman who bedded men on a whim, no matter their origin. A wicked woman.

Just as she, Frederica, had bedded Robert, because she couldn't seem to stop it from happening. Because she was wicked. Like her mother.

Her hands were clenched so hard, her nails dug into her palms. She opened her fingers and resisted the temptation to wipe them on her skirts while the butler methodically deposited a silver tray loaded with a teapot, pretty china cups and a plate of iced cakes on the table in front of her chair. She wanted to scream at him to go.

She needed to hear the whole story.

'Thank you, Creedy. That is all,' Lady Radthorn said. 'We are expecting Mrs Phillips shortly. Have Digby help her in with her swatches and fabrics.'

'Yes, my lady.' He bowed and left.

'Where were we?'

'A v-viscount.'

'Ah, Endersley. Gloria married the old gentleman under duress.'

'Old?'

The dowager nodded. 'His only son died unexpectedly

and he desperately needed an heir. Gloria had been in
and out of love with several young men during her first
Season. Her father was in despair, thinking she would
never settle on one. Then rumour had it she'd fallen hard
for someone he absolutely refused to countenance.'

'Like a coachman? Or a criminal?' Or an assistant
gamekeeper.

'Well, as to that, I couldn't say. There were rumours.'
Lady Radthorn frowned. 'All the gentlemen adored her
and if they knew this man's identity, they never said.
Gentlemen are like that. But your grandfather, Wynchwood, saw Viscount Endersley's suit as the answer to a
prayer. He was rich, you see, and as usual the Bracewells
were balanced at the edge of financial disaster. He bore
the expense of your mother's come-out with the idea
she would catch a wealthy man. It was her duty to save
them.'

'So she was forced to marry Endersley?'

'Nobility marries for duty,' the dowager countess
pronounced. 'If one is fortunate, as I was, love grows
after a time. If not...' she shrugged '...one endures.'
She let go a sigh. 'Gloria was not the enduring kind,
I'm afraid. Endersley knew the child she carried wasn't
his when you were born three months early.'

'I was born in wedlock?' She could scarcely believe
it. All these years she'd been lectured about her place
in life. Lowest of the low. Fortunate the family hadn't
cast her off.

'Few men will accept another man's love-child as
their own. Endersley put the word out that the child
Gloria bore was stillborn.'

They'd said she'd died? She felt sick. 'And my mother
agreed?'

'Gloria was in no case to agree to anything. Milk

fever, you know. It killed her soon after you were born.'

Well, at least that part of the story matched what she knew about her mother. Everyone at Wynchwood saw it as justice for her wicked ways. 'I don't know why they didn't drop me off at an orphanage.'

Lady Radthorn's brow crinkled. 'I wondered about that myself, to be honest. My guess is Endersley paid the financially strapped Wynchwood off on condition he keep you. As a sort of punishment. It would have been like him to exact some sort of payment. Or Wynchwood might have done it for Gloria. He loved the gel. He was deeply saddened by his daughter's passing. Went into a complete decline. When he died, the title passed to Mortimer, a distant cousin of his, along with your guardianship.'

The thought of her grandfather grieving for her mother was a shock. It gave Frederica an odd sensation in her chest to think that someone actually cared for her mother. It made her feel a little less of an outcast.

'If Endersley was not my father, who is?'

The dowager's wince made Frederica's heart clench. 'No one knows.' Lady Radford shook her head. 'Gloria couldn't have been more than eighteen when they announced her betrothal.' Her old eyes misted. 'It really wasn't fair. She rebelled. Said she was going to enjoy herself while she could. Things were different in those days. More free and easy. My son John said there was talk in the clubs. Masquerades at Ranelagh. Footmen. Even a highwayman. It seemed unlikely, but who can say.'

Criminals and servants? No wonder she'd earned the horrid sobriquet from her family. Nor had she given a thought to the result. An unwanted child. 'She was wicked.'

'Spoiled, I think. Too adored. I always thought her too finicky to have an affair with a man who was not a gentleman.'

Robert was a gentleman for all his rough ways. It was possible for a man to be of low birth and gentlemanly. Could her mother have fallen for that kind of man? Or was she completely wanton as Uncle Mortimer said?

She desperately wanted to believe Lady Radthorn, but feared Uncle Mortimer, a member of the family, was more likely to be privy to the truth.

The dowager countess was looking at her sadly, as if she felt sympathy for her mother, which was really rather sweet.

Frederica sat a little straighter in her chair, felt a little less guilty about who she was. An odd feeling filled her chest. 'Thank you,' she said. And she meant it. 'You've answered questions I never dared ask.'

'And added some too, I'll warrant,' the old lady said kindly.

Not added, just increased her curiosity and dread. Who was her real father?

The widow tucked her handkerchief away and smiled. 'And now it seems your family has decided to let bygones be bygones and bring you out. You know, I never had a daughter and here you are, attending your first ball, and I am to bring you up to scratch. We are going to have such fun spending your uncle's blunt. Now, young lady, serve the tea—we have a great deal to do before the seamstress arrives.'

Frederica poured milk into both cups.

'Ah,' Lady Radthorn said, 'a very good start.'

* * *

The next hour proved less arduous than Frederica expected despite Lady Radthorn's constant verbal stream of instructions.

'Now to deportment,' Lady Radthorn announced after the butler retired with the tea tray. 'Let me see you walk across the room.'

It wasn't her walking that would cause her trouble, it was her speech, though Lady Radthorn hadn't said a word about her hesitations. The thought of talking to a herd of strangers made her quake in her shoes.

None the less, Frederica rose and walked to the window through which she had an excellent view of the park's formal gardens. They seemed to stretch for miles. If only she could be out there, instead of in here, even if the grey lining to the large fluffy clouds did portend rain.

'Straighten your shoulders, Miss Bracewell. Keep your chin up. Breeding shows in every step. Walk as if you are floating on air, not tramping through a field.'

On air? She felt like she was sinking into a quagmire. Still, who could resist Lady Radthorn?

'Turn,' the doughty lady said. 'No, no. Not like that. As if you had a book on your head. Try again.'

Frederica did.

'Much better, gel. You've your mother's grace if nothing else.'

The compliment almost sent her to her knees.

Her taskmaster tsked. 'Now you are sagging again. Straighten your spine. Imagine a chord from the top of your head to the ceiling and it is too short. Glide, gel. Glide. As if you were waltzing. You do know how to waltz, or course.'

Oh, God. More evidence of her lack of breeding. 'I d-d-d—'

'Do.' Lady Radthorn flicked her fingers. 'Of course you do. All young ladies do these days. Wait until you see John, my grandson. He is a wonderful dancer.'

Another knock at the door diverted Lady Radthorn's attention and cut off Frederica's words.

'Mrs Phillips is here, my lady,' the butler said.

'Show her in at once.' Lady Radthorn rubbed her blue-veined hands together. 'Now we will truly enjoy ourselves.'

And they did, much to Frederica's astonishment. But who would not be charmed by the array of muslins and laces brought by the seamstress? Best of all, the two ladies consulted Frederica about each item selected, often praising her taste and sense of style. She put it down to her artist's eye, though she didn't say that to the two women.

Informed of the urgency, Mrs Phillips had brought several ready-made gowns from which to choose with the idea of altering them to fit. The riding habit was to be made new, as well as an evening gown.

'Do you think you can manage all of that in three days, Mrs Phillips?' Lady Radthorn asked, leaning against the sofa back and fanning her face.

The bird-like Scottish lady smiled. 'Oh, I think so, your ladyship. I'll gain some help from a couple of lasses I know.' She turned to Frederica. 'And it is pleasure, I assure you, to dress such a lovely young lady.'

Frederica's heart jumped. Lovely? Not possible. It must be flattery because they'd spent so much money. Although Robert could not have found her completely unattractive or he wouldn't have… Oh, heavens. If Lady Radford guessed at the direction of her thoughts, she'd probably dismiss her as worse than her mother and toss her out on her ear. She didn't want that. She liked the dowager countess. She was the first person who had taken any real interest in her, apart from Robert. She'd do anything to keep her friendship.

'Thank you, Mrs Phillips,' she said. 'There is one thing we haven't yet discussed.'

'Nonsense,' Lady Radthorn said. She counted off on her fingers. 'Three morning dresses, two afternoon dresses, a pelisse, an evening gown and a riding habit.' She frowned at Frederica. 'That was all your uncle asked for.'

'The m-masked ball?' Frederica said.

'Oh, my,' Mrs Phillips said, her eyes widening. 'That's right. A costume. Oh, mercy.'

'Masked?' Lady Radthorn said. 'What flummery.'

Frederica wanted to giggle at her disparaging tone. 'Simon requested it.' She rather liked the idea of pretending to be someone else for one night.

'Well,' Mrs Phillips said, 'if the young lady is wanting to go as Mary Queen of Scots or some mythical beast, I truly will not have time to make all of these other things as well. A poor body can only do so much, your ladyship.'

'Let me think,' Lady Radthorn said. 'I dressed once as Guinevere, and Radthorn was Arthur. All that metal clanking around quite gave me a headache.'

'I had thought of something less complicated,' Frederica said. 'Perhaps a Roman lady. It needs no more than a long length of white sheeting.'

'Too plain,' Lady Radthorn said, narrowing her eyes on Frederica as if she was an exotic weed that had shown up in a bouquet. 'But, yes, something simple.

Something to show off your delicate skin and lovely figure.'

There was that word *lovely* again. Frederica felt heat in her cheeks and a bubble of something pleasant in her chest, as if life suddenly held a great deal of promise. Was this part of Uncle Mortimer's plot? Woo her with gowns and balls, so she would go like a lamb to the slaughter?

'What about Titania?' Mrs Phillips said. 'From *A Midsummer Night's Dream.* A wisp or two of fabric, some wings and daisy crown. Sure, I could do that in an hour or two.'

A wisp of fabric? Frederica shivered. 'I prefer the sheeting.'

'Nonsense. My word, gel, it is the very thing. Caroline Lamb would have eaten her heart out for curves like yours. Titania it is.'

'I—'

'I'll hear no more from you, miss.' Lady Radthorn laid the back of her hand against her high forehead. 'I am exhausted. Ring the bell for Creedy and a footman to help Mrs Phillips out and then take yourself off.'

When Frederica didn't move, she sat up. 'No arguments. Go along, child. Come back tomorrow and we will continue our lessons.'

In short order, Frederica found herself bundled out of the house and into her uncle's waiting carriage.

She collapsed against the squabs. Titania. And she had hoped to spend the ball hiding out in a corner, avoiding Simon. She would have to hide if all they gave her was a wisp of fabric. And Lady Radthorn thought she knew how to waltz.

There was one person she trusted who knew how, but he had forbidden her to call.

* * *

For Robert, the New Year had come and gone with barely a mention. The next day, collar turned up against the wind, he walked to Wynchwood. The faint grey of dawn was already dimming the stars to the east. He'd grown to love the peace of the early mornings, but today he felt tired. Once again, thoughts of Frederica had kept him tossing and turning on his cot and now if he didn't hurry he'd be late. Damn the girl for plaguing his nights. The lost look she'd given him when he told her not to come back had been a hard bed mate, particularly when all he'd wanted to do was pull her close and offer comfort.

As well as seek his own.

He should never have drunk so much.

Damnation, he should never have dallied with the girl, innocent or no. But he just couldn't resist, could he? A wastrel, Father had called him. Dissolute. Perhaps the reason it hurt so much was because he'd been right.

Making love to her had been incredible, but he still couldn't believe he'd jeopardised his position here at Wynchwood for the fulfilment of transient lust. From now on, he must ignore her, or better yet frighten her off.

The trouble with that plan was that she seemed hard to scare. He'd thought she'd run a mile when he called her bluff, but she'd accepted his challenge and he'd forgotten his intentions in the pleasure of her arms.

Never again.

The decision lay on his chest, cold and hard, as he strode across the stable yard where the impending visit of London gentry had already made its impact by way of freshly washed cobbles and repaired stable doors.

Young Bracewell had not been part of his circle of

friends, thank God, so there should not be anyone in the party of guests he knew well. For added security, he'd let his beard grow for the past couple of days.

He knocked on Weatherby's office door and ducked inside at the gruff permission to enter.

A lantern on the bench relieved the gloom and gave Weatherby's weatherbeaten face a rather saturnine cast. 'I'd almost given you up, Deveril,' the old man growled. 'Did you catch our poacher?'

'I think I scared him off when I removed his traps last week. It was likely some poor sod from the village adding a bit of meat to his cooking pot.'

'You are too soft-hearted, my lad. It's his lordship's game they're stealing. If you find him, you'll deal with him.'

Robert nodded obediently. *If I find him.*

'Ah, well, these are the plans for the guests' hunt. Think you can handle it?' Weatherby handed Robert a map and gestured him to take a chair.

Robert pored over the map. Weatherby intended to draw out the fox from Gallows Hill and give the hunters a fair run. So Miss Bracewell's fox had been spared his traps only to end up fleeing the hounds. She would hate that.

Damn. What the hell was he doing, thinking about her likes and dislikes instead of his work? 'When?'

Bushy brows lowered, Weatherby bent over more maps. 'Two days from now.'

'We'll need beaters from the village.'

'Right. Let them know. They won't want to miss his lordship dropping of a bit of blunt their way, or the chance of a stray rabbit or two. Pass the word down at the Bull and Mouth, would ye.'

'Be glad to.'

Weatherby reached for another plug of tobacco and stuffed his clay pipe. Robert braced for the choking smoke while Weatherby went over the rest of his duties for the day.

A half-hour later, he stepped out into a gusty north wind with the brace of pheasant Weatherby deemed ready for his lordship's table. Storm clouds gathered overhead. Another day, he'd go home soaked to the bone. But at least he had employment.

He glanced up at the back of the mansion. The diamond panes stared back like empty eyes. Was she up there somewhere, tucked up warm in her bed dreaming of foxes? Or dreaming of him? His body responded instantly.

Damn it. Why could he not get it through his thick head, she was not for him?

He strode across the courtyard and through into the kitchen where a rush of heat enveloped him. The scent of new-baked bread made his mouth water.

Maisie lifted her head from her churn and grinned. 'Morning, Rob.'

'Good morning.'

Cook bustled out of the scullery and he handed her the rust-coloured birds. 'I suppose you are looking for breakfast, lad?' She set the birds down on the table and planted her hands on her ample hips.

'If you've any to spare.'

Once in a while, Weatherby sent him in here first thing in the morning, knowing he'd be offered a hot meal. Another of the crumbs offered by the higher servants to the lower orders, a greasing of the wheels of servitude. The old gamekeeper had a kind heart beneath his gruff ways.

'Sit you down, then. Maisie, fetch the butter.'

Robert drew up a wooden chair to the scrubbed pine table. While Maisie scurried about setting him a place, Mrs Doncaster tossed two eggs and a thick slice of bacon onto the griddle hung over the fire, then cut off two thick hunks of bread from one of the cottage loaves cooling by the window.

Moments later, she slapped the bread down in front of him and pointed her knife at the pat of butter set out by Maisie. 'There you go, then, you big lummox. Eat hearty if you want to keep that frame of yours from caving in.'

Maisie giggled, then grimaced when the cook glowered in her direction.

Robert pretended not to notice. He stemmed his anticipation of a decently cooked breakfast by slowly buttering the bread. 'It's getting right busy around here.'

'Aye. T'ain't so much the master's guests,' she went on in a low grumble. 'They's bad enough in theirselves. ''Tis all them stuck-up maids and valets what'll want feeding and waiting on. The master makes no allowance for that.' Her pudgy hand worked swiftly over the griddle. Deftly, she scooped up the eggs and bacon and dropped them on a plate. She set his plate down with a sharp bang on the table.

At the sound of a throat being cleared from the doorway, the cook turned to face the butler framed in the doorway. 'Good morning, Mr Snively.'

Another battle in the offing?

The grim-faced butler acknowledged the greeting with no more than a flicker of an eyelash. 'Maisie, Miss Bracewell is in the breakfast room looking for tea and toast.'

Not in bed dreaming, then.

'In this house, breakfast above stairs is at eight o'clock,' Cook muttered, handing Maisie a slice of bread and the toasting fork.

'Family is served when they want to be served. I will return in fifteen minutes for the tray,' Snively uttered in awful accents. Receiving no reply, he left.

'Family,' the cook uttered with scorn. 'Hardly. Making out like she's real family. Well, she ain't. Mark my words, she'll come to a bad end.'

A flash of anger shot through his veins. Hot words formed on the tip of his tongue. He swallowed them.

'Good Gawd, Maisie,' Cook yelled. 'Watch what you're doing. You've burned the toast again. Scrape it off quick and slap some butter on it before old Iron Drawers returns and finds nothing ready.' She turned back to Robert. 'You mark my words, blood will out. The mother was no better than she should be, and the daughter will turn out the same. Now, if you're finished, Rob, I gots work to do.'

Seething with rage, he clenched one fist under the table, taking one slow breath after another, angry at her. But worse. Anger he could say nothing in her defence. It was not his place to defend Miss Bracewell. Any sign of interest would fan the flames of gossip.

The sight of congealed egg on his plate turned his stomach. Either that or the vicious words had stolen his appetite. He pushed the plate away. 'Quite finished, Mrs Doncaster. Thanks.'

He rose and picked up his hat and coat. For once he couldn't wait to leave the warmth of the kitchen and get back to his labours.

Outside in the passage, where the servants' stairs led to the bedrooms above, he took a deep breath and fastened his coat buttons, residual anger making his fingers clumsy.

'Rob?'

He turned at Maisie's breathless call. 'Don't you have a breakfast to prepare?' he asked. 'You'll be in trouble if it's not ready.'

'Snively came fer it right after you left.' She closed the gap between them. He backed up until he hit the newel post.

'Cook meant to give you this.' She waved a small package. 'Tea.' She made a dive for his pocket.

He snatched the packet from her hand. 'Give her my thanks.'

Still blocking his path, she peeped up at him from beneath stubby lashes. 'They'll be right busy when the guests arrive. No one will notice me and thee.' She nudged him with a generous hip. 'Perhaps we can have our own party. Ee, but I do fancy you, Rob.' Scarlet blazed on her plump cheeks as she aimed a kiss at his mouth. Jerking back, he fielded her moist lips on his cheek at the same moment he heard a gasp from farther along the passage.

Maisie lifted her chin and glanced over his shoulder. Smirking, she bobbed a curtsy, then sauntered away with an exaggerated sway to her hips. 'Enjoy yer tea, Mr Deveril,' she called over her shoulder.

Wincing, Robert turned to face Frederica, feeling just a little too warm for comfort.

Frederica regarded him gravely from eyes swirling with grey shadows. A silent considering stare. He had no idea what she was thinking. A little jealousy would have been nice.

'She kissed *me*,' he said at last.

'I saw. You are certainly popular.'

Robert huffed out a breath. 'I thought you were eating breakfast?'

'Cook forgot the jam.'

Probably on purpose. He gestured for her to pass and turned to leave.

She grabbed his sleeve, glanced up the hallway and back to him. 'Snively mentioned you were in the kitchen. I wanted to ask you something.'

A pot clattered. They both jumped. Robert raised his eyes to the ceiling and saw no help forthcoming. 'We cannot talk here.' They would put two and two together and unfortunately would make four.

'I'll come to your house,' she murmured. 'Later.'

'No!' he whispered.

'Where, then?'

'Down there.' He caught her elbow, feeling once more the delicate bones beneath his fingers. A shimmer of awareness over his skin. He sucked in a breath and released her. 'The cellar.'

With a nod, she whisked along the hall and down a few steps into the dark. He ducked in after her. 'What did you want?' he murmured, aware of her scent mingling with the smell of coal and mildew.

'I need your help.'

'Ask your uncle.'

'He can't help me in this.'

'What makes you think I can? I told you it is best we not meet again.'

'Y-you s-said…' She gave a little moan of distress. She sounded desperate. His body strained in response, the desire to defend and protect rising rampant.

What the hell? He never let women get to him this way. Yet he couldn't help it with this one. He softened his tone. 'Take a deep breath, then tell me what is wrong.'

Her quick, indrawn gasp was like a knife to his heart She sounded terrified.

'I need to learn to waltz.'

He retreated up a step, unaccountably disappointed. 'A dancing lesson?'

She touched his arm. An unexpected sensation in the dark. The heat of it travelled straight to his chest. He flinched.

She snatched her hand back as if she too felt scorched. 'I must learn to waltz or I will make an idiot of myself. Can't we still be friends?'

Friends, when the thought of holding her in his arms stirred his blood and drove his brain to the brink of madness?

Somehow he kept his voice calm, glad the dark hid his expression. 'There must be someone else who can teach you.'

She stilled. He felt her stillness as if her heart had stopped beating and had thus stopped his own.

'I'm s-sorry,' she whispered, her voice full of ache, as if her only friend in the world had let her down. 'I was wrong to ask.'

Now he felt guilty, a pain that bit all the way to his heart. 'All right.'

'I beg your pardon?'

'I'll teach you. One lesson.'

He heard her sigh of relief. 'Thank you. When?'

'Tonight. My house.' Footsteps sounded in the passageway. He moved deeper into the dark of the stairwell, protecting her from casual sight with his body. One of her breasts pressed against his arm; the scent of her hair, vanilla and roses, a heady combination, filled his nose.

His body quickened. Demanded more. Somehow, he kept his hands off her. Breath held, he waited while the footsteps passed them by. No outraged shout of surprise broke the silence. Nothing but her rapid breaths against his neck. One move that even suggested she wanted to kiss him and he wouldn't be able to resist. She drew him, more than any woman he'd ever met. He worried about her, when he didn't want to care. People he cared for always let him down. He knew that and yet he could deny her nothing.

He was in over his head and drowning.

The sounds faded. He leaned close to her ear. 'Whatever you do, do not let anyone see you leave the house tonight.'

She nodded.

His body shaking with the effort of not kissing her senseless, he released her, strode up the stairs and, with a quick look to make sure all was clear, made the two steps to the back door and out into the yard. He released a shuddering sigh of relief.

Was he mad? Had he actually agreed to meet her again?

She'd looked so vulnerable, so afraid, he couldn't say no. Not and sleep at night.

He'd promised. One dance lesson, but nothing more.

God save him, he'd seek other work. Somewhere far away.

Wrapped in sacking, Pippin's hooves made little sound on the frosty earth. Thick clouds obliterated any light from above, but Frederica found her way to Robert's cottage with ease.

A faint chink of light shone through the shutters.

She slid from Pippin's back and tied him to a tree. His hot breath warmed her chilled cheeks as she patted his neck. 'I won't be long.'

Her heart set up a steady thud in her ears. Suddenly unsure, she crept to the door and tapped softly.

Nothing. Perhaps he'd gone out and left a candle burning. Or perhaps he'd changed his mind.

She rapped louder and backed up into the shadows. If the door didn't open by the count of three, she'd leave.

The sound of a bolt being drawn through metal held her suspended between fleeing and staying. Her heart-beat drummed against her ribs.

Light spilled onto the ground in front of the door from his lantern.

God. He was just so beautiful. His shirt, open at the throat and tucked into tight-fitting buckskins, revealed a glimpse of crisp, dark hair at the base of his throat. The dark shadow on his jaw gave him a disreputable air. Frederica swallowed, trying to find enough saliva to speak.

Shaking his head, he started to close the door.

'It is me,' she croaked, stepping closer.

'I'd begun to think you weren't coming after all. Come inside before you are seen.' He leaned forwards, clasped her hand and pulled her over the threshold, and she stumbled into the room.

He'd tidied up. The bed was neatly made, no sign of supper dishes or clothing. The chair and table were pushed back against the wall, leaving an open space in front of the merrily blazing hearth. He'd been waiting for her. Her heart gave a little lurch of happiness.

She twirled around.

His face held a pained expression. He was looking at her legs. His eyes widened as he took in her attire, a pair of Simon's old breeches and one of his shirts. 'What in hell's name are you wearing?'

'I rode. I thought it would be easier than skirts.'

'Good God.'

'I borrowed some of Simon's breeches. He's grown out of them. And one of his shirts,' she said. 'I had to saddle Pippin myself and I need help to mount a lady's saddle. I know I look dreadful.'

'I wouldn't say dreadful.' His gaze reached her face and in the firelight, his eyes seemed alight with embers. 'Certainly…unusual.'

A giddy swirl hit her brain as if the air in the cottage had turned to steam and she laughed, albeit a little breathlessly. 'I always ride astride when I can. I can go so much faster without fear of falling off.'

'You ought to be spanked.' He looked as if he might like to undertake the task himself.

She felt hot all over. He wouldn't, would he? 'You promised me a lesson.'

'In waltzing.'

She eyed him warily. 'Yes.'

His jaw flexed and his mouth flattened. 'Then let us begin. First, have you ever seen a waltz performed or tried it yourself?'

She shook her head.

He huffed out a sigh. 'Then we will begin with the basics. A waltz is a gliding dance in three-four time. When danced well, it is a sensual experience for dancers and watchers alike. Performed badly, and it is simply two people galloping around in circles.'

He ran his eyes from her heels to her head. No doubt expecting her waltz to be of the galloping variety.

'Where did you learn?' she asked.

Her question seemed to catch him off guard. He

blinked a couple of times as if trying to come up with a story. He gave a small dismissive gesture with his hand. 'In my misspent youth.' His smile was bitter.

The waltz was considered scandalous by many. He must have had a misspent youth. A flitter of excitement skated through her abdomen. 'Show me.' Her body trembled, awaiting his touch.

He narrowed his eyes. 'First, let me see you move. Go and sit down in the chair by the hearth.'

Puzzled, she strode across the room and dropped on to the seat.

'No,' he said. 'Forget you are dressed like that. Pretend you are wearing the most elegant of gowns. Do it again. This time don't swagger, glide.'

She went back to the centre of the room and walked slowly to the chair and lowered herself into it.

'Better,' he said. 'You are the most beautiful woman in the room. You do not dance with just anyone. Your partners have to be worthy.'

She batted her eyelashes at him and smiled. She didn't feel particularly beautiful, only rather silly.

He shook his head. 'No. Ignore me. Feel it inside yourself. Feel light. Ethereal. Beautiful. Calm. Be completely unconscious of anyone except the person seated beside you.'

'There isn't anyone.'

He glared at her. 'Pretend you are talking to someone.'

When she shook her head, he growled something under his breath. Seconds later he had picked up a broom and stood it next to her chair. 'You are an artist. Use your imagination. This is Lady Stuck-up. You are not visibly aware of anything but her gossip. Yet you know the world is looking at only you.'

She closed her eyes for a moment, imagined a ball-room full of glitter and members of the nobility. She straightened her spine, opened her eyes, but let the images remain. Her companion, a luscious blonde in a diamond tiara and sky-blue gown, spoke in soft tones. Music played in the background. Eyes followed each nod of her head. Aware of Robert's approach, she pretended not to see him, but smiled at something Lady Stuck-up said.

'Miss Bracewell,' Robert said, 'may I ask you to honour me with the next waltz?'

She slowly turned her head to look up at him. A small, devastating smile curved his lips. He held out a hand.

She hesitated for a moment. Would she, the most beautiful woman in the room, dance with this man? Perhaps she would do him the honour, this once. With a slight incline of her head, she rested her hand on his palm.

He stared at her for a moment, as if lost. He was certainly a good actor, playing to her role of *coquette*.

He raised her to her feet, placed her hand on his sleeve and drew her into the centre of the room, his guiding hand almost imperceptible as he steered her to her place, yet full of energy and demand.

How did he do that? She tried to look unconscious of his powerful presence.

He swirled her around, then placed one of her hands beside his lapel, and kept the other firmly grasped. She felt pressure from his other hand between her shoulders. 'The orchestra plays the opening bars,' he murmured. 'Listen to the rhythm. One, two, three. One, two, three. Feel it inside your body.'

He hummed a tune in a light tenor and a shiver raked her shoulders.

'Step back, step side, step around,' he said as he moved in a circle.

Stiff and awkward, she tried to follow his movements. She stumbled. His strong arm held her up.

'S-sorry,' she said.

'You are fine. Follow my lead. Relax.'

'If I could just see what you are doing with your feet…'

An eyebrow went up and he gave her a rueful smile. 'And I used to envy the dancing masters their job.' He released her and she stepped back. After a second's pause, he crossed the room and bowed to the broomstick. 'Dear Lady Stuck-up, would you be so good as to demonstrate to Miss Bracewell?'

Frederica giggled.

He shot her a warning glance. 'Remember, you are a haughty diamond of the first water, not a schoolroom miss.'

Frederica lifted her chin and stared down her nose at him. His look of approval gave her confidence. She maintained her indifferent expression as he picked up the broom and twirled around the room. At first, she wanted to laugh, but as she watched his lithe body and manly grace, her blood quickened and her insides fluttered in a rush of pleasurable thrills.

Silly girl. He isn't interested. He'd made it quite plain. She wiped her palms on her breeches. Watch his feet. Learn.

Gradually the pattern became clear, and she tapped her foot in time to his soft hum.

He stopped and cast poor Lady Stuck-up to the corner. He grinned at her. 'Do you see?'

'I think so.' Oh, she hoped so, or he'd think her such a dolt.

'Very well, we will try again.' Once more he encircled her in his arms. A tremble shook her frame.

'Don't be nervous. Remember, you are a willow, you are elegant, you glide, you do not hop like a frog.'

She chuckled at the image.

He frowned and she resumed her haughty pose.

'Above all, you are bold and confident,' he instructed.

As bold as her mama. The thought bolstered her courage. She took a deep breath.

'First the opening.' He hummed a few bars, then with the gentlest touch, he led her into the dance.

This time, she felt his directions, subtle tugs and pushes of hand and arm and body guided her steps. She floated as if immersed in the River Wynch's swirling eddies.

'Very nice,' he said.

She stumbled.

He laughed. A wonderful, warm sound. It touched her heart with the sweetest echo of pain.

'Next lesson,' he said. 'How to converse with your partner. Keep the music in your mind, let your feet listen to it.'

Now her feet had ears?

'You dance divinely, Miss Bracewell.'

'As do you, Mr Deveril.'

'Uh-uh.' He shook his head at her with a smile. 'A mere gracious thank you will do. And if you make a misstep, never apologise. After all, the man is in charge of the dance. If you falter, his is the error.'

And so it went, over and over, his chiding and guiding, her occasionally stumbling until a ridiculous conversation about the price of corn escalated to nonsense.

And she was doing it. Dancing the waltz, gliding and twirling and talking nonsense.

They laughed as he swirled her around in a complex set of steps and brought her to a breathtaking halt.

He stared down at her, his dark eyes full of laughter, his handsome face the most relaxed she'd ever seen it. Her breath caught in her throat.

His expression softened, eyelids lowered, his lips took on a sensuous cast. Unable to bear the uncertainty, she slipped her hand up to his neck and raised her mouth to his.

Who kissed whom, she wasn't sure, but the kiss was blissful, gentle and infinitely sweet. His chest rose on a deep breath and the pressure against her mouth increased. His tongue traced the seam of her lips and she opened for him.

The taste of him filled her mouth, the scent of him invaded her pores and, swept up on a tide of sensations, she clung to him.

Strong hands caressed her back, her hips, her ribs. So delicious. Her skin warmed and cooled as his touch trailed a sensual path of delight. One hand cupped her buttocks, pressed her against the evidence of his arousal, while the other strayed to brush the underside of her breast, then slid up to cup her fullness. Her breasts tightened.

She gasped.

On a groan, he broke away.

She clung to his shoulders. 'Don't stop. Not now.'

He held her close, cradled against his chest. 'We must not.'

She stroked his jaw, felt the springy beard, which

softened its angular lines. 'How can it be wrong when it feels so wonderful?'

In the old days, the words would have been all the permission Robert needed. But this wasn't the old days. She was too young, too inexperienced and he was the wrong man. 'No. You came here to learn the waltz. Now you must go.'

'But I want you, Robert.' She flung her arms around his neck, ran her tongue around the edge of his ear.

His body shivered. She'd learned his sensual lessons too well. 'You say that now. But what about later, when ardour cools?'

'I don't care about later.'

This was desire talking, her newly discovered feminine power. How many times had he seen it happen to débutantes in their first Season? Not that he had ever partaken of such forbidden fruit. No matter what she said, she was still innocent in so many ways. While she might have lain with some youth without experience, or some blundering man, she'd not yet been jaded by sordid affairs.

'Please, Robert.'

The agony of denial made his body clench unbearably. Lust for a woman had never ridden him this hard. There had always been another waiting in the wings. This one was out of bounds.

She'd lain down with him once, a small voice whispered. Why not again? One last time. What difference would it make? The insidious whispers drove a wedge between his conscience and his desire. Only the growing sense that if he succumbed he would never want another woman held him back. Was she indeed some other worldly being who held his soul enthralled? The devil's spawn.

My God, was he losing his mind? He pushed her away. 'Answer me this, then?'

Eyes hazy, she blinked. 'What?'

'Who was your first lover?'

'My f-f-first...' Her mouth, red from his kisses, trembled.

'You said you were ruined. By whom?'

Her lashes lowered, hiding her eyes. 'A lady doesn't tell.' Her voice was a low seductive murmur. 'Why do you want to know?'

'Did he break your heart? Is that why you are so reckless? Are you using me to...to get back at him?'

'No.' Her shocked denial rang true. Tears glistened. 'If you don't want me, just tell me and have done.' But now there was heartbreak in her voice.

He'd been too harsh, his tongue too rough. Unable to bear the pain and confusion in her gaze, he pulled her close, kissed the top of her head, inhaled the scent of her hair, her unique essence, soothed her back and shoulders with his hands. 'I confess I find you irresistible.'

At last she relaxed and he tipped up her chin to look into her face. 'I'm sorry. I should not have asked. I'm trying to do the right thing, instead of what I want.'

She smiled. 'Right for whom?'

'For you, of course.' He cupped her face in his hands and took her lips with his and felt his soul rise to meet hers as she returned the kiss.

When he finally broke the kiss and pulled away to look into her face, she smiled. 'I want this,' she whispered.

After such a declaration, she'd be hurt if he refused. He could see it in her face. She'd feel scorned. Rejected. He couldn't do it. He took a deep breath. Then he would bring her pleasure she sought without taking his and let her go in good conscience. It was the only thing to do and retain a shred of integrity.

Mentally, he shook his head. The right thing to do would be to bundle her out of the door, but it was as close to right as he could get without destroying his fragile little elf. He picked her up and carried her to his cot.

He lay her down on the bed and stretched out beside her.

He captured her sweet mouth in a kiss. She responded by sweeping his mouth with her tongue, then drawing his into her mouth with a gentle suck. His member throbbed a demand.

He unbuttoned her shirt and exposed one perfect breast. God. No stays. Had she planned his seduction? Did he care as he gazed upon her breasts, a perfect fit for his palm? He rubbed the nipple with his thumb and watched it tighten to a rosy bead, heard her indrawn breath with a surge of blood to his loins.

He bent to suckle and she squirmed beneath him, arched her hips against his thigh in silent demand for more. Not so silent. The little cries in the back of her throat, the sounds of wanting, of desire, filled his mind, stole his thoughts, robbed him of control.

His shaft strained against his trousers, pressing for escape, seeking a far sweeter, hotter confinement.

To survive this torment, he'd have to bring her to a climax fast. Still sucking and nipping at her breast, he skimmed his hand between her open thighs, pressed down hard and circled.

At once she cried out, wove her fingers in his hair and quivered. Almost there. Please, God, let her be almost there.

He sucked her other breast, pressing and grinding

against her woman's flesh, the heat of it burning his hand, dampness seeping through to his fingers.

So hot. So wet. He needed to be inside her.

His fingers tore at the buttons of his falls. One side undone.

No. He squeezed his eyes shut. He'd lost control with her the first time. This time he would master his urges. He went back to his firm massage of her, only to discover her fingers finishing the job on his buttons, her hand burrowing beneath his shirt and cupping him.

Her nails grazed his balls and his body tightened. Her fingers wandered, explored the base of his shaft. He thought he would explode in her hand.

'It feels so hot,' she said. She curled her hand around him. 'And so hard here. When you are so s-soft under—'

He reached down and grabbed her hand and pulled it free.

She stared up at him. 'Don't you l-like me to touch you?'

Heaven preserve him when she looked at him with those huge, seductive eyes. 'Touch me elsewhere.' His voice sounded harsh, but only because he was hanging by a thread. Her wince cut him to the quick.

He kissed her fingertips. 'I love it when you touch me there, but it will end too soon. For both of us.'

'Oh. I see.' She rubbed her hand over his chest. Through his shirt, his skin tingled with need to feel her skin to skin.

Dear God, he hoped she didn't see how much power she had in the palm of that little hand to bend him to her will. 'Yes. Like that.'

He swooped in for a kiss, anything to take her mind off her exploration of him, and resumed his ministrations with his hand. She sighed and moaned into his mouth. Her teeth grazed his tongue and she sucked his bottom lip. Ah, no. He was too close to the edge. He drew back.

'What are you doing?' she asked.

He shook his head. He no longer knew what he was doing. 'Pleasuring you.'

'Take your clothes off,' she whispered. Her breaths came short and fast. She undid his shirt buttons and tugged the fabric free of his breeches. He whipped the shirt off over his head. Her fingertips traced the contours of his chest, then circled his nipples. 'Now your breeches and boots.'

He inhaled a deep breath, saw the heat in her gaze, the anticipation in her tongue licking her lips and sighed.

Why fight it? It would be the last time. He swore it. In seconds he'd stripped out of his clothes. When he turned back, she had her shirt off and was wriggling out of her breeches. In the light from the fire, the triangle of light brown hair at the apex of her thighs glistened with her moisture. For him.

His wood nymph, his exotic, wild woodland creature, glowing in firelight, begging for his touch. An unexpected blessing. A pure light in his blighted life.

Lost. He was lost. And he never wanted to be found.

He tugged her breeches over her feet and flung them aside. Ripped off her stockings in feverish haste. He covered her with his body, thrust inside her. Her heat, the tightness of her flesh, squeezed around the pulsing of his blood inside her body.

A sigh of fulfilment whispered hot breath in his ear.

Pleasure ripped through him, unbearable, the tension

too hard and too fast. He surged against her, holding his weight with trembling arms, aware of her joy in the far-off reaches of his mind, but stretched to breaking point with his need for completion.

He came into her, hard and fast and rough, and she met each stroke with a thrust of her own that sent him spiralling to the stars. Together they rode all the way to heaven and the abyss beyond.

He collapsed beside her, face down, and finished against the rough blanket, blissfully satiated, yet wanting more. Disgust welled up inside him. He was what he had always been. A seducer. A rake.

She snuggled into the crook of his shoulder.

'Happy now?' he murmured for something to say, to divert his thoughts from his own sense of disappointment that he was not a better man.

'Very happy,' she said softly.

Moisture leaked from his closed eyes and he brushed it away. Because she was happy? Or because he might never again experience such joy?

While Frederica slept, her even breath a symphony to his ears, Robert watched shadows and licks of flame dance on the ceiling. How to extricate himself without doing her damage? More damage, he thought bitterly. In the old days, he would have sent round a string of pearls with a footman. Jewels were his speciality. This child of nature had no need for baubles and trinkets to enhance her beauty; she needed protection from a cruel harsh world.

And he wanted to be the one to fight her dragons. Even if he was not her first, he wanted to be her last.

Marriage.

Shocked, he inhaled a deep breath. Surely not. He'd never wanted to wed. Never wanted to be tied down to one woman. Was this simply a case of him not being ready to let this one go?

He didn't recall ever feeling this need for possession. Or the urge to protect.

Frederica stirred.

Robert glanced down and found her looking up at him. 'Time to go?' he asked.

She sighed. 'Soon. Robert?'

'Yes, love?' He liked the way the word tasted on his tongue, but it was as far as he dare go for the moment.

'What if I can only dance the waltz with you, here in this room? What if I trip over my feet?'

He pulled her close, felt her fear in the faintest tremor beneath her skin. He kissed her forehead and the tip of her nose, inhaled the musky scent of their loving and the essence of her, outdoors and fresh air with a trace of vanilla. 'You will be fine.'

He'd find a way to make sure of it. 'Come, let us get you dressed.'

The next morning, still feeling blissful, Frederica strolled into the breakfast room and found Snively hovering over the sideboard.

She lifted the lid of a silver platter and helped herself to a couple of gammon rashers. Goodness, she was hungry this morning. Today she would see the results of the dressmaker's efforts at Lady Radthorn's. The riding habit and the gowns would be a boon for her travels. Poor Uncle Mortimer. All that expense for nothing. One day, she would find a way to pay him back. In the meantime she'd do her best to make sure the ball went off without a hitch and keep her own plans a secret.

'Is everything ready for our guests, Snively?' she

asked. 'Do you have all the extra help from the village you need to decorate the ballroom?'

'Yes, miss. All is arranged, as we discussed.'

Frederica smiled. There was no one as well organised as Snively. Or so willing to aid her over the years. She would be sorry to leave him behind. 'Thank you so much for your help. You will let me know if you have questions, will you not? Lord Wynchwood will have an apoplexy if we run into problems.'

He afforded her a quick smile. 'All will be well. Oh, I should let you know that his lordship asked that we move your things to the second floor in the morning.'

She stared at him. 'My things?'

'Yes. Next to the other lady who will be staying here. He thought it made more sense with company in the house. I'll set someone on it in the morning.'

So they felt a little guilty at hiding her away. 'I do not want my desk moved. Or my easel.'

A twinkle lit his eyes. 'Don't worry, miss, I'll see to that part myself.'

She grinned back. 'You are a dear. By the way, is there any mail for me this morning?'

'Michael is not yet returned from the village. If there is anything for you, I will see it reaches you directly as always.'

'Thank you.' She selected a slice of toast and went to her usual place at the table facing the window. Beneath a clear blue sky, a hoar frost sparkled like crystals on the lawn. Impossible to catch that glitter with a paint brush. She sighed.

Snively brought her a cup of tea. He glanced at the door and back to her. 'Miss Bracewell, are you thinking of leaving Wynchwood?'

Her heart jumped, heat flashed under her skin,

followed by cold. She stifled her gasp and tried to look
unconcerned. 'Whatever d-do you m-mean?'

'I've known you a long time, miss. I've watched you
grow up. I know what goes on in this family and I've
never seen you so happy, or so excited. Not since your
uncle let you ride the gelding. You are up to something.
And it's my opinion that you are planning to take the
money from your drawings and run.'

Heart pounding, she folded her shaking fingers in
her lap. Snively had always been her ally in this house,
but as her uncle's employee, would he see it as his duty
to betray her? His eyes remained kindly but concerned.
Dare she give him her trust?

'L-leave? Why would you think so? For the first
time, I am to attend a ball and I am to have a whole new
fashionable wardrobe in honour of our guests. What can
you mean?'

He frowned and stepped back, shaking his head. 'If I
spoke out of turn, miss, I beg your pardon. I just wanted
to be sure you will be here for your birthday. I have a
gift for you, you see.'

She narrowed her eyes. 'For me?' No one ever gave
her gifts on her birthday. Unless you counted her annual
new gown as a gift.

He shrugged. 'I understood it to be a special day.
Your age of majority, so to speak.'

He looked so uncomfortable she wished she'd told
him the truth. 'How kind of you, Mr Snively.' The birth
of an unwanted child had never been a cause for celebra-
tion. She couldn't help her sarcastic little laugh. 'I think
my uncle prefers we not make too much fuss.'

A sheen of perspiration formed on his wrinkled brow.
He looked as if wild horses were tearing him in two.
He once more glanced at the door and leaned forwards

and lowered his voice in a conspiratorial manner. 'If by some chance you change your mind, Miss Bracewell, promise me you won't go without speaking to me first. Please? I swear I'll tell no one else.'

He'd never ever let her down. She gave him a reassuring smile. 'If I were to leave, I promise I will tell you beforehand.'

'That is all I can ask, miss.' He bowed and stalked out of the room, and somehow she had the sense she'd hurt his feelings.

Dash it. She'd told him of her longing to study in Italy. He must have guessed she would use the money from her painting to achieve her ambition.

Surely he wouldn't interfere. He'd always helped her in the past. Still, she needed to be careful. She didn't want her uncle guessing her purpose before she was ready. And if Snively had guessed, someone else might too.

The following day, the drawing room after dinner seemed eerily silent. Even the walls seemed to be listening for the sound of the carriage. Frederica let go a long breath.

'Stop your sighing, girl,' Uncle Mortimer said. His eyes gleamed over the top of his book, softening the stern words. 'It is good to see you so anxious to meet your cousin again, I must say. You are going to make a fine couple. Do this family proud.'

If only he knew. 'Simon said they would be here this afternoon. He's late.'

'They'll be here. The hunt is tomorrow.'

She frowned. 'We don't have enough horses for two extra people.'

'Don't be absurd, child. They will bring their own.

Behind the carriage.' He made a sound in his throat like disgust. 'We'll have the stabling of them for a week, though, I'll be bound. They won't think to leave them at the inn in the village.'

'We have lots of room.'

'It isn't the space, girl, it's the cost. And there will be grooms to feed as well as valets and ladies' maids.'

'Just one of each I should think, Uncle. At least, that is all I have provided for.'

'Hmmph.' Uncle Mortimer returned to his book.

About to let out another deep sigh, Frederica stopped herself just in time. She picked up her embroidery and eyed the design. It would have made a lovely addition to the drawing room. It would never be finished. Working right-handed just took too long.

The sounds of wheels on the gravel and the crunch of horses' hooves brought Uncle Mortimer to his feet. 'Here they are at last.'

'Will you greet them at the door, Uncle?' she asked, putting her needlework aside.

'No. No. Too draughty. Snively will bring them in here.' He stood, rocking on his heels, his head cocked to one side, listening to the front door opening and voices in the entrance hall.

The door flew back. 'Uncle,' Simon cried, his round face beaming. 'Here we are at last. Did you think we were lost on the road?'

Uncle Mortimer shook his nephew's hand and patted him on the shoulder. 'I knew you'd come, dear boy. Eventually. I just hoped you'd not be too late. Need my rest these days, you know. Not been quite the thing.'

The instant gravity on Simon's face was so patently false, Frederica wanted to laugh.

'I know, Uncle. The ague. You wrote to me of it.'

He turned to Frederica. He had to turn his whole body, because his shirt points were so high, his head would not turn on his neck. In fact, he didn't appear to have neck or a chin. His head looked as if it had been placed on his shoulders and wrapped with a quantity of intricately knotted white fabric to keep it in place. It made his face look like a cod's head. His valet must have stuffed him into a coat two sizes too small to make him so stiff and rigid.

He bowed. 'Coz. I hope I find you well.'

Good lord, he had put on some weight around the middle, and was that a creak she heard? Some sort of corset?

'Y-yes, Simon. V-v—'

'Very well,' Simon said. 'Splendid.'

Frederica's palm tingled with the urge to box his ears.

Simon turned himself about and looked expectantly at the door. 'I want you to meet my friends, Uncle. Great friends.'

Snively appeared in the doorway. 'Lady Margaret Caldwell and Lord Lullington, my lord.' He promptly withdrew.

Pausing on the threshold, the lady glittered. Dark curls entwined with emeralds framed her face. More emeralds scintillated in the neckline of her low-green silk gown as well as at her wrists and on her fingers. Her dark eyes sparkled as they swept the room, seeming to take in everything at a glance. Lady Margaret held out her hand to Mortimer, who tottered forwards to make his bow.

All Frederica could do was blink. It was like looking at the sun. Compared to this elegant woman she felt distinctly drab even with her new blue gown.

Lady Caldwell sank into an elegant curtsy. 'My lord. How kind of you to invite us to your home.'

Uncle Mortimer flushed red. 'Think nothing of it, my lady. Nothing at all.'

The lady turned to Frederica. She tipped her head to one side. 'And you must be Simon's little cousin.' She held out her hands and when Frederica reached out to take one, Lady Margaret clasped Frederica's between both of her own. 'How glad I am to make your acquaintance. I vow, Simon has told us all about you, hasn't he, Lull?'

The viscount, a lean, aristocratic and tall man in a beautifully tailored black coat, finished making his bow to Uncle Mortimer, then raised his quizzing glass and ran a slow perusal from Frederica's head to her feet. 'Not all, my dear, I am sure,' he said with a lisp.

Frederica felt her face flush scarlet.

'Simon,' exclaimed Lady Margaret, 'Lull is right! You didn't tell us your cousin was so charming. Absolutely delightful.'

Simon stared at Frederica, opened his mouth a couple of times like a landed fish, then nodded. 'By jingo, Lady Caldwell, you are right. New gown, coz?'

'A whole wardrobe of new gowns,' Uncle Mortimer mumbled.

The burn in Frederica's face grew worse.

Viscount Lullington lounged across the room and took Frederica's hand with a small bow. His blue eyes gazed at her from above an aquiline nose. She had the sense he was assessing her worth. 'Delighted to meet you, Miss Bracewell. Simon has indeed been a songbird regarding your attributes. And I see his notes were true.'

Oh, my. Had he just issued a compliment? And if so,

why did his soft lisping voice send a shudder down her spine as if a ghost had walked over her grave?

Swallowing, Frederica curtsied as befit a viscount. 'I am very pleased to make your acquaintance, my lord.'

He patted her hand. 'Call me Lull. Everyone does.'

Not she. She backed up a step or two, looking to Simon for guidance.

He rubbed his hands together. 'Here we are then. All ready for the ball. It will be such a grand time.'

'Oh, it is sure to be, isn't it, Lull?' Lady Margaret took the seat by the fireplace and Frederica returned to the sofa. The men disposed themselves around the room, Lullington beside Lady Margaret and opposite Frederica, Simon beside the window and her uncle in his favourite armchair.

'Without a doubt,' Lullington said, his gaze fixed on Frederica.

Frederica took a slow deep breath. 'W-would you like t-tea?'

'We were waiting to ring for tea until you arrived,' Uncle Mortimer added. 'Didn't expect your arrival so late.'

'By Jove,' Simon said. 'What a good idea. Tea. Just the thing.' He looked at Lullington. 'If you think so, Lull? Do you?'

It seemed Viscount Lullington now pulled Simon's strings. Not a pleasant thought.

'Oh, yes, please,' Lady Caldwell said with a brilliant smile. 'We stopped for dinner when we realised the hour was far advanced, but I would die for a dish of bohea.'

All eyes turned to the lean viscount. He nodded his

head. 'Very well. Tea for the ladies. For myself, I'd prefer brandy.'

'Me too,' Simon said.

Frederica got up and rang the bell.

Lady Caldwell smiled up at her. 'I wonder if, while we wait for the tea, you could show me my room. I am desperate to freshen up.'

Oh, dear. She should have thought to ask. 'S-s-s—'

'Surely, she will,' Uncle Mortimer said. 'Show our guest upstairs, Frederica. Don't take too long. My head aches if I drink tea too late in the evening.'

Aware of Lady Caldwell's rustling silks, her lush curves and exquisite face, Frederica found her tongue tied in knots. She would have liked to ask the woman about London, about the museums and the academy of art, but feared her words would only make her a fool. So they walked side by side in silence until they reached the bedroom.

Frederica opened the door and Lady Caldwell breezed in. 'Ah, Forester,' she said to a stiff-looking grey-haired woman standing over a brass-bound trunk, shaking the creases from a gown of a soft rose hue. 'Here you are.' She turned to Frederica. 'Come in, my dear. Fear not. Forester's bark is much worse than her bite.'

Forester played deaf.

Since the words of a polite refusal escaped her, Frederica stepped inside. She perched on the upholstered chair by the door, while Lady Caldwell headed for the dressing room.

'Do you need help, my lady?' Forester asked.

'Fiddle-de-de. If I cannot make water at my age, you best send me to Bedlam.'

Forester's lips pressed together, but she made no comment, continuing to remove items from the chest and put them away, opening and closing drawers, putting scraps of lace here and handkerchiefs there. Such delicate items and so many? Had their guests come for an extended stay? Uncle Mortimer would not be happy.

A soft chuckle made her turn. 'You are gazing at my wardrobe in awe, Miss Bracewell.'

'You have a g-great many gowns.'

Her ladyship laughed. 'So I do. Lullington and I are on a progress, do you see? We are going to visit everyone we know for the next month or two, until the Season starts again. London is flat, there is absolutely nothing to do.' She sat down at the mirror on the dressing table, patted her hair and pinched her cheeks.

'Are you engaged to be married, then?' Frederica asked, then turned red and was glad Lady Caldwell had her back to her as she realised just how impertinent her enquiry sounded.

'La, but you are a country miss,' Lady Caldwell said with a musical laugh. 'I left my husband in London. I am travelling with several companions. I have my maid, as do the other ladies who make up our party. The rest of them are staying at Radthorn's house, as you know, and so for now you are my chaperon. Not a breath of scandal, I assure you.'

The thought of trying to chaperon the sophisticated Lady Caldwell made her want to giggle. The whole arrangement sounded odd, but then Lady Caldwell was clearly a woman of the world.

From out of the trunk Forester pulled a dark blue riding habit with gold epaulettes and lots of frogging.

'Do you ride out with us tomorrow, Lady Caldwell?' Frederica asked.

'Oh, my dear, you must call me Maggie or I vow I shall feel like an ancient crone.'

Put entirely at ease, Frederica laughed. 'No one would use that word to describe you. And thank you. Please call me Frederica.'

Maggie clapped her hands. 'To answer your question, yes, I will join the hunt. Do you go too?'

She nodded. That had been a bone of contention between her and Uncle Mortimer. In the end, she'd agreed, but only if she could stay well to the rear and avoid being present for the kill.

'I shall look forward to keeping you company.' Maggie rose to her feet. 'I can't wait for this masked ball. I love dressing up, don't you? Of course you do. What woman wouldn't? And wait until you see the wonderful men Radthorn has brought with him.' She put a delicate hand to the centre of her chest and gave a languid sigh, then laughed and held out her hand. 'Come, let us go downstairs. Tea must have arrived. I think you and I are going to get along famously.'

Oh, yes, they'd be great friends. Maggie would talk and Frederica would listen and everyone would be happy.

What would her new friend think if she learned that Frederica was an artist? A wanton? And about to go out into the world alone?

Robert tightened Pippin's girth and looked up at Frederica, the first of the riders out of the stable. No longer the secretive little mouse she'd been a day or so ago. The sea-green riding habit was of the very best quality. Its tailored lines suited her slim figure and matched the colour of her eyes. He'd never seen her look so elegant or so happy. She looked utterly charming. Glowing.

Bloody alluring.

He wanted to drag her back to his cottage and hide her away.

'Th-thank you, Robert,' she whispered.

Aye. She'd whisper, with her London guests nearby. And that was just how he wanted it. He touched his cap and pulled it lower on his forehead, keeping a wary eye out for Lullington. Of all the cursed ill luck, he had to be one of the guests. And Maggie, too. He was still having trouble believing it.

He shouldn't have reported for work this morning. He should have sent word of some infectious disease the moment he'd realised who young Bracewell had brought along as guests. But that would have left poor old Weatherby in the lurch.

A visiting groom led out the next animals, a sweet little chestnut mare called Penny and a large black gelding. The mare whickered a soft greeting to Robert. He bit back a curse. Who'd have thought the horse would remember him? Maggie, in a dark blue habit, strolled into the courtyard on Lullington's arm. Robert watched covertly as a groom threw her up. She was too busy conversing with the viscount to notice him, a mere servant. Thank God.

Instead of leaving the task to the groom, Lullington saw to Maggie's tack, his hand touching her thigh lightly in an intimate gesture as he finished. So Maggie had gone to Lullington. Perhaps that's why the viscount had been keen to see Robert disgraced. They had often vied for the same females, usually to Lullington's disadvantage. But unless things had changed, he'd not be able to afford the kind of baubles Maggie liked to add to her collection.

Lullington sprang into the saddle unaided. 'Hey, you

there.' He pointed his crop at Robert. 'A stirrup cup for the lady.'

Head lowered, Robert touched his hat and went for the tray of pewter cups set on a bench by the door. Normally Maisie would be out here passing the good cheer around, but something had happened in the kitchen and Snively had assigned Robert the task.

He handed a cup up to Maggie, who nodded a thank you.

Lullington looked down only long enough to grasp his goblet. He leaned closer to Maggie. 'God,' he lisped in a low voice, 'did you see the hack Bracewell is riding? A slug.'

Maggie's answering laugh struck a chord in his memory. It was what had attracted him to her in the first place. Merry and meaningless laughter. Now it left him cold.

He took a cup to Frederica, who bestowed thanks by way of an intimate little smile.

Robert prayed Lullington didn't notice. Damnation, but this was hell.

The last rider out of the stable was the young master on a showy bay. It was Robert's first real look at Frederica's cousin. Clearly greener than grass and still with his mother's milk on his lips, he was just the kind of youth dangling at the edges of society to be impressed with Lullington's smooth style of address. Still, even the daring viscount would not dare gull the lad under his own roof.

Bracewell jobbed at the horse's mouth. It reared in protest. Its wicked flying hooves narrowly missed Pippin. Frederica manoeuvred neatly out of the way. 'Take c-care, Simon.'

Robert caught the bay's bridle and soothed it with

some whispered words. 'Stirrup cup, sir?' he asked Bracewell, who seemed unconscious that another had taken control of his mount.

'Yes, by Jove. Good man.' Simon beamed. 'I say, Lullington. Good hunting weather, what?'

'Is it?' Lullington replied, looking up at the clear blue sky.

'You wag,' Bracewell said. 'Always ribbing a fellow. What do you think, Maggie? Are you ready to take the first brush today?'

Frederica winced, causing Pippin to dance side-ways.

Lullington, who had drawn close, caught her bridle. 'Steady there,' he said to the horse, his gaze fixed on Frederica. 'My word, Miss Bracewell, you look simply ravishing this morning. I am quite determined not to leave your side—you present such a pretty picture.'

Robert gritted his teeth and handed the last of the stirrup cups up to Bracewell. If he had known Lullington was to be ensconced under the same roof as Frederica, he might have whisked her off to Gretna Green and to hell with the consequences.

No, he wouldn't. Any more than Lullington would. The man was simply enjoying himself putting a pretty miss to the blush. Robert knew, because he'd done it himself. The last thing the viscount wanted was a wife as poor as himself.

He just hoped Frederica would see through the vis-count's charm to the rake beneath.

She hadn't seen through Robert, though. The thought gave him a cold feeling in his chest.

Gun over his shoulder, Weatherby marched into the courtyard and approached Bracewell with a touch to his hat. 'Hunt is meeting at the Bull and Mouth, Master

Simon. Ye've a half-hour to get there. Deveril here will send the beaters off ahead. You'll have a good day's sport, I promise ye.'

Robert ran around, collecting the goblets from the riders.

'We're off,' Maggie said, her face a picture of eagerness. 'We don't want to miss the start.' She trotted out of the courtyard and down the drive, with Bracewell right behind.

Frederica grimaced as if she'd like to miss the whole thing, but the viscount still retained his grip on her bridle. He gave it a jerk. The little gelding tossed his head, then broke into a canter with Lullington at Frederica's side.

Ire boiled in Robert's gut. How dare he touch her horse? It was as if he'd taken possession. Robert kept a tight grip on his urge to shout a protest. Lullington couldn't do her much harm if the party stayed together.

When Frederica leaned back and gave the viscount's black a sharp slap on the rump with her crop and the black took off at a gallop, he couldn't hold back his smile. For all her appearance of frailty, his Frederica was a woman to be reckoned with.

His? What the hell was he thinking? That was one thing she could never be. Not in any way, shape or form. And there were going to be no more midnight visits.

He'd made certain. He still felt a sharp pain between his ribs every time he recalled the hurt look on her face. What if they could be friends, as she'd asked? Would it ever be enough? Would he be able to resist her appeal? Damnation, he missed her like the devil already.

It wasn't as if he'd seduced an innocent, he reminded

himself, but there were different kinds of innocent. And she was the most vulnerable to a man like him.

'Don't stand there daydreaming,' Weatherby growled. 'Get off, lad. You need a half-hour start on the pack or they'll overrun the fox before midday.'

'We don't want that,' Robert said wryly and set off through the kitchen garden at a jog. He'd take the short cut and be gone from the inn long before the Wynchwood party appeared.

The hounds and red-coated hunters streamed up Gallows Hill far ahead of Frederica and Maggie, but Frederica didn't care.

'Hurry up, Frederica,' Maggie called back, twisting in her saddle. 'We are falling behind.'

That's the idea, Frederica thought, but she urged Pippin to a greater burst of speed. The gelding, who'd fretted at being held back, took the bit and surged forwards. Frederica kept a sharp eye out for rabbit holes.

Fortunately, her slow pace had annoyed Viscount Lullington. He'd galloped ahead, promising to return to see how she was doing the next time the hounds were at a stand.

She caught Maggie up and matched Pippin's speed to the chestnut. They rode side by side over the brow of the hill. Hopefully, they would not see her particular fox this morning.

Far ahead, the hunt master blew the view halloo. It seemed her wish was not to be granted.

'Here we go,' Maggie yelled, her eyes brimming with excitement. 'Come on, if you want to be in on the kill.'

Ugh. 'You go ahead. Pippin is lame. He must have

picked up a stone. I will need to dismount and take a look.'

Maggie gave a little grimace of disappointment. 'I'll send Lull or your cousin back to find you if you don't catch us up.'

Frederica waved her crop and watched Maggie fly off down the hill.

Pippin's ears pricked forwards. He strained at the bit.

'I know, old fellow. But we don't want to be there when they catch the fox. Wait a few minutes and then you can gallop.'

A lady in dark green and two men in hunting pink, members of Mr Radthorn's party whom she'd met at the village inn, straggled up to her. She waved them on. The last thing she needed was some well-meaning gentleman poking around in Pippin's hooves. He'd soon realise her excuse was a hum.

She had Pippin walk slowly down the hill, listening to the retreating sounds of baying hounds and the hunting horn. Leaning forwards, she patted her mount's neck. 'What do you think? Are they far enough ahead?'

He tossed his head as if he understood every word.

She laughed. 'Very well.' She dug her heel into his flank and he sprang forwards into a gallop, straining at the bit. Oh, dear. He seemed determined to catch the other horses. The hedge at the bottom of the hill came up fast. Too fast. She hauled on the reins, trying to turn his head. Too late. They were going to have to jump it. Not a good idea in a lady's saddle.

Her heart picked up speed. She eyed the closing distance, judged the horse's pace and steadied herself. Not that the saddle provided much support.

Pippin gathered himself. And they flew. She was

going to make it. Beautiful jump. Clean. Clear. The horse landed. Frederica hit the saddle with a bump and jolted sideways. She was flying again. Straight at the ground.

Ouch. She landed on her bottom. Hard. She couldn't breathe. She'd crushed her ribs. Panicked, she clutched her chest. She couldn't inhale. She was dying.

'Steady,' a deep voice said. 'Take it easy.'

A huge rush of air filled her lungs. Her head swam. For a moment she didn't know where she was. Then Robert's anxious face filled her vision. 'Where are you hurt?'

Grateful to feel the air sawing in and out of her lungs, she managed a weak smile. 'Winded.'

'Are you sure that is all?' His hands, gentle, clinical, ran over her arms, legs, back. 'Does it hurt when I touch you?'

'No. It feels lovely.'

He repressed a quick grin. 'Not another word.'

'Why aren't you up front with the villagers?'

'I was. I noticed you hanging back, then Lady Caldwell showed up without you. One of those idiots should have stayed behind.' He sounded furious.

'I'm not a child, you know. I've ridden these fields alone all my life.' She glanced around for Pippin. Not a sign of him.

'Still chasing the leaders,' Robert said.

'I don't know what got into him.'

'Overexcited, I suspect.' Robert held out a hand and pulled her to her feet. 'Can you walk?'

She took a couple of steps. Her legs felt like blanc-mange and her bottom hurt, but she wasn't injured. 'A little stiff and sore, but I'm fine.'

'Too bad.' His dark eyes sparkled. 'I was hoping for the excuse to carry you in my arms.'

'Now why didn't I think of that?'

'Because you don't play those kinds of games,' he said. 'Good thing too.'

There was no one in sight. The only thing in the middle of the field was them and an oak tree. An oak tree with a very wide and gnarly trunk. As they passed it, a wicked thought popped into her mind. 'Oh, I'm not feeling quite the thing.' She headed for the tree trunk and leaned against it with her arm covering her eyes.

'Are you feeling faint?' he said, peering into her face.

She let her arm fall and laughed up at him. 'No.'

He cursed softly. 'Do you know how beautiful you look?'

'No. But I'm hoping you are going to tell me.' Had she said that? Was it he who made her recklessly wanton, or was it all her bad blood?

He gave an unwilling laugh, his white teeth flashing in the black of his curly beard. 'It seems you do play those games.'

'Why have you given up shaving?' she asked.

He stroked his chin with strong square fingers. Mischief shone in his eyes. 'Don't you like it?'

'I'm not sure.'

He placed his hands against the rough trunk, his broad forearms bracketing her head. She drew in a quick breath at the jolt in her stomach. He leaned in for a kiss and she flung her arms around his neck and melded her body to his. After the strain of the morning, it felt wonderful to be in his arms.

He groaned and deepened the kiss, his mouth working magic against her lips, his hands crushing her close.

He broke away, and she was pleased to see he was breathing just as hard as she. 'Robert—'

'Someone is coming. Listen.'

Hoof beats approaching fast. 'Dash it all,' she muttered.

His dark eyes gleamed. 'You owe me the rest of that kiss, but for now, start walking.'

They stepped out from behind the shelter of the tree as a black horse and rider leading Pippin stopped to open the gate to the field.

'Your rescuer arrives,' Robert said drily.

'Viscount Lullington.'

He nodded. 'Watch that man, Frederica.' His voice held such deep loathing, she couldn't help but glance at his face. His eyes were narrowed and his shoulders tense.

'Do you know him?'

His lip curled. 'I know men like him. He'll take any advantage.'

'Oh, he's not interested in me. He's in love with Lady Caldwell.'

'That kind loves only one person. Himself.'

'Why, Robert,' she said, her smile growing, 'are you jealous?'

He glanced at her, his eyes dark, almost bleak. 'What right do I have for jealousy?'

With a sinking sensation, she realised he'd made no promises to her. 'Just do not trust that man.'

The viscount was almost upon them. She turned to face him as he leaped from his horse and strode to her side. He appeared not to notice Robert. 'Are you all right, Miss Bracewell?'

Wishing him elsewhere, she forced a smile. 'Perfectly fine. Pippin decided I needed a walk.'

He grinned. 'I am all admiration. Your spirit does you credit. I expected tears and gnashing of teeth.'

Federica could almost hear Robert grind *his* teeth. She gestured towards him. 'I was fortunate Mr Deveril came along or I might be less sanguine.'

'Good man,' the viscount said. He dug into his pocket and flipped a coin to land at Robert's feet.

Robert stared at it, his face rigid, pride in his eyes, in the set of his shoulders, then he bent to retrieve the coin from the dirt. He touched his cap and walked away.

She felt sick and faint. As if he'd been shamed and it was all her fault. She longed to call out an apology, but Robert's long legs carried him off at a rapid pace.

Meanwhile the viscount was all kind concern. 'Are you sure you are not hurt, Miss Bracewell?'

Heart aching, she forced herself to answer calmly. 'P-perfectly sure.'

Lullington looked at her face and then at the retreating Robert. 'Has he been with your family long?'

'Just a few weeks,' she said.

'He seems like a competent fellow, if rather bold.'

She glanced up to find him staring at her intently, his pale eyes seeming to see into her mind. His gaze dropped to her mouth and he gave a tight smile. 'Now, Miss Bracewell, do you think you can re-mount this beast?' He pointed to Pippin.

Aware of prickling heat creeping up her face, she nodded. 'I can.'

'Pluck to the backbone. Let me give you a hand.'

He led her to Pippin and she noticed how soft the leather of his gloves and how long and languid his fingers were. A shudder ran down her spine as if she'd brushed past a cobweb in the dark. Such nonsense. He was a dandy. A nobleman. She was wrong to compare him with the hard-working Robert.

With Maisie looking on, her face a picture of envy, Frederica twisted to look at her back in the mirror. Wings. Made of the sheerest material and dusted with sequins, they looked almost real. The gown made her look taller, more shapely. 'It is supposed to represent Titania from *A Midsummer Night's Dream*. Mrs Phillips did a wonderful job.'

'You look like a fairy an' all, miss,' Maisie said. 'My ma used to tell me about them. Don't walk in the fairy circle, she always used to say. Toadstools, they was.'

With a smile, Frederica ran her hands down the front of her sheer gown of browns and soft greens.

Maisie went to work with the hairbrush and Frederica let her thoughts wander. What would Robert think if he saw her now? Would he approve? Or would he stare at her with those fathomless dark eyes and tell her that she looked like a damned peacock? Pretty, but useless.

She couldn't prevent a small smile. Yes, that was indeed what the blunt, unpolished man would say. And after tonight, after her one and only ball, she would never look like a peacock again. Why, she might even dance the night away on the arm of a handsome gentleman. She sighed. If only that gentleman could be Robert, it would be the best night of her life.

A knock sounded on the door. 'Who is it?'

'Maggie. May I come in?'

'Please do.'

Maggie looked simply ravishing. A vision. Frederica felt quite dull and plain as she took in the gauzy trousers and soft veils of midnight-blue covered in sequins. The dress of an exotic eastern harem girl. Bangles jingled on her wrists and around her ankles, and a heavy gold choker fringed with coins hugged her elegant neck. Her eyes, rimmed with kohl, peeped over the top of a gold-edged veil.

The brush was held suspended over Frederica's head as Maisie let her mouth hang open.

'You look beautiful,' Frederica said.

The dark-eyed siren ran her gaze over Frederica. Her finely plucked brows shot up. 'Oh, my dear. You are simply divine.' She floated across the room to finger the fabric. 'Look how cleverly she dags the hem and so much fabric. If I had only thought of it.' She shook her head. 'But no. My curves were never meant to play a wood sprite. I would look like a gnome. My dear, you will be the belle of the ball.'

'Fine feathers make fine birds,' Frederica said with a laugh, quoting one of Mortimer's favourite sayings.

Maisie began brushing again.

'And modest too. So refreshing. My dear, you must come to London. They will adore you.'

Until they discovered who she was, then she would be ostracised. Uncle Mortimer had made that very plain. And that was why she did not understand why Simon's parents were going along with his uncle's betrothal plans. But apparently they were. There was only one way out, she'd realised in the dark of her room late last night. She'd have to tell Simon she was a fallen woman. He'd be so disgusted, he'd have to cry off.

She'd offer to save him a whole lot of embarrassment by disappearing.

She could do it without getting Robert into trouble. No one would need to know who had debauched her, any more than they knew who had debauched her mother.

All she needed was a few private words with Simon and she would be free to live her own life.

Unfortunately, Simon spent all his time glued to the viscount's side while Lord Lullington looked bored nigh unto death.

Tomorrow, after the ball, she'd find a way to get Simon alone.

While Maisie finished brushing Frederica's hair, Maggie wandered around the room, touching the bed, pulling open the curtains to stare out of the window, strolling back to the dressing table. Restless energy rolled off her in waves.

She spun about. 'How will you wear your hair?'

'Miss always has it in a knot,' Maisie said.

Maggie tilted her head to one side. 'Wear it down.'

'Too fine,' Frederica said. 'It doesn't have a scrap of curl.' Unlike the older woman's luxuriant waves.

Maggie picked up the headdress, a simple wreath of silk flowers in yellow, pink and white, wound around with ivy leaves. 'You are wrong. Pin it up at the sides so it falls down your back and leaves your neck and shoulders bare.' With a hairpin, she caught one side up, then added another. She popped the circlet on Frederica's head so it settled high on her brow. 'Like so. What do you think?'

It made her look young and vulnerable, and...well almost pretty. 'I like it.' She smiled at Maggie's reflection. 'I really do. But it will not stay.'

'More pins,' Maggie cried. 'Fasten those pieces we pulled back to the circlet. That will hold them in place.' Once more she looked at Frederica like a bird eyeing a worm. 'Earbobs.'

Frederica blinked. 'I don't have any.'

Maggie looked surprised. 'No? I know. I will lend

you some of mine. Sapphires?' She shook her head. 'Diamonds. Nothing but diamonds will do. You will provide the colour and they the light.'

'Oh, no, I couldn't.'

'But you shall.' The lady had a determined gleam in her eye and a stubborn set to her jaw.

And Frederica could not think of a reason to refuse. She smiled. 'Then thank you.'

'Oooh. This is so exciting. Wait a moment while I fetch them.'

'What a nice lady,' Maisie said as Maggie scurried out of the door. 'And pretty too.'

How nice to have a friend for the first time in her life. There had been a lot of firsts just lately. 'Very pretty. Thank you, Maisie, for your help. I am sure there are lots of things you are needed for downstairs. You can go now.'

'Aye. Mrs Doncaster is fair fit to burst she's that busy.' Maisie packed up the pins and tidied the dressing table.

'I suppose Cook did not want to lose you to me this afternoon.'

Maisie grinned. 'Mums the word on that, miss. Oh, and by the way, I was to tell you that your uncle wants to see you in the library before the other guests arrive.' She bobbed a curtsy and headed for the door, standing back for a moment to allow Maggie to enter carrying a leatherbound case, before she hurried away.

'Here you are, my dear Frederica.' She set the case down on the dressing table, and pulled forth a string of the most gorgeous diamonds, a delicate strand of little teardrops with earbobs to match. She fastened the necklace around Frederica's throat and stood back to admire. 'Perfect. Now the earrings.' Frederica turned back to the mirror and gasped. 'It is lovely, but I can't wear something so valuable.'

'Nonsense. It is not half as lovely as you, my dear. You will outshine everyone.'

Frederica swung around to face her. 'Oh, no! How can you say such a thing?'

The other woman sighed and patted her hand. 'I'm not much prone to think of others, but for some odd reason I like you.' She laughed. It sounded a little brittle. 'And Lull will be so proud of me when I tell him, he will no doubt buy me the pearls I have been after.'

Frederica couldn't help laughing at her naughty grin.

'And now I must be off,' Maggie said. 'My poor Forester is quite in a fit about my headdress. Apparently, it needs work.' She stood in the doorway and blew a kiss. 'I will see you downstairs.'

Frederica felt rather as if a whirlwind had blown in and out of the room. She took a deep breath. Time to visit Uncle Mortimer. Hopefully he would not be too shocked at this gown.

Simon and Uncle Mortimer rose on her entry into the study. They looked quite splendid. For once, Uncle Mortimer was not wearing his old-fashioned frock coat. Although not in costume, he looked magnificent in a black coat with silver buttons and satin knee breeches. He'd even powdered his best wig. She made her curtsy. 'You wanted to speak with me, Uncle?'

As Mortimer looked her up and down, his pink nose quivered. Oh, dear. Perhaps she would not be attending the ball after all.

'I say, coz,' Simon said, his eyes bulging worse than

usual above his mountain of neckerchief. 'You look splendid. Where did you get the jewels?'

'Lady Caldwell l-l—'

'Lent them to you,' Simon said. 'Most obliging. Is she not the most delightful of creatures?'

Uncle Mortimer grunted, but gestured her to sit. 'We need to talk about this evening.'

She perched on the chair. 'Yes, Uncle.'

'Mind your manners and behave as you ought. Do not mention your mother and things should come off well enough.'

She stiffened. 'I don't know why Simon wishes to marry me, when you are all so ashamed of my connections.'

Simon's mouth opened and closed. He gulped. Small beads of perspiration lined his loose top lip. 'Really, coz. A pleasure.'

If that was the truth, why did he sound so anxious?

Uncle Mortimer glowered at him before turning his attention back to Frederica. 'You should be grateful he is willing to make the sacrifice.'

'Good for the family name,' Simon added, looking as grave as an undertaker.

'Gratitude is in the eye of the beholder,' Frederica said, her anger making the words come out in one go.

Mortimer's mouth dropped open. 'Damn stupid saying.' He pointed a shaking finger at her face. 'Listen to me, young lady. One wrong word out of you, one syllable astray, and you'll find yourself in the workhouse. Do I make myself clear?'

'I say. By Jove, Uncle. A bit harsh, what? I'm sure m'cousin don't need reminding of our charity. She knows her place.' Simon gave her one of his pleading

looks. He hated a fuss. Frederica wanted to take each
end of his stupid cravat and pull hard.

She certainly wasn't going to get any sense out of
him at this moment. He always did what Mortimer said,
but if he thought he had any say in her life now or in
the future, he was in for a surprise.

She bowed her head to hide her thoughts. 'I understand, Uncle.'

Mortimer looked her up and down. 'What is Lady
Radthorn thinking? You are almost naked. I've a
damned good mind to lock you in your room.' If truth
be told, he'd probably like to drag her into his under-
ground tunnel and feed her worms. Or feed her to the
worms.

'No need to make a fuss, Uncle. I'm sure it's all the
crack,' Simon said, surprising Frederica. 'You should
see what the ladies wear in London.'

'I doubt they are ladies,' Uncle Mortimer grumbled.

She wasn't exactly a lady either. She pressed her lips
together to stop from smiling.

Finally composed enough to raise her gaze, she
caught both men looking at each other with a sort of
satisfied smirk. Now what were they up to? 'Will there
be anything else, Uncle?'

'I'll be watching you, girl. Closely. Behave well, and
who knows, perhaps Simon will take you to London to
see the sights one day.'

Never.

'Off you go. Be downstairs in the hallway ready to
meet the guests at seven o'clock with Lady Radthorn.'
He flicked his fingers in dismissal.

Doubts about her plan assailed Frederica as she left
the room. Simon was so far beneath Uncle's thumb, he'd

probably accept her despoiled state without a murmur, if Uncle Mortimer insisted.

In that case, there was nothing else she could do but run.

Robert cut across the Wynchwood lawn. Light streaming from the downstairs windows made it easy to see his way. Clearly Lord Wynchwood intended to impress his neighbours and his London guests.

Preferring to check out the lie of the land before venturing into the lion's den, Robert pushed through the shrubbery beneath the ballroom windows and from the shadows peered into a room packed with every imaginable creature and assorted figures from history.

All the local gentry were invited, according to Weatherby, as well as the guests down from London. A few years ago he would have been one of them, though he rarely attended such dull affairs. Now here he was, an outsider skulking in the bushes.

Invitation or not, they ought to be honoured by his attendance. He'd found the perfect costume, too—a highwayman. The only person he feared might see through the disguise was Maggie. She might recognise his voice. He'd practised keeping it coarse and rough and with the beard and the waxed moustaches he'd devised from locks of his hair, he defied even his mother to recognise him.

The scrap of black silk he had fashioned for a mask covered the top half of his face. He pulled his borrowed tricorn hat down low on his brow for further concealment.

He took a deep breath. Now or never.

Careful to avoid attracting attention, he worked his way around to the front door, timing his entrance with the arrival of a carriage full of guests. Out stepped a Roman dignitary and his toga-clad lady, a male dressed as an Oriental in loose, flowing robes, who he immediately recognized as Radthorn, and a woman in a Tudor ruff and enormous skirt. Robert followed them in. Snively didn't give him a second glance as they were directed to the antechamber where the ladies could change their shoes and leave their cloaks.

'Really, John,' the Tudor lady whispered having passed off her wrap to Maisie, 'are you sure the Bracewells are quite the thing?' She wrinkled her nose at the faded wallpaper above grimy panelling. 'It is a little dingy.'

Lady Bentham, Robert realised. A merry young widow and John's long-time mistress. John always said his grandmother was up for a lark. She had to be if she permitted him to house his mistress under her roof. If the old lady knew, that was.

Radthorn glanced around, his gaze passing over Robert without a gleam of recognition. 'Old friends of the family. I haven't been here in years.' A smile flashed from beneath his drooping moustache. 'It hasn't changed a bit.'

Robert let his breath go. If his erstwhile best friend didn't recognise him, then it appeared he was safe.

'Why on earth was Lullington so insistent we all come?' Lady Bentham asked. 'It is going to be dreadfully dull.'

Radthorn shrugged. 'You know Lullington. Young Bracewell owes him money and he's not going to let him escape without paying up.'

Robert felt a flash of embarrassment. He'd left a great many debts in his wake. Devil take it, he would pay them no matter how long it took.

John took his lady's arm and with many curses from him and much laughter from her, he helped her tilt her enormous hoop to allow her to pass through the doorway and they headed for the ballroom.

His heart racing more than he liked, Robert trailed them. The Roman tribune and his lady followed hard on his heels.

'Oh, my,' Lady Bentham said, stopping at the entrance to the grand room that ran the length of the back of the house.

Robert wasn't surprised at her reaction to the swathes of cloth draping the walls and hundreds of candles. He'd spent most of the day helping with them.

'She's beautiful,' Lady Bentham continued. 'Who is she?'

Robert's jaw dropped as he saw that she referred not to the decorations, but to the lady. A vision of loveliness, a glittering queen of the fairies. Frederica. He choked back a gasp.

Dressed in something floating and sheer, she looked enchanting. It didn't take much to imagine the slender limbs beneath the skirts, or the high, pert breasts skimmed by the low-cut bodice. An ethereal queen of the fairies. He half-expected her to use the gossamer wings cunningly attached to the back of her gown and fly off on a breeze.

Every man in the room had the look of a rabid dog as they gazed at her. Only by dint of will did he stop himself from rushing to her side and covering her with his highwayman's cloak.

Her face glowed. Beneath her mask of silk and sequins, her lips were parted in excitement. Yet her eyes held the shadows of absolute terror. Pride filled him. Pride at her beauty and her courage. The beast inside him wanted to proclaim her as his own.

He clenched his jaw instead.

'I had no idea she was so lovely,' Radthorn said, in an awed whisper. 'Simon's cousin. I met her on the hunt this morning. She is making her début under my grandmother's guidance.'

Lady Bentham dug him in the ribs. 'Stop salivating.'

Robert had never seen John look so besotted. He wanted to strangle his friend with his bare hands. He kept them loose at his sides.

The Roman couple pushed forwards. 'I say there, what's the hold up?'

The last thing he needed was an altercation. Robert extricated himself from the little knot at the door and swaggered in best highwayman style to his chosen location behind a pillar. From here he would observe yet remain unnoticed.

Like every man in the room, he found his gaze drawn to the slight figure in earth tones and diamonds. Like every man in the room, she filled his heart with a strange kind of wonder. He could see it in their eyes. How could any woman look so lovely, so pure, so unattainable?

A sprite come to taunt them all.

How could the man at her side, a cherub-faced idiot in a lion suit and a foolish grin, think himself good enough? Hell. Robert wasn't good enough, but he wasn't going to let that stop him from claiming the first waltz.

He knew the moment she saw him, because she smiled brightly enough to outshine the hundreds of candles. A dozen men around him gasped and clutched their assorted chests of steel and wool and silk, but only he caught the full force of her wide-eyed astonishment.

He bowed and gave a slight shake of his head.

She covered her laugh with her fingers and looked away. His heart thudded wildly. The music started. A cotillion. The lion held out his arm. She placed her hand in his paw.

A growl of protest rumbled in Robert's chest. He almost stepped out from his pillar. Mine. The possessive thought reverberated in his mind, yet he held still, narrow eyed, watching.

The scent of violets wafted beneath his nose. A voluptuous maiden in a veil and the garb of a sultan's consort drifted to his side. 'Oh, my,' she said. 'I do like a tall, strong highwayman. Who are you? Ten String Jack?'

Damnation. Maggie.

'No, yer ladyship. I be the ghost of Mad Jack. Hung I was, up on Gallows Hill yonder.'

Maggie recoiled. 'Lud! How gruesome.' She eyed him up and down. 'You know, I have the strangest feeling I know you from somewhere.' She smiled her radiant, sophisticated, charming smile. A smile as bright as the gold coins on her bangles. The smile she used to hide her disappointments in the life she'd been handed by her parents. Married to an old man as a girl.

He grinned back. 'No, yer ladyship. I live in these parts. You ain't never heard of me.'

'Oh, you foolish creature. I know we have met. Who are you?'

He flashed her a leer and waggled his brows. 'If ye guess right, I'll kiss you. Else ye'll wait until the unmasking.' When he'd be long gone.

'Maggie?' Lullington's imperious voice jerked her head around.

The viscount, splendid as the Sun King in a gold mask and his lean body tightly encased in a suit of white embroidered with gold, crooked a finger. 'Dance, my lady?'

'Coming, Lull.' She hurried off, but not before she cast a glance over her shoulder at Robert. He couldn't resist. He bowed his appreciation. She really was a lovely sight. The loveliest woman in the room save for one.

Not that Frederica's partner did her justice. Pompous ninny. The man knew the steps and performed with dignity, but without grace or feel for the music. The idiot spent most of his time nodding to the other members of the set, or shouting raillery to the other square when all his attention should have been fixed on his partner.

Popinjay.

The back of Robert's neck prickled. Someone was watching him. Nonchalantly, as if seeking refreshment, he turned away from the dance floor. A swift glance found Radthorn's puzzled gaze fixed on his person. Robert pretended not to notice and, walking with a limp, headed for the refreshment table. Glass in hand, he looked again. John's attention was now wholly engaged with a grey-haired lady in the full regalia of the last century and looking as if she had simply pulled out one of her old gowns and wigs. Her long chin reminded him of John's. This must be the doughty grandmother of whom John had spoken often and with great affection. The woman who had taken Frederica in hand.

Thank God the old dear hadn't spoiled Frederica's natural grace and spirit and turned her into a simpering miss like the one dressed as a shepherdess, crook in hand, heading his way.

Robert swung away. He prowled the circumference of the ballroom, avoiding Maggie and the shepherdess with spectacular success until Maggie cornered him beside the orchestra.

'Dance with me,' she said, batting her kohl-rimmed eyelashes.

'Nay, lass,' he growled.

She pouted. 'La, sir. You are very rude.'

Flags of colour flew in her cheeks, a sign of her rare temper. Not good.

He pointed to her flimsy sandals. 'I are mortal afeared of stepping on your pretty little toes.'

She pointed her foot. 'They are pretty, aren't they?' She gazed at his feet. 'And you are wearing very large boots.' She reached up and tapped his chest with her flail. 'But I'll not take it as an excuse, sir.'

He grinned his defeat. 'Then, my lady, your wish is my command.'

He led her into a set still in need of couples and she spent the whole of the dance throwing names at him. When they promenaded down the set, she laughed up at him. 'Why won't you tell me?'

'It's a masked ball. You ain't supposed to know.'

'Infuriating man.' She narrowed her eyes. 'That voice… Are you related to a member of the *ton*?'

'Arr, missy. I'm related to the King of Thieves. Aladdin.'

She shook her fist at him, then groaned as the music concluded. 'I give up, but I will see you later.'

Chuckling at her boldness, Robert stalked back to his pillar. Nearby, Lady Radthorn was engaged in a heated discussion with the master of the house.

'Of course it is necessary. Do you want the world to think the Wynchwoods are country bumpkins?'

'I have no reason to care what the world thinks,' Lord Wynchwood said, wiping his brow. 'You are giving me a headache.'

'Then do as I ask. You requested my help, now you will accept it. We invited all these people from town. They expect to waltz.'

'No.'

'Oh, you are past bearing.'

'And you are overbearing. And foolish.'

The two of them stared at each other in silence. Any man with an iota of common sense would have known Lady Radthorn would not be gainsaid.

Lord Wynchwood sagged. 'All right. I'll give the instruction. But my niece will not waltz. She will stand right here beside me.'

'Nonsense. The gel must dance.'

Robert permitted himself a small smile and positioned himself within easy range of his lordship. The Roman, with whom Frederica had danced the last set, returned her to her spot beside her uncle and Lady Radthorn, who continued to argue that Frederica must dance.

Before anyone could instruct her either way, Robert strode forwards and led her on to the floor to the opening bars of the waltz.

'I say,' her uncle called out.

'Too late,' Robert murmured.

Frederica laughed up at him. 'True to your profession, sir?'

'Aye,' he murmured finding her laugh enough to set wild music soaring in his blood. What was left of his mind he needed for dancing.

She glided in beneath the light touch of his fingers. In his hovel, she'd been earth, grounding him in the here and now. In the ballroom, with the candles playing rainbows among her diamonds and shimmering in the ocean colour of her eyes, she was pure sprite. She floated beneath his fingers, her lips curved in a smile of joy. He felt as if he could fight demons and win.

'R-Robert?'

'Hush,' he murmured into hair scented with vanilla and roses. 'I'm Mad Jack tonight.'

Her smile grew. 'Mad indeed.' Her eyes sparkled. 'You remembered my story.'

'I did.'

Her face dropped. 'But the fox…'

'Safe and sound. Probably up on Gallows Hill, watching the lights and the dancing and wondering whose chickens to steal.'

A gurgle of laughter curled around him. 'How?'

'I trapped the other fox down in the meadow.'

They circled the floor. Despite feigned indifference, he noticed eyes watching him and wondering. Fans fluttered as people asked who he was. He dare not request more than one dance.

'You will be in d-dreadful trouble if you are discovered, but I'm so glad you are here. I had quite decided not to waltz. But I would have been sorry.'

'Me too, sweetheart. You deserve to dance all night.'

He swung her in a dizzying circle, her body, as pliant as a willow, moved in perfect harmony. She felt right in his arms, as if they'd been made for one another. Why had it taken so long to find her? And why now, when he could do nothing about it? After tonight she would be the toast of London. The *ton* despised anything different, except the truly unique. Those they embraced with fervour. For a while. Look at Byron and Brummell. His little wood nymph might well be next.

He caught sight of John watching her with a smile of admiration. His gut clenched. Before long some smooth-talking dissipated rogue would sweep her away with soft words and flattery.

He had no way to prevent it. He could not ask her to give up her life of privilege.

She sighed sweetly. 'I'm so glad you came here tonight.'

He inhaled her scent. 'I couldn't stay away.' He would have been worried knowing how nervous she was.

She glanced up at him and he saw shadows in her gaze. His gut clenched. Something was wrong.

'Meet me in my room, when this dance is over,' she whispered.

He stared at her, startled. 'Are you mad?'

'I owe you the rest of that kiss, remember?'

Arousal gripped him fast and hard. 'It's too dangerous.'

'Please.'

Her husky voice sounded so full of longing, he wanted to kiss those lips right at that moment, lose himself in her magic. He fought the urge to crush her close and smiled down at her instead. 'For a few moments with you, I'd dare anything.'

'My room is on the second floor.'

'I know. I helped with the move this afternoon.'

Her cheeks turned a delicate rose. 'I will make some excuse. Say I need to pin my gown. But R-Robert. Please. Be very careful.'

'Always.'

For the last few moments of the dance, he lost himself

in the depths of her sea-witch gaze and allowed himself to dream it would never end. The music came to a close all too soon.

His arms ached when she stepped out of their embrace. His heart felt empty. Yet he must let her go. He led her back to her uncle.

'Where did you learn to waltz?' the old man asked, his chins wobbling and his face a furious red. 'Disgraceful dance. I am shocked.'

'Oh, my dear,' Lady Radthorn said. 'You looked lovely. Quite lovely.'

Other men approached. Robert could smell their interest. Soon she would be surrounded. Flattered. He wanted to draw his ancient pistol and hold them at bay. Instead, he bowed to no one in particular and withdrew.

On his way across the room, he sidestepped the shepherdess. Fortunately, since Lullington had Maggie's full attention on the dance floor, he strolled out of the ballroom unnoticed by anyone but Frederica.

The promised kiss had him hot with lust. Careless of who saw him, he ran up the stairs and slipped into her chamber.

Would she dance a set with another of her admirers before she joined him, or would she come right away? He paced around the bed and back to the fire. Five minutes passed. Then another. Damn it. It was all a tease.

The door opened. He dove for the shadows at the head of the bed.

'R-Robert?'

Joy flooded his veins. He stepped forwards and held out his arms.

She rushed into them and put her mouth up for his kiss. And kiss her he did. Long and sweet, full of his heart and his soul. It wasn't enough. 'Oh, sweetling,' he murmured against her mouth, 'I have wanted to do that all night. You ran a terrible danger meeting me here.'

'It is all right. No one thought anything of it.'

He led her to the chair by the window and sat with her on his lap. He kissed her again, sincerely, tenderly, fiercely.

'R-Robert,' she gasped, when he at last permitted her to take a breath. 'What is the matter?'

He forced himself to speak. 'I just had to tell you how beautiful you look tonight.'

She wound her arms around his neck. 'Thank you. And thank you for being the first to waltz with me. I wasn't nervous at all.'

He smiled down at her. 'I had to see my pupil's début.'

'Thank you.' She kissed his cheek.

He stroked the silky tresses floating down her back. 'I'd risk anything for a moment alone with you. I felt so bad sending you away, but if your uncle ever found out about us, I fear what he might do to you. I can't bear the thought of bringing you harm.'

'I know.' There was sadness in her voice. 'And if my uncle finds out you've been meeting me, you will lose your position.'

He felt like he'd destroyed something precious, but he had no choice. 'I don't care about that, but our worlds are too far apart. I can't offer you the life you deserve. We have to end this here.'

She rested her head on his chest, her sigh a balm to his heart. 'Run away with me.'

Shock ripped through him. And longing. He almost said yes, then he imagined the kind of life he could provide, dragging her from one estate to another, never sure of a roof over their heads. 'You'd lose everything—position, your family. I have no means to support you.'

'I don't care. I hate them.'

God, why was refusing her so hard? He'd never before felt as if he was cutting off his right arm when he gave a woman her *congé*? What was it about this one that had buried itself so deeply under his skin? 'I care.'

'Why don't you just admit that you are tired of me?' Her voice was husky with emotion, but when she gazed into his face her eyes were hard and bright. 'If I hadn't come to ask you teach me to dance, you would not have sought me out, would you?'

He squeezed his eyes shut for a second. He considered asking her to wait until he was well established and become his wife.

A wife? Had he lost his reason? He never stayed with a woman for more than a month or two. It wasn't in his nature. No. He had to be cruel to do the right thing. 'No. I never would have sought you out.'

She pushed away from him.

He let his arms fall away. Felt the chill as she slipped off his lap to stand before him.

'Fine,' she said. 'If that is what you want, then there is nothing more I can say. I wish you well, R-Robert Deveril.' She headed for the door.

For a single mad moment, he considered telling her his story. Of unburdening himself. Oh, hell. What kind of man placed his problems on a woman's slight shoulders? A weakling. 'You'll thank me one day,' he said.

She paused with her hand on the doorknob, not looking back. 'Will I?'

He cracked a hard laugh. 'Probably not. Go ahead. I will follow in a moment or two.'

She turned then, her eyes drinking him in as if for the last time. 'Take care, R-Robert.'

He grinned. 'Don't worry about me. Enjoy the rest of your ball.'

'It won't be the same.' On that wrenching admission, she slipped out into the hall and closed the door.

His heart felt as if someone had torn it in two and stamped on the pieces.

Chapter Eight

Five hellish minutes passed with Robert listening at the chamber door for sounds in the hallway beyond. All he could think about was getting as far away from Wynchwood as possible and drowning himself in brandy. Only a shred of sanity kept him from storming down the stairs.

Heart thudding slow, he continued to listen, angry he'd hurt her. Angry he didn't have a choice.

Hearing nothing, he stepped into the hallway, closed the door swiftly behind him and sauntered for the staircase as if he had every right to be wandering the upper chambers.

A soft click behind him made the hairs on the back of his neck rise. Had someone seen him leave her chamber? If they had, they'd not raised an outcry. Resisting the temptation to turn and look, he continued on his way. A couple in medieval garb ascended the stairs giggling and laughing, clearly looking for privacy. The joys of a masked ball.

Nodding politely, though he doubted they saw him, Robert continued on down the wide staircase, his footsteps drowned by the noise of revelry. The guests had spilled out into the entrance hall where tables sagged beneath punch bowls and glasses. He pushed through towards the front door, narrowly missing treading on Bracewell's lion's tail and dodging a wildly waving tribal spear.

He caught sight of Frederica standing in the doorway to the ballroom, smiling brightly at Radthorn and a couple of his cronies. Too brightly. God, she looked lovely. Something dark rose up in his chest as John smiled down at her, his gaze fixed on her face in undivided attention. An overwhelming desire to snatch her away, to ride off with her, made him clench his fists.

He didn't have the right to take her away from everything she knew and he'd finally convinced her he no longer wanted her. Longing hung around his neck like a chain.

He'd never stop wanting her.

With an effort, he turned away. He'd have to leave Wynchwood. He would never be able to stand in the shadows watching her, seeing her with men like Radthorn and Lullington, and not commit murder.

He stopped at a refreshment table and grabbed a bumper of brandy. It went down in one gulp, burning his gullet. Trust Wynchwood to buy cheap brandy. He needed fresh air. Needed to clear his head. Get a grip, Robert.

There were hundreds more women waiting to be plucked.

Except he didn't want any of them. For his sins, he only wanted one.

He continued his progress to the door.

'Ladies and gentlemen.' A voice rang out above the hubbub of talking and music. 'May I have your attention?' Lord Wynchwood's voice. 'I have an announcement. Please gather in the ballroom.'

The crowd around Robert craned their necks in the direction of the voice, pressing closer, surging forwards.

Robert pushed against the tide.

'I say,' said a pirate. 'You are going the wrong way.'

'You stepped on my skirts,' a queen said crossly, tugging at her train.

'Excuse me,' he said, shifting his foot.

Someone shoved him. His hat and wig slipped. He grabbed at it. Other faces turned his way, curious.

Damn. Any moment now, his behaviour was going to garner unwanted attention. He let himself be carried along with the flow into the ballroom, slowly inching his way closer to the bank of French windows, which he'd earlier made sure were closed but not locked.

He looked up to see Frederica standing on the orchestra dais beside her uncle. She looked mutinous and worried. What the hell was going on?

Jammed between a Roman senator and a black cat and blocked by Queen Elizabeth's enormous hoops, he wasn't going anywhere without causing a stir. He remained still, watching Frederica, who looked more unhappy than when he'd left her upstairs, if that was possible.

Someone bumped him. He braced himself to withstand the shoves of those around him.

'Quiet, please,' Lord Wynchwood yelled. The buzz of conversation died away. A trickle of sweat ran down

Robert's back as the temperature in the room increased along with the level of curiosity.

'Thank you,' Wynchwood said. 'It is my very great pleasure to announce the betrothal of my ward, Miss Frederica Bracewell, to my heir, Mr Simon Bracewell.'

Betrothed? All around him, people shouted their congratulations and exclaimed their surprise, while Robert felt as if a black hole had opened in front of his feet and he was falling in. His vision darkened, his heart seemed to still in his chest. Betrothed?

The cold steel of betrayal knifed through his chest, an edge so finely honed, so cold and sharp, the pain almost drove him to his knees.

Why hadn't she told him? Had she tried, just now, and lost her nerve? Is that why she asked him to run away with her?

Was that the reason she'd come to him in the first place, as a means to escape an unwanted marriage? Would she now confess her sins? At any moment he expected to hear her inform her uncle that she was no longer chaste.

Not that she'd been chaste when she came to him, but they were not to know that.

God, she'd even offered to pay him. To sit as a model. Was that all she had wanted to pay for? Was it? Was she like every other woman in his life, simply using him? She'd certainly betrayed his trust by not telling him the truth.

He pushed blindly through the crowd, squeezing between hot bodies, his nose filled with the stink of perfumes and powdered wigs. The crowd parted with cross looks and grumbles. His stomach roiled with self-disgust. He'd allowed himself to be used.

He felt sick.

A scream rang out.

Once more silence reigned in the ballroom. The room seemed to hold its breath. Nothing moved, except Robert, pressing steadily ahead, the doors filling his vision like the Holy Grail to a Templar Knight.

'My emeralds,' a woman's voice cried. 'I've been robbed.'

Exclamations of horror rippled around the room. People looked at each other in shock, checked their jewels, glanced at each other in suspicion.

Barely aware, and uncaring, Robert drew the curtains aside. He needed air. Something to clear his head, something to stem the tide of icy blackness rising up from his chest and threatening annihilation.

'Stop the highwayman,' a male voice cried out from behind him. Lullington?

A crocodile with a fat belly barred his path.

Surprised, Robert shouldered him aside and grabbed the door handle. The crocodile gripped his wrist. Anger rose up. Robert swung his fist. It connected to bone and soft flesh with a satisfying crunch. The man landed on his tail with a howl. Robert pulled open the door, only to have it slammed shut by the weight of the oriental man and an enormously fat monk.

'Oh, no, you don't,' John Radthorn said, breathing hard beneath his conical hat. 'No one leaves until we find the jewels.'

Jewels? Right. Someone had yelled something about stolen emeralds. He glanced around at the suspicious faces, John's, Simon Bracewell's, his lion head gone, Lord Wynchwood's. 'I don't have your bloody jewels,' he said. 'But I do have an urgent appointment.'

'Search him,' someone said.

'Go to hell,' Robert growled.

John Radthorn raised a brow. 'No one leaves this house until they are searched and unmasked.' His voice was quiet, but full of determination.

His disguise wouldn't hold up in front of John. Not unmasked.

He pulled his pistol from his belt. 'Stand back, damn you. I haven't got your jewels. I'm leaving.'

People gasped, men muttered, but as one the crowd pulled back, leaving a glittering Lullington in the empty space, with Maggie a few feet behind him. The viscount's lip curled. 'A highwayman. How appropriate. 'Tis my belief he is our thief.'

Bloody hell and damnation. 'I've stolen nothing. I'll let you search me. Then I'm going.'

Lullington minced forwards. 'Perhaps he handed his ill-gotten gains off to an accomplice.' He moved to check Robert's pockets despite the pistol.

The man had courage. But Robert already knew that.

'Not you,' Robert growled and shoved the pistol in Lullington's face.

The viscount halted with a nasty smile on his lips and recognition in his eyes.

He knew.

Robert's heart picked up speed. He glanced around, caught Radthorn's intense stare and nodded at him. 'You do it. I've nothing to hide.'

Men in the crowd surged closer. Robert waved his pistol. 'Who wants a ball in their head? I'll drop the first of ye like a stone.'

'My God,' Wynchwood said. 'That man works for me.'

Inwardly, Robert groaned, even as he smiled and

bowed. 'My lord. Thank you for a very pleasant evening. I would recommend a little less water in the punch.'

A half-smile kicked up John's mouth as he moved in. Robert held his hands away from his body, watching the men crowding closer. Off to his right, still on the dais, a small figure in green-and-brown earth tones stared down at him. Her eyes were huge in her pale face.

Radthorn would find nothing and Robert would leave her to her betrothal ball. His lip curled. Once he was gone, she could announce her ruin with his blessing.

John patted the pockets in his coat, ran a hand across his waistcoat and his hips. 'No jewels,' he said.

'Then why is he holding us at bay with a gun?' Lullington lisped, waving a languid hand. 'I suggest we call the magistrate and have him searched properly by the local constable.'

A man dressed as King Charles the First, but looking more like a spaniel, popped through the throng. 'I am the magistrate. You,' he said to Robert, 'will put down your pistol and submit to a proper search of your person.'

'That was a proper search,' John said, his voice strained.

Robert glanced at him, saw concern in his friend's eyes and his stomach hit the floor. John had found something.

A hiss of steel whipped his head around. It was Lullington pulling a sword from his costume's scabbard.

He held the sword tip against Robert's throat. 'It is my guess the rogue's pistol isn't loaded.' He showed his teeth. 'Is it?'

'Do ye dare to find out?' Robert said, pressing his pistol's muzzle against Lullington's chest.

Several men lunged forwards.

'One more step,' Robert said. 'And this man is dead.'

They stopped cold.

Lullington gave a soft laugh and pressed the blade to Robert's throat. He felt the sting as the blade nicked his flesh. 'Shoot, then.'

Curse him. Robert tossed the pistol aside. Loaded or not, he'd not shoot a man in cold blood.

He held his arms wide. 'Search me again, then, if you must.'

'Oh, I think I must,' Lullington said softly. He raised his voice. 'I saw him upstairs a while ago.'

Hades.

The crowd around them muttered.

Robert kept his face impassive and let Lullington pat him down. The moment the viscount announced he did not have the emeralds, he would dive through the glass. But he needed space. He needed Lullington clear of the door. He moved into the semicircle of watchers, putting John between him and the door. John would let him past.

Lullington slowly ran his hands down Robert's body, his legs, his arms, checking the cuffs on his coat. Robert lifted his gaze and saw how Frederica clung to the music stand. She actually had the gall to look worried. As if she actually cared.

Or was she worried he'd give her away?

Lullington swung him around and felt through the folds of his cloak. 'Aha,' he cried.

Robert froze. It couldn't be. He could not have found the jewels.

Maggie put her hand over her mouth and shook her head.

Lullington pulled forth a strand of emeralds and

diamonds. Robert recognised them. Maggie had worn them often in his company.

'A strange thing to keep in your pocket, sir,' Lullington lisped.

'Someone put them there,' Robert said. 'I did not take them.'

'What were you doing upstairs, then?' Lullington asked. 'In the same wing where Lady Caldwell's chamber is located.'

Robert clenched his fists. The bastard. He must have seen Robert in the upstairs hall and then planted the necklace in his pocket in the crowded ballroom. He recalled the bump. Robert glanced around. Every face stared back with an expression of suspicion. It was White's all over again.

'It is possible that the real thief hid them on this man's person, meaning to claim them later,' Radthorn said. The pity in his eyes made Robert feel sick, but at least John wasn't abandoning him.

He glanced towards the podium, dreading Frederica's reaction. She was gone. No doubt she thought him guilty.

'Arrest him,' Lullington said to the magistrate. 'There is no doubt he is guilty.' He held the necklace high to the gasps of the crowd. 'You really should be more careful whom you employ, Lord Wynchwood.'

His sneering gaze rested on Robert. The bugger was enjoying himself. Robert eyed the door two steps away. A fist in the viscount's gut might make him a little less smug and give him enough time to escape.

'Someone fetch a rope,' the magistrate said. A footman scurried off. People turned to watch him go.

Lullington handed the necklace to Maggie, whose pallor had taken on a greenish cast.

The momentary distraction was all Robert needed. He leaped for the door handle, wrenched the door open. Lullington grabbed at his cloak and yanked. Robert tore the damned thing free. Too late. Three men leaped on his back. He hit the ground chest first. The air rushed out of his lungs as all three men sat on his back.

'Bring the rope,' one of them yelled. The other two grabbed his arms.

Robert shook off one, kicked another in the groin and struggled to his feet with the third hanging on to his sleeve.

'Hold him,' someone yelled. Three more men latched on to his arms and dragged him to the floor. His hat went skidding across the tiles. Robert, gasping for breath beneath the pile of men, stared at a gap in the tangle of arms and legs where John's face appeared. 'What the deuce is going on, Robin?' he whispered.

Robert shook his head. 'I did not steal that necklace.'

John winced. 'Hold still, then, man. Don't make it worse. I'll see what I can do.'

Submit to the final indignity. Rage welled up inside him. Blast it, John was right. The odds were against him. There was no sense in getting beaten as well as arrested. Robert took a deep breath and lay still.

'Stand him up,' the magistrate said, his flowing wig all askew, the footman at his side, rope in hand. 'Let me have a look at him.'

The men hauled Robert to his feet. He came face to face with Frederica. Robert pretended not to see her. He kept his chin low in hopes of hiding his face from those that might know him.

The footman fastened a rope around his wrists and pulled it tight.

'An emerald necklace isn't the only thing you are hiding is it, my lord?' Lullington murmured in Robert's ear so no one else could hear.

'Shut your damned mouth,' Robert muttered.

Lullington smiled. 'If you don't want your family name dragged through the mud,' he whispered, 'you'll proclaim your guilt like a man.'

'I'll see you in hell,' Robert whispered.

Lullington held his scented handkerchief beneath his nose, muffling his words. 'I'm sure you will. But you will arrive first.'

'What is he saying?' the magistrate said, leaning forwards.

'Think about it, Robert,' Lullington murmured. 'I'll give you 'til morning to admit your guilt. If not, I'll really unmask you.' He used his forefinger and thumb to pull Robert's mask over his head.

Maggie stared at him. 'Robert?' she whispered in disbelief. Her eyes rolled up in her head and she collapsed in a heap beside the magistrate's high red heels.

One of the ladies near her, a dark-haired woman in a toga, bent to chafe her hand. Robert saw all of that from the corner of his eye, but it was Frederica's reaction holding him captive and rigid.

At the moment Maggie fainted, the pallor of her skin blanched to translucent white, as if every drop of blood in her veins had drained away, but instead of fainting or screaming, she backed away with an expression of terrible hurt.

Even at this distance he felt her shock and horror. Revulsion oozed from her pores and made his skin feel slimy.

He wanted to deny the theft, but Lullington's threat

held him silent. It really didn't matter what she thought. He had far more pressing problems.

She shook her head, stumbled over the crocodile's stupid tail, then turned and fled up the stairs.

He watched her disappear until someone tapped him on the shoulder. John, looking as sick as a horse. 'I'll take my grandmother home and come back later.'

Robert nodded, feeling a little less isolated.

Everyone else, except the triumphant-looking Lullington and the two footmen clenched on Robert's arms, huddled over Maggie's inert body, proffering smelling salts, vinaigrettes and fans. What a bloody farce. If his position weren't quite so desperate, he might have laughed.

'Take Lady Caldwell into the drawing room,' Lady Radthorn directed. She raised her head and peered through her lorgnette at Robert. 'Fine mess you are in, young man.'

'Grandmama, please, let us go home,' John said.

'Throw that vermin in the cellar,' the magistrate said. 'We can't have a fellow like him ruining our evening.' He puffed out his chest. 'I will get to the bottom of the matter in the morning.'

'Ain't got no cellar,' Michael the footman said, looking blank.

'The coal cellar,' Wynchwood said, mopping his brow with a handkerchief. 'Oh, my lord. I feel faint. My health cannot stand the shock. Where are the smelling salts?' He staggered after Maggie's entourage.

'Did you really think by posing as a gamekeeper you could hide from me?' Lullington murmured into Robert's ear.

Robert said nothing.

'Pay your debt or it will either be the gallows,'

Lullington said with an infuriating smile, 'or transportation.'

A cold chill settled on Robert's shoulders. In that case, he'd count himself lucky to be hanged.

'The only question is,' Lullington continued, 'under which name do you want to be tried?'

Lullington knew Robert would do anything to protect his family's name—he could see it in the other man's face. He knew Lullington had never liked him, but he'd never thought the man so vindictive as to accuse a man of a crime he didn't commit and make it impossible for him to deny it.

'You bastard. I'm working to get your money.'

Lullington's thin lips curled in a sneer. 'I think I prefer this method of settling your debts, my friend. I shall enjoy telling my cousin.'

Michael, the footmen and a man from the village swung Robert around, hustled him down the back stairs and in short order shoved him into the cellar. Lumps of coal rolled beneath his feet. Stumbling forwards, Robert slammed into the wall head first. Stars circled in front of his eyes. Thick dust choked his throat. Coughing, he struggled to remain upright.

The door banged shut. A bolt slid home. The key turned in the lock.

Damp chill seeped through his coat and into his skin. He waited for his vision to adjust to the dark. It didn't. Not one crack of light penetrated his cell.

The beating of his heart filled his ears, a slow steady thud. His ears rang from the blow to his head.

What an idiot he was to have given Lullington such an easy opportunity. If he'd been thinking with his brain instead of what was in his trousers, he would never have risked coming here tonight. And for what?

A woman who was betrothed to another man.

* * *

Why would Robert steal from the guests of his employer? She felt as if the ground beneath her feet rocked and swayed to a rhythm she didn't know. She'd thought him perfect, a down-to-earth man, honest and straightforward. She'd trusted him.

It was her fault he'd gained entry to the ball. Her fault he had access to Lady Caldwell's chamber. He never would have been tempted if she hadn't allowed him come to her room. Unless he had planned it all along.

Her heart clenched. She didn't want to believe it. *Men are ruled by their needs,* she'd heard.

Apparently their needs included priceless gems.

And why had Lady Caldwell said his name and then fainted? Did she know him? She kneaded her temples.

At first, he'd denied his guilt. He'd stared at her, willing her to believe him. Was it the truth? Or was he hoping the spell he'd spun would keep her entranced?

If so, sadly he was right. She couldn't bear the thought of him locked up in the coal cellar. She got up from the bed and paced to the window.

Lady Caldwell had her jewels back, so no real harm had been done, had it? Perhaps she could convince her to let the matter drop.

But first, she wanted to hear what Robert had to say. He owed her the truth.

Chapter Nine

Robert cursed and gripped the shovel hard between his knees and once more began grinding the ropes against the dull edge of the blade.

He allowed himself a wry smile. The magistrate had done him a favour, putting him in a place he knew only too well. With a bit of luck, he'd be long gone before they came to fetch him in the morning. He huffed out a breath. His escape wouldn't help prove his innocence. It would probably make matters worse, but without the evidence, namely Robert's person, the viscount would be unable to prove the identity of the so-called thief. And John would deny it, Robert was sure, even if Maggie supported Lullington.

What would it matter once he was gone? He'd lost any chance of a future here and this way, his family would never know for certain that the man arrested was him. They'd only have Lullington's word.

He sawed back and forth. The first strands of the rope gave way. He still half-expected Wynchwood to stomp down here accusing him of debauching his niece. Well, if it got her out of a marriage she didn't want, good luck to her. Her cousin was an idiot. He wasn't going to stay around to find out if she succeeded. The last thing he wanted was for his father to hear his son was not only a debaucher of innocents, but a thief to boot.

He'd thought she was different from all those other women he'd known. That she liked him for himself, not what she could get from him.

It didn't matter. He was leaving. He would never see her again. Just as he'd planned.

One thing was sure, he wasn't going to let Lullington get away with his ridiculous accusation. Once free, he'd find Maggie and get her to withdraw the charges. He was not going through the rest of his life with this hanging over him.

He sawed harder and faster. The edge of the shovel scored his wrist.

Pain tore up his arm. He clenched his jaw, bit back a curse, blinking away the welling moisture in his eyes. He did not want his guard lured down here by a noise.

Awkwardly, he wiped his face on his upper sleeve. The shovel fell to the flagstones with a clang.

Hell.

He listened. A muffled silence greeted his ears. It was like being entombed alive, or how he imagined being entombed alive. Dark, silent, damp and cold, with the only noise his rasping breath and pounding heart.

Don't think, you idiot. Just get this bloody rope off. He scrabbled among the lumps of coal for his shovel.

The back stairs creaked beneath Frederica's feet as she felt for each step with her foot. Creeping around Wynchwood in the dark was something she had done as a child, looking for food when sent to bed without supper for some transgression or other. Tonight it seemed far scarier, far more risky with so many strangers in the house and something other than food on her mind. Robert.

A thief. He hadn't offered one word of explanation after the gems' discovery, once Lullington muttered something in his ear. He'd stood there, sullen and angry, the very picture of guilt.

Her stomach heaved again. Was that why he'd befriended her, made love to her? So he could steal from her family?

Had she been so utterly taken in?

And here she was planning to set up on her own. If she was so easily duped, here in a house where she was protected, how would she manage on her own?

Whatever he was, whatever he'd done, she wanted the truth. Deep in her heart, she prayed there was some explanation.

Frederica tiptoed along the passage toward a sliver of light cast on the flagstones by the ajar kitchen door. Knowing William, she'd find him taking his ease by the fire instead of standing on guard outside a locked cellar door. Her tale of noises below her chamber window and fears of a possible accomplice should send the footman out into the night chasing shadows, wanting to satisfy her foolish womanly fears.

If she played her part right.

With shaking fingers, she pulled her wrap closer about her and pushed the door open. The figure on the settle by the hearth straightened. Sharp eyes observed her over a tankard.

She stared at him, mouth agape. 'Mr Snively?'

'I wondered how long it would be before you put in an appearance,' Snively said.

She winced. 'I thought William was guarding the prisoner.'

He set his mug down on the hearthstone. 'I sent him to bed with a belly full of his lordship's best porter.'

'Oh.'

'Come to see Robert, have you? You've been getting far too close to that young man, you have.'

Nothing slipped past Mr Snively. 'I wanted to speak to him. Ask him what happened.' She twined her fingers together. 'I just can't believe he would do such a thing.'

'No more do I,' Snively said. 'That there lass and the viscount are up to something.'

'Lady Caldwell, you mean?'

'I do, Miss Wynchwood. There have been some late-night visitations between those two. And the way his lordship looked at Robert Deveril, I could see there was bad blood between them. Old bad blood, or my name's not Joshua Snively.'

A little bud of hope unfurled in Frederica's chest. 'Do you think they put the jewels in his pocket to make him look guilty?' She frowned. It didn't make sense, or answer the question of how they knew Robert. Or why they would deliberately incriminate him? Or why he'd let them? But it was a relief to know that Mr Snively shared her doubts. She plunked down on to a chair. 'What should we do?'

'If he runs, he'll never prove his innocence. If he is innocent, that is. He'll be a hunted man.'

Frederica's blood chilled. 'What is the alternative?'

'Damned if I know,' Snively said, scratching at his chin. 'If he stays, he'll hang for sure.'

She couldn't bear the thought of Robert being hanged, even if she was his dupe. 'Then we must set him free.'

He nodded. 'We've another matter to discuss too, miss. This business of your betrothal. You don't want to marry Master Simon, do you?'

Even though she'd hinted to Snively that she had no desire to marry her cousin, astonishment didn't begin to describe the emotion whirling in her head to hear Snively speak so boldly of family matters.

He narrowed his eyes. 'If you do, I'll say no more.'

Frederica found her tongue. 'No. I do not want to marry my cousin.'

'Ah. Fair shook the wind out of my sails when I heard the announcement, it did.' He glowered. 'Something's gone wrong. Your uncle received a letter from Bliss two days ago. I'm thinking it's behind this rush to marry you off.'

'Who is Bliss?'

'A London lawyer with information of interest. I can't say any more.'

Could he sound any more mysterious? 'I don't have time for this now.'

'It's important.'

'I can't see how it is more important than a man's life.'

'You would if you knew,' Snively muttered.

'Knew what?' She felt like screaming—he was being so secretive.

'I'm not at liberty to say, miss. Not yet. But something has to be done.'

It did and it would. She was leaving for London. Tomorrow. She'd use the first instalment from her drawings and buy a passage to Italy. The publisher could forward the rest of her money to Florence.

In the meantime, she had to do something about Robert. 'Can you saddle Pippin and leave him at the gate? I will talk to Robert and explain that running is his only course.'

'I doubt he'll need any encouragement,' Snively said. 'I'll do as you bid, miss, but you and I needs to talk after.'

'First thing in the morning.'

'You'll need these.' He handed her a candle, a knife and a key. 'Tell him to be as far from here as possible by morning. And he's to keep mum about your part in letting him go.'

Frederica felt her jaw drop. This was not the man she knew, the stiff and starchy Wynchwood butler. Not only had his accent changed, his personality had undergone a metamorphosis. It was all very odd. But right now she didn't have time to think of anything except Robert and securing his freedom.

She dashed down the cellar steps to the coal room. At the door she paused to listen.

'R-Robert?' she whispered through the keyhole.

A metallic clang and then a crunching sound emanated from the other side of the door.

'R-Robert. It is Frederica. Can you hear me?'

'I can indeed.' He sounded impatient. 'Go back to bed.'

'I'm going to open the door.'

'All right,' he said slowly.

The key turned easily in the lock. The bolt was stiff in its hasp and she flinched every time the metal squeaked, despite knowing no one could hear. The moment it shot back, the door flew open.

Blinking, Robert stood in the doorway illuminated in the light of her candle. Coal dust streaked his face and his eyes were red-rimmed.

'I-I... Are you all right?'

A wry smile twisted his lips. 'Aren't you taking rather a risk, Miss Bracewell? Opening the door to a desperate criminal?'

'Did you really steal the necklace? You denied it at first.'

He stiffened slightly, so imperceptibly it almost seemed a trick of the wavering light. He lifted an arrogant brow. 'And if I told you I did not steal it, would you believe me?' He leaned one shoulder against the dusty wall, the picture of arrogance and insouciance. The picture of a rogue.

It was as if he didn't care if she believed him or not. She glared at him fiercely. 'If you tell me you are innocent, then, yes, I believe you.' She realised it was true. Despite everything, she trusted him, as she had trusted few others in her life.

He stared at her for a long moment as if trying to decide whether or not to believe her. 'I have a question of my own. Why did you say nothing about your betrothal?' While the expression was still uncaring, she heard an edge in his voice.

'I had no idea it would be announced tonight.'

'That wasn't my question.'

How could she possibly explain? 'I'm not going to marry my cousin Simon.'

'You'll forgive me if I say the arrangements looked pretty firm from where I was standing.'

'How could I denounce poor Simon in front of all those people? I couldn't make him a laughing stock, even if he is an idiot.'

'Poor Simon indeed.' The corner of his lip lifted in a mocking smile. 'When did you plan to tell him of his cuckolding, before or after the wedding?'

A trickle of shame slid through her belly. He must have seen it in her eyes because his smile grew all the more cynical.

'Why are you being so horrid?' she said.

'Am I being horrid? Then run away, Frederica.' He jerked his chin. 'Back to your noble friends. To your betrothed. You should not be here with the likes of me.'

She gasped.

A shadow passed across his eyes. Bleakness. The announcement of her betrothal must have hurt him. Could that be reason enough for theft? So he could depart Wynchwood with money in his pocket? Lord, she hoped not.

'I told them repeatedly I would not marry my cousin. But they wouldn't listen.'

'Really.' He tilted his head, his dark eyes intent on her face. His jaw flexed. 'Did you think to use me to make them change their minds? Tell them I'd stolen your virtue?'

She winced. Put like that it sounded cold and calculating. Still, he deserved the truth. 'I thought of it afterwards. And only as a last resort.'

He flattened his back against the wall and stared up into the dark above his head. 'Do you think it will work?' He sounded dreadfully tired.

She stooped and set the candle on the floor. 'Actually, no. I have another plan.' She reached into her pocket and pulled the knife she'd taken from the kitchen out of her pocket. 'I'm booking a passage for Florence.'

He looked down at the knife and up at her face. 'Italy?

Was that where you wanted to go when you asked me to run away with you?' He sounded bemused.

'An art teacher I've been writing to has offered to take me as a student if he likes my work. We could go together.' She shrugged as if it didn't matter either way. 'If you wanted to.' She didn't want him to know how hurt she'd been at his rejection. 'Turn around. Let me set you free. If they find you guilty, they will hang you.'

He jerked his hands from behind his back. 'I used the shovel to cut the rope.'

The lace at his wrist was black and bloody. 'And hurt yourself in the process.'

'It's nothing. You should go now before someone finds you here.'

'But what will you do?'

His face became grim. 'I need to speak to Maggie.'

Something sharp pierced her ribs at the familiar name. 'You do know her.'

He cursed under his breath 'Yes. I do. And I didn't steal her damned jewels.'

'Then why say nothing?'

He cracked a bitter laugh. 'You don't want to know.' He grasped her shoulders and turned her around, pushed her towards the door. 'It's time you left.'

He preferred Lady Caldwell's help to hers. The realisation cut her to the quick. And he still hadn't given her any answers. She whirled around. 'I'm not going until you tell me what is going on. What is Lady Caldwell to you?'

The Robert she knew seemed to disappear; another man, relaxed, charming, at ease, took shape before her. He had a dangerous smile on his lips. A smile warm enough to melt a woman's heart. Another woman's heart, for this was not her Robert.

He raised a cocky brow. 'Little girl, you couldn't get much closer than Maggie and me at one time.'

'Lovers.'

He bowed. 'A gentleman never tells.'

The pain almost knocked her off her feet. She clenched her hands, felt the skin tighten over her knuckles and the breath held in her chest like a hard lump of coal. She forced herself to ignore it, to focus on his words, not her hurt. 'And yet you stole her necklace?'

'Let it lay, Miss Bracewell. Forget we ever met. Get married. Have children. Or go to Italy if you must. Be happy, but for God's sake go.' He turned away, his shoulders set and stiff as if he was angry. But the note in his voice wasn't anger, it was bleakness.

'You are a gentleman, aren't you?'

'Once. No more.'

'How can that be?'

'I did something dishonourable. I seduced a lady and refused to wed her.'

The words hung in the damp, coal-dust-laden air.

Robert had never said those words out loud. Never. They were like daggers to his heart, nails in his coffin. But as she'd gazed at him with hope in her eyes, he knew he didn't have the right to drag her down into the hell-pit that was now his life. Better she hate him than follow him into the abyss.

He turned, expecting to see disgust in her elfin face. Instead he saw puzzlement.

'W-why?'

The stutter was back, betraying her nerves. Good. She should be nervous. 'I didn't want to get married.'

'Oh.' She looked shocked.

As well she might. He took a deep breath and found his chest tight. 'I am a rake.'

'But not a thief.'

'No, but nor am I a good man. And after tonight I will be a wanted criminal.'

'But you didn't take the necklace. They have to tell the truth.'

He shook his head, his throat too full of something hot and hard for speech.

A fissure cracked in the ice that seemed to encircle his heart. The pain of it sent him spinning away, made his eyes blur, his heart feeling too large for his chest. It was as if the coal piled at the end of the cellar had been lifted from his shoulders and been put back where it belonged. She trusted him.

He grabbed her shoulder. Tipped her chin so he could look in her eyes. 'Don't get involved.'

'Then stand up for yourself, R-Robert.'

'The evidence is against me, I'm afraid. Who will believe me, a gamekeeper against a peer of the realm?'

She winced. 'How did the necklace get in your pocket?'

All questions he'd asked himself. He took a deep breath. 'I believe Lullington put it there.'

'Because he hates you. I saw it in his face. He is jealous of you—' her voice caught and she took a deep shaky breath '—because of Maggie.'

He narrowed his eyes. 'What do you know about Maggie?'

'That she spoke your name, just before she fainted. She knows you.'

If she trusted him enough to believe him about the necklace, he had to do the honour of telling her some of the truth. 'It was Lullington's cousin whose virtue

I stole.' Not that she'd had any, but that was the way it appeared.

She pursed her lips. 'It isn't a very honourable way to punish you.'

He cracked a laugh, couldn't help it. 'He's a clever man. This is the one way he can do it, without sullying the lady's name.'

Her beautiful eyes stared at him. He tried to maintain dispassion, tried not to let the trustful gaze suck the truth about his banishment from his throat even as it ate through every defence he'd built over the years. He didn't want her pity.

He caught her around the shoulders and pressed a brief kiss to her lips. 'You must go now. Forget we ever met.'

A noise sounded out in the passage. They both swung around to face the intruder. Hell. Now he'd never be able to speak to Maggie. He pushed Frederica behind the opening door and picked up the shovel.

'Robert?'

He let his weapon fall. 'Maggie?'

Her buxom figure glided through the door. She paused when she saw Frederica frozen in the light of the candle.

'La, Robert,' she drawled, 'I see you haven't changed. But isn't she a little young even for you, darling? On the other hand, you always did have an eye for something special and this one is quite unique. I'm madly jealous.'

Frederica backed up a step, her gaze flickering back and forth between them, her eyes large and hurt and grave.

'How did you get down here?' Robert asked.

'There was no guard in the kitchen. I hoped to find

you alone.' Maggie looked shamefaced and, now he looked more closely, rather pale.

'Why?'

'Dash it, Robert, there's no need to look so Friday-faced. I wanted to apologise. I had no wish to get you into trouble.'

'*You* planted the necklace on me? Not Lullington?' He felt as if those he cared about most were bludgeoning him from all sides. He clenched his fists. 'God damn it, Maggie. Why?'

Maggie flinched. And so did Frederica. She must have heard the shock in his voice, the note of betrayal. Naturally, she wouldn't understand that he and Maggie had been friends as well as lovers. In some perverse way, Maggie's betrayal hurt worse than Father's. At least that hadn't surprised him.

'I had no idea it was you,' Maggie cried. 'Oh, I saw through your highwayman disguise, but I thought you were the saucy gamekeeper. How could I know you were my Robert out for a lark?'

Frederica gasped. Robert inwardly winced. 'I'm not your Robert.'

'You know what I mean. I thought you were a cheeky servant. I knew you'd leave before the unmasking.' She tossed her head. 'Dash it all. This is so confusing. What are you doing playing at gamekeeper anyway?' She cast a sidelong glance at Frederica. 'Or shall I make my own guesses?'

'That's enough,' Robert snapped. 'Even if you didn't know it was me, why incriminate an innocent man? A theft like that means the gallows.'

'The necklace wasn't supposed to be found. You were to walk outside where my groom was waiting to relieve you of the necklace. He was to engage you in a bit of a scuffle, or get you drunk or something. Then it was to disappear. Lull ruined everything.' She sounded distraught.

'So Lullington is not in on your little scheme.'

'It was his idea.' She caught her bottom lip in her teeth. 'The emeralds are paste. They have to disappear before my husband finds out. I don't know why he changed the plan.'

'Lullington always plays his own game. You know that.'

Her chin thrust forwards. 'He's been good to me. Kind and generous since you left.'

Robert snorted. 'He's a rake.'

She stamped a foot. 'So were you.'

Robert recoiled from her vehemence. He held up a placating hand. 'How came you to be in such a fix that you needed to steal your own necklace?'

Frederica moved forwards, as though she too wanted to know the answer. Her face was white and pinched. He wanted to hold her. To offer comfort. He didn't dare. Maggie had already guessed about them. He didn't want to give her proof.

'You know what Caldwell is like about my gambling. I had a run of bad luck. Lull would have given me the money, but he was short of funds.'

'So you pawned it.'

She nodded.

He glanced at Frederica, standing silently in the shadows, her thoughts hidden by an unusually blank expression. 'Were you planning to claim the insurance?'

Maggie gave a bitter laugh. 'My husband is the only one who could benefit from that. No. Just before I left to come here, he told me he'd noticed the clasp needed repairs and promised to send it to the goldsmith on my return. I was terrified. If he discovers I pawned it to pay off gambling debts, he will lock me away in the country. He threatened it last time. This time he will do it.'

Robert stifled a curse. 'Well, you are in a pretty fix now. The emeralds are recovered. And very publically, too.'

'I know.' She twisted her hands together.

Frederica moved into the circle of light. 'You must t-tell the magistrate the t-truth,' she said. 'You cannot allow R-Robert to take the blame.'

Her fierceness took him by surprise. The sense of being swept up out of harm's way by the arms of an angel was strangely uplifting to say the least. He wanted to hug her. Instead, he raised a brow at Maggie.

She wrung her hands. 'I'll tell the magistrate I don't wish to prosecute,' Maggie said. 'I can't tell him I planted them on you, but I can convince Lull to let the matter drop.'

'I don't need Lullington to do me any favours, but dropping the charges would work.'

'Is this a private party?' said a drawling voice from the doorway. 'Or can anyone join?' A lithe, tall man leaned against the doorpost, a bottle in one hand and two glasses dangling from the other.

John. Robert groaned. How many more people from his past would join him in his cell? All it wanted was Lullington to complete the nightmare. 'Radthorn, what are you doing here?'

'I dropped the ladies at home, then returned to see if you needed help.'

'By giving me enough brandy so I won't notice when they hang me?' He gave a hard laugh. 'I'm surprised you are prepared to acknowledge you know me.'

John stiffened. 'Er, Robert...about that afternoon.

You took me by surprise. I didn't expect to see you out in the street. We were meeting at White's.'

'What are you talking about?' Frederica asked, her eyes suspicious.

'The day he got sent to Coventry,' Maggie said. 'Lull told me all about it.'

'He would,' Robert said.

'It was all over Town,' Maggie said. 'The son of one of the most powerful dukes in the land thrown out of the fold?' She shrugged. 'It was on everyone's lips.'

'A duke's son?' Bemusement dawned on Frederica's face and then horror.

'A second son, Frederica,' he said, reaching out a hand. 'I'm banished. My father disowned me.'

She spun away, avoiding his touch. Then she turned back, her soft mouth twisted in pain. It almost killed him to see her hurting even if he couldn't understand the source of her pain.

'You have to leave here tonight,' she said, clearly anxious to be rid of him. 'If Viscount Lullington deliberately implicated you, there is no guarantee he will back down.'

Maggie opened her mouth to protest.

'Miss Bracewell is right,' John said. 'Lullington would love to spear you with his proverbial rapier. Come home with me and we'll find a way to sort out the mess. The duke—'

'No,' Robert said.

'What about Charlie?' Maggie asked.

Charlie had been less than charitable the last time they met. He shook his head. 'Forget about my family.'

A grating noise had everyone looking up.

'Snively,' Frederica said. 'Unbarring the trapdoor. Pippin should be waiting at the end of the drive.'

John looked startled. 'Enterprising young lady, I see. Robert, let me offer you refuge until we get this sorted out. Do you think you can find your way to Radthorn Grange? You can stay in the east wing.'

Another person who believed in his innocence. His best and oldest friend. A man he would trust with his life. Robert let go a breath. 'All right. I'll meet you at the gate. Then we can decide on what to do next.'

'Let Pippin go when you are done with him. He'll find his way home,' Frederica said. She looked at him for a long moment, moisture glistening in her eyes. 'I just want you to know, I am not getting married.'

Amid the tears he saw hope. Yet he could not be swayed by those eyes or that lovely mouth. He could not tie her to a man without honour. He could not let the ache to fill his empty nights be her downfall, no matter how much he desired her. 'You are safe here,' he said softly. 'Get married, have children and be happy.'

She stared at him as if he'd handed her a death sentence.

'You had better get going,' John said. 'Who knows who else might decide to visit you?' They all knew he meant Lullington.

Frederica turned away, but the pained expression on her face sliced through his chest like a sword. At that moment he would have much preferred to face the viscount's blade.

She was better off without him. He might never clear his name. He'd certainly never be accepted back into society. He forced himself to scramble up the coal heap, holding his breath against the clouds of dust, and pulled himself out into the fresh air.

Chapter Ten

Frederica turned back to see his legs disappear through the trapdoor. Tears she hadn't wanted him to see stung the back of her eyes. Obviously, he couldn't wait to see her married to Simon. He'd said she belonged here.

Of course she did. He was a duke's son. One step from royalty. Far above her touch.

And all this time she'd thought him no better than herself. One of the lesser mortals. A man within her reach. How he must have laughed behind his hand at the way she'd fallen for his charm.

The tears threatened to well over again. To hide them, she picked up the three-cornered hat lying at her feet, then rounded on Maggie who was talking in a low voice to Lord Radthorn. 'You will do as you promised, won't you?' Her voice sounded damp.

Lady Caldwell's wide eyes darted a glance at Lord Radthorn before she answered, 'Robert is not the man for you, my dear. He's a charming rake, but a rake all the same.'

Radthorn shook his head. 'But he's too much of a gentleman to betray you, Maggie. I'm damned if I'll let you make him an outlaw.'

Maggie folded in on herself, her shoulders hunching, her hands twisting at her waist, her pretty face looking years older. 'I already said I would withdraw the charges. But my husband is going to murder me.'

Radthorn put an arm around her shoulders. 'Don't worry, Lull with think of something.'

Maggie wiped her eyes with the heel of her hand. 'Yes.' A tremulous smile curved her lips. 'He usually does.'

'Of course he does,' Radthorn said cheerfully. He patted her shoulder.

She smiled up at him ruefully. 'I never meant for anyone else to be harmed, John. You know that, don't you?'

Such endearing sweetness curved her lips, Frederica could see why Robert had loved her. Her heart squeezed pitifully, but she forced a practical smile. 'That's it, then. We are d-done here. I'll lock the d-door. With luck it will be morning before anyone notices he's gone.'

Radthorn nodded. 'Good idea. You need to get back upstairs, Maggie. I've no wish for pistols at dawn if Lull finds you missing and comes looking.'

Maggie laughed and fluttered her lashes, no doubt cheered by the thought of men fighting a duel over her. She took Lord Radthorn's arm and the two of them walked out of the cellar.

All's well that ends well. Not quite. Maggie would be fine. Robert would be fine. And she was betrothed. Hah. In a pig's eye.

She dropped the hat on the floor.

The son of a duke and the Wynchwood Whore's

bastard daughter—he must have thought her such a fool.

Suddenly, she felt drained. Empty. As hollow as a drum in her chest, and yet there was a hard ball of something else in there making it hard to breath. A sense of loss.

She didn't want to think about it or she might start crying in earnest. And never stop. Tears never did the slightest bit of good.

Frederica left the cell and locked the door behind her. The affair with Robert must be viewed as one of life's lessons. She would never again give her heart to a handsome man. She had no heart left to give. Robert had taken it with him.

She marched up the stairs. With Robert rescued, she needed to know what her uncle was about, announcing the betrothal without warning. Did it have something to do with a letter from the London lawyer as Snively had hinted? Perhaps she should find out in case there was more bad news in the offing.

On silent feet, she stole along the corridor past the drawing room and crept into her uncle's dark study. If there was a letter from this mysterious lawyer, it would be here.

She lit a candle. The desk was cluttered with paper. A quick search turned up nothing. She pulled on the right-hand drawer. It was locked. If Uncle kept to old habits…yes, here was the key in the inkwell. It turned in the lock.

The drawer was full of papers. She unfolded the one on the top, an official-looking thing with a seal. She almost dropped her light. It was a special wedding licence. Made out for her and Simon, dated the day he left London. She picked up the next sheet of paper. A letter. From the vicar. Agreeing to perform the ceremony—tomorrow. She gulped.

They couldn't force her to marry Simon. Could they?

Did she dare stay and find out?

Umm. No. She needed to leave. Now. Tonight. And there was only one person she trusted to help her.

Raindrops ran down the nursery's diamond window panes. Low-hanging clouds hid Radthorn Grange's acres from Robert's view. He swung around at the sound of the door opening.

'Only me,' John said, tossing a pile of clothes on the cot on which Robert had spent a restless night. 'Why you insist on wearing these rags is beyond me. I would happily lend you some of mine.'

'Because no one will give me work if I dress like a damned dandy,' Robert said.

John winced.

Robert focused on undoing the buttons of his frilled highwayman shirt to avoid seeing his friend's embarrassment and softened his tone. 'Thank you for fetching them. I'll be off as soon as I'm dressed.'

'You might want to hear the latest.'

Robert glanced up. John's face was half-puzzled and half-amused. 'What?'

'Wynchwood Place is in utter turmoil. You are a wanted man.'

'Hardly news.'

'It's not what you think. Maggie worked her magic on Lull. He agreed that the jewels in your pocket weren't Maggie's at all and said they must have been part of your costume. For a moment I thought all would be well, until they discovered you missing, along with Miss Bracewell. Now you are wanted for kidnapping.'

Robert's stomach pitched. 'The little fool.'

'It gets worse. The silver plate has gone. They found signs of a struggle in the butler's pantry and the butler is also missing. Apparently done away with by a desperate criminal. You.'

Robert's jaw dropped. 'Bloody hell? Are you saying he stole the silver and ran off with Frederica?'

'It looks like it.'

Robert's mouth went dry. 'My God.'

'I know.' John gave him a pained looked. 'They found your hat in the butler's pantry. It seems your Miss But-ter-never-passed-my-lips Bracewell neatly took a leaf out of Maggie's book and left you to carry the blame for her abduction. No wonder she was so keen to set you free.'

'She wouldn't do that.' She couldn't have.

What did Snively have to do with it? Was he the one who'd had her virginity? That old man? Disgust rose like bile in his throat even as he shook his head in denial.

What other explanation could there be? She'd seen her chance and used him to take the blame. The cunning little witch.

He struck out with his fist at the wall. Felt pain in his knuckles, felt the vibration up his arm and all the way to his chest.

Damn it all. After Father's betrayal, he'd sworn to trust no one. To rely only on himself. He'd forgotten his own rules.

But Snively! How could she? Jealousy pricked like the point of a knife. He forced himself to think. Where would they have gone? She'd talked of Italy, which meant a port. Or was that a smokescreen? A lie to put him off the scent, if indeed he had any ideas of following her.

One thing was certain, they would have to fence the silver. And London was the most likely place.

'Where does Wynchwood presume we are headed?'

'Ah, that's where things start to get interesting.'

'Out with it, man. I don't have time for puzzles.'

John sighed. 'You spoil everything. Listen to this. Young Simon was in such a dither when I found him in his room packing he muttered something about finding them at a Mr Bliss's office near Lincoln's Inn Fields.'

'A lawyer?' It made no sense at all.

John shrugged. 'I was just about to question him further when Lullington joined us. He hustled me out of the door.'

'Meaning he is in Bracewell's confidence.'

'I assume so. Even old Wynchwood is headed for town and he hasn't been there for years. It all sounds a bit like a Minerva novel, don't you think.' John chuckled, clearly vastly entertained.

'If Wynchwood's for London, I am too.'

'What I don't understand is why Lullington is tagging along?' John mused.

'Lullington is short of funds.'

'I don't see how this would help.'

'I really don't care about Lullington. If Wynchwood thinks Mr Bliss's office is the place to look for the runaway pair, I am going there too. I have to clear my name, John. I won't let anyone turn me into a criminal.'

John clapped him on the shoulder. 'Nor you should. Come with me to the magistrate and we can clear the whole thing up.'

'Can we? Or will they accuse me of doing away with her too?'

'Ouch.'

'Quite. I'll catch the first stage that goes through Swanlea.'

'I think not,' John replied. 'I'll take you up in my carriage, as my groom.'

Robert raised a brow.

'You insisted on dressing like that.' John grinned. 'I'm going to enjoy giving you orders.'

'Bastard.'

'Numbskull. Why the hell didn't you come to me before?'

For the first time in a long time Robert didn't feel completely alone. But his growing rage at Frederica's dirty trick left little room for softer emotions.

'Right. Let's be off.'

A duke's son. Again the realisation twisted Frederica's insides painfully. It was as if her mind refused to believe what she'd heard. Standing at the window of the private parlour Snively had procured at a down-at-heel inn near Lincoln's Inn, she took a deep, calming breath. Dash it. She kept letting thoughts of Robert creep into her mind the way shadows creep into a valley at night. Thoughts of what she'd hoped.

If wishes were horses, then beggars would ride. She had many wishes. But horses were in short supply.

From one side of the mullioned window, she peered into the narrow street, careful to ensure no one would see her from below. Snowflakes floated past the window, turning grey when they hit the cobbles, then melted away. It would make an interesting drawing. If only she could settle.

After visiting the publisher to arrange for the payment of her money, Snively had gone to find a friend he thought might prove useful. She paced to the blazing hearth on the other side of the room and held out her hands to its warmth.

Robert *had* tried to warn her off. She just hadn't wanted to hear. She'd thought he was trying to protect her because he thought her too good for him. Quite the opposite. In the end, she'd seduced him. Used his wicked male urges against him. Her body flashed hot, then cold.

What man would resist a wanton? He'd tried to be honourable and she'd behaved with all the morals of a barn cat. If only he'd told her who he was, she would never have harboured such foolish ideas. It had to be his lack of trust that made her chest ache as if her breastbone was pressing against her heart.

The door flew open.

Frederica jumped. She swung around.

'I told you to keep this door locked,' Snively said, hanging his hat on the hook on the back of the door and shooting her a glare under his brows much as he'd done when she was a child tracking mud across the hall floor.

'What did you discover?'

'None of the Wynchwoods have called on Bliss as yet.' He dropped into a chair beside the hearth. 'An old friend of mine is watching the place.'

They'd arrived in London yesterday and so far there had been no sign of pursuit. 'Perhaps you are wrong about Uncle Mortimer,' she said, sitting opposite, clenching her hands in her lap to keep them still.

He wiped his brow with a large white handkerchief and stuffed it back in his pocket. 'I'd be right glad if I was, miss. My nose tells me otherwise. 'Tis my guess he knows your father left a letter to be opened on your birthday.'

'My father?' Her chest squeezed. She couldn't breathe. It was like falling off Pippin, the ground rushing up to meet her. 'My father left a letter?' she gasped. 'You know who he is? Why didn't you tell me?'

Snively's face turned red. Beads of sweat broke out on his brow. 'A slip of the tongue, miss. Forget it.'

'No. I need to know what this is all about.'

'I can't tell you.'

She had never seen Snively sweat as he was doing now.

She voiced her greatest fear. 'At least tell me he is not some horrid murderer.'

'I've said more than I ought, but I'll say this. You needs to find out for yourself. Tomorrow at the lawyer's office.'

'And if I don't?'

He pressed his lips together. 'You'll be sorry.'

Pieces of a puzzle fell into place in her mind. 'You said you went to see Mr Bliss because he could arrange an account on which I could draw. It isn't true, is it? He is the lawyer who wrote to my uncle.'

He tugged mightily at his stock. 'Yes.'

'Then where is the money for the drawings?'

'Waiting for you at the publishing house,' he squeezed out.

'Then we don't need to see this Mr Bliss. I will book passage to Italy immediately.'

'Don't, miss. Please. You must read the document Mr Bliss has for you.' His jowls wobbled. He dabbed at his brow. 'Sworn to secrecy, I was. But I assure you, you will not be sorry.'

'I'm sorry I trusted you.'

He gazed at her with hurt eyes.

'Dash it. If my father wanted to contact me, he could have done so years ago.'

Snively cringed. 'It's all explained in the letter.'

She huffed out a breath. 'I don't even know his name.'

'He swore me to secrecy.'

Because of who she was? She felt sick. 'I don't need to know and I need to be on a ship before Uncle Mortimer finds me.'

'You'll regret it,' he said.

She glared at him.

He let out a sigh. 'Joshua Snively don't blab. Not with a thousand pound on the line. And Bliss will not see it paid to me if I say one word. Your father trusted me. Now so must you.'

Life had seemed much simpler less than a week ago. Did she really want to know the identity of her father? Lady Radthorn's talk of her mother's wildness before her marriage meant this man could be anyone. A shiver ran down her spine. Perhaps the man was a criminal. Or married and ashamed. Or…what? And why should she care when her father had never paid her the slightest heed until now?

Should she trust in Snively's assurances that all would be well or her own instinct to run?

This was like one of Shakespeare's plays where everyone pretended to be someone else. The only thing she knew for sure was that if she didn't leave England she might never have her chance to learn her craft. And yet Snively had always been a good friend and right now he looked terribly upset.

She huffed a sigh. 'Very well. I'll wait one day to read

this letter. But no matter what happens, I am leaving right afterwards.'

'Fair dos,' Snively said, looking hugely relieved. 'I'll go find us a ship. In the meantime, lay low.' He pushed to his feet with a grunt.

'Thank you.'

He rubbed his chin. 'Your pa paid me well for this job, miss. But after all these years watching over you from a distance, I've come to think of you as one of my own.'

She reached out and squeezed his hand. 'Thank you, Mr Snively. I do wish you'd tell who my father is so it won't come as too much of a surprise.' Or a horrid shock.

'I gave my word. Tomorrow is soon enough, never you fear.' His dark eyes twinkled. 'Now when have I ever steered you wrong?'

She took a deep breath. Tomorrow it would be.

'Radthorn!'

On his perch at the back of John's curricle, Robert cringed at the sound of his mother's voice. His heart plummeted. 'Pretend you don't see her,' Robert hissed in John's ear, careful to keep his head low.

'Can't,' John muttered, neatly pulling into the curb on Bond Street. 'Take their heads, Parks,' he said in a louder voice.

Robert leaped down, and, keeping the horses between him and the diminutive lady on the footpath, ran to the bridles. He shifted so he could see his mother as she raised her face to look at his friend. She looked elegant as always, but beneath her jaunty red-plumed bonnet her face seemed more lined than Robert remembered. More careworn. Damn Charlie. Or was it the girls running her ragged? He prayed she didn't look hagged because of him.

'I didn't think you were due in town for another week, John?' she said, her voice calm and cool. 'How is your grandmother?'

'Very well, your Grace.'

'And you, Robert?' she said, raising her voice. 'Why have you not called to see me?'

Startled, Robert jerked the bridle. He must have been mistaken. She couldn't possibly recognise him like this. He patted the horse's flank.

'You jobbed at the bits,' Mother scolded, appearing at the curb in front of him.

John's rueful chuckle carried above the noises in the street while Robert drank in the sight of his beloved mother's face, her fine grey eyes holding sadness and pleasure, her lips curved in an encouraging smile.

His throat burned and his arms longed to hug her slim shoulders. 'Father won't like it if you acknowledge me,' he said roughly, bitterly.

Her eyes widened. She drew in a quick breath. 'I knew you'd had an argument, but I thought it was you who left in a temper. Charlie hasn't looked me in the eye since.'

Charlie wouldn't. He'd agreed with Father. 'You had best move on,' he said, seeing her footman lingering a few yards farther down the pavement.

'Come home with me, to Meadowbrook, and I'll talk to the Duke. Sort it out.'

A lump rose in his throat. He swallowed and shook his head. 'Please go, your Grace, before someone sees you talking to a groom and gets suspicious about the low company you keep. I certainly don't want another episode like the one at White's.'

Her gaze took in his garb and her eyes filled with pity. He felt ashamed to cut such a disreputable figure in her presence. 'I'm so angry with your father,' she said softly. 'How you must have suffered. Come home. I'll make him put it right.'

He stiffened, the events of that day rushing through his veins like poison. 'What happened was my own fault, Mother. I must be the one to make it right. But what Father said…well, I'm sorry, it was unforgivable.'

'As proud as ever.' She shook her head sadly. 'We cannot talk here. Your father is still at Meadowbrook. I came to town to visit an old friend who is ill. Call on me in the morning at the town house.'

'I'm in a bit of a scrape. I will not bring more disgrace to the family.' He couldn't help his smile. 'Are the girls well? How is Hal?' The youngest son, born long after the other children and most beloved by his father.

Her eyes misted. 'All are well. They miss you.'

His throat felt raw and full. 'I miss them too. And Charlie?'

She shook her head. 'He went to Durn on business.'

'Good God.' Durn was the gloomiest of the Duke's properties, located in the wilds of Yorkshire. No one ever went to Durn willingly.

Mother smiled wearily. 'I worry for him. He is not happy.'

A chill entered Robert's chest. 'I'm supposed to feel sorry for him?' He headed back to his seat.

Mother looked up at John over the horses' backs. 'I'm glad you found him for me, John. Keep him safe.'

'Always at your service, your Grace,' John said. He flicked his leader with his whip and the curricle moved out into the traffic. Robert stared straight ahead, not daring to look back in case he did something rash like leaping down and giving her a hug. No doubt some bright spark would take him by the collar to the nearest constable for assaulting a lady.

'Damn,' he muttered.

'Quite,' John said. 'Bloody well, quite.'

And damn him for a fool for getting tangled in another woman's toils. And still he kept not wanting to believe what she'd done.

They left Mayfair and entered the city. Here the bustle was all about commerce, the businessmen purposeful and the poor more ragged. John pulled up outside a well-maintained bow-fronted office with a sign proudly proclaiming the name of Mr Edward Bliss. A fellow leaning against the wall on the opposite side of the street ran a knowing eye over the horses. 'Hold 'em for you, mister?'

'Get a move on, Parks,' John chortled.

Robert glowered. 'Ask if either of them have visited,' he muttered and leaped down to take the nags' heads.

John stabbed his whip in the holder and stepped down. In the unhurried saunter of the polished gentleman, he entered the solicitor's office.

The wall-lounger sloped off.

John was back in less than a moment. He shook his head imperceptibly. Robert wasn't surprised. Neither Snively nor Frederica was a fool. Still, he'd had to try.

'You didn't say who was asking?' he said, when they were on their way again.

'As we agreed,' John said. 'Where now?'

'Drop me off at the Angel. I'll start by looking in all the inns within walking distance of here. And then try farther afield.'

'I'll come with you.'

'There isn't a prig in the City who will talk to you looking like that,' Robert said. 'And besides, I want you to check on ships to Italy. See if any left in the last day or two and if any are due to sail within the next few days.'

'Do you want me to look at the list of passengers?' John said, grinning over his shoulder, then executing a nice weave between a baker's van and a hackney.

'Thank you,' Robert said with feeling.

'What are friends for? You don't know how I kicked myself after that meeting outside White's.'

'Water under the bridge and far out to sea,' Robert said, clapping him on the shoulder, then cursing as he realised his *faux pas*.

John laughed. 'I'll leave these tits with the groom at the inn and we'll begin the hunt.'

A knock sounded at the door. Mindful of Snively's strictures, Frederica approached it cautiously, listening. 'Who is it?'

'Chambermaid, miss. To make up the fire.'

The voice was familiar. Betty had been in and out several times during the day. Frederica turned the key and stepped back.

The maid bustled in with a coal scuttle. 'A man was asking after you and the other gentleman, miss. Described you he did.'

Frederica's heart gave a warning thump. 'What man?'

'Young 'un. Handsome too.'

'What did you tell him?' They had given false names at the inn.

'Nothing, miss. As your friend requested. Thought I

better let you know.' The girl emptied half her bucket on the embers in the grate and poked at them vigorously.

The thumping in her chest picked up speed. 'Yes. Thank you.' She fumbled in her reticule and found some coins. Her fingers encountered Snively's pistol primed and ready to fire.

The girl rose to her feet. 'Will that be all, mum?'

Frederica nodded and pressed a sixpence in the girl's ready palm.

'Tell no one I am here.'

'No, miss.'

Frederica opened the door and the girl and her coal scuttle slipped out.

Frederica swung the door closed. It stopped short of the frame. The toe of a scuffed brown boot appeared in the crack.

Frederica backed away, watching the door swing open.

'Miss Bracewell. This is a pleasure,' said a voice full of anger.

Chapter Eleven

'R-Robert?' Frederica sat down heavily on the sofa instead of running and throwing her arms around his neck as she wanted, because this was the Robert of weeks ago. Dark. Aloof. He looked as if he wanted to throttle her. 'What are you d-doing here?'

He stalked in, his eyes raging, his expression murderous. 'You didn't think you'd get away with it, did you? That I'd accept your blame?'

He kicked the door shut with his heel and crossed his arms over his chest. 'Or did you think I wouldn't find out until they had me clapped up in prison?'

Her heart thumped madly against her ribs. 'I don't know what you mean. I helped you escape.'

His lip curled in disgust. 'While you and Snively helped yourself to his lordship's family heirlooms.'

She gasped, shocked by the fury in his eyes as much as his words. She gulped a breath. 'Don't be r-ridiculous.'

'Then you won't mind coming with me to the magistrate and clearing this whole thing up, will you?'

She clutched her reticule against her chest, felt the weight of the pistol inside. Snively had warned her that she had enemies in the Bracewells, but she hadn't expected Robert to be one of them too. Trying to look natural, unconcerned, she tucked the reticule between her and the sofa arm, fiddling with the strings as she spoke. 'You are talking in riddles. Isn't it rather dangerous for you here in London? Or did Lady Caldwell keep her promise and have the charges dropped?'

He snorted. 'You know very well there is little Maggie can do about what you and your partner in crime have laid at my door. You are coming with me to Bow Street and you are going to admit the whole wretched scheme. Where is the silver? Have you sold it?'

'Silver?'

'The Wynchwood family plate you and Snively ran off with.'

He was talking nonsense, but she did not doubt his intention to hand her over to the authorities.

She eased her hand inside her reticule and gripped the pistol firmly. 'I took nothing that was not mine.'

'Don't play the innocent with me. I know better, don't I?'

Heat rose to her cheeks. He made everything sound so horrid. Sordid. She might have known he'd use her past against her. Everyone did.

She drew out the pistol and cocked it with her thumb, just as Snively had shown her.

Robert started back. Then he grinned, an unpleasant curl of his lips. 'You don't think I'm scared of that little pop?'

Her hand shook. Her heart galloped. She felt hot all

over. Shoot Robert? She couldn't. She just needed to hold him at bay until Snively came. She levelled the pistol at his chest and swallowed. 'In the r-right spot, it will do significant d-damage,' she said, her voice shaking.

He took a step towards her.

'Stay where you are.' *Don't make me do this.*

He lunged and knocked the pistol aside, then wrenched it from her hand. 'If you are going to threaten a man with a pistol, you had better fire it right away.' He released the cock and slipped the pistol in his pocket.

She crumpled against the sofa back, a little ashamed of her cowardice and a lot relieved. She couldn't have shot him, no matter what. 'I won't go back. I would sooner you shot me than marry Simon.'

He narrowed his eyes. 'Damn Simon. Where is the silver? Tell me the truth or I swear you are going straight to Bow Street. You and your accomplice.'

She glared down her nose at him. 'We did not take any silver.'

'Are you telling me Snively did this without your knowledge?'

He was shouting. She struck the sofa cushion with her fist. 'You are mad. I'm no thief, any more than you are. And anyway, what concern is it of yours if I did take the silver?'

His jaw hardened. His voice lowered to a growl. 'You made it my business when you let them think I'd taken you with me. I am charged with abduction.'

She gasped. 'What?'

'When they found me gone and you gone, they assumed I had stolen you away, just as you planned.'

'No!'

'They found the evidence you left, my hat, blood, and the silver gone. You must have taken it.'

'We didn't.' She stared at him. 'Why would Uncle Mortimer make it look as if we had stolen the silverware?'

A startled expression crossed his face. 'Your uncle lied?'

'What else can it be? I swear to you, I came away from Wynchwood with nothing but the clothes on my back and my portfolio.'

Anger leached from his face, leaving only mortification, his cheekbones stained red. 'Oh, hell,' he said. He passed a hand over his face. 'I thought... Forgive me.'

He looked so devastated that she nodded, though she wasn't sure how she felt after his accusations.

He sat down beside her on the sofa, his eyes full of regret. 'Could Lullington have taken it to pay Maggie's debts?'

Maggie. As before, the casual use of his lover's name made her chest squeeze. Jealousy, when she had no right to be jealous. She forced herself to think, instead of feeling hurt. 'The silver isn't worth much at all. And he could have had it without stealing it, too. Simon would have been only too glad to settle his debts with some old plates and cutlery.'

'Bloody hell.'

She frowned. 'They are saying you abducted me?'

'It appears so.' He laughed softly, and shook his head. 'You know my father always predicted I'd come to a bad end.'

He sounded so resigned it hurt her to hear it.

'I will go to Bow Street,' she said bravely. 'Tell them I'm safe and say I stole the silver.'

He picked up her hand and kissed the back. The brief

brush of his lip sent a hot shiver down her back. 'If you do that you'll be forced back to Wynchwood. I thought you might be on a ship to Italy by now.'

And she would have been, if Snively hadn't been so excised about her father's letter.

'Where does Snively fit into all of this?' Robert said. 'Is he another of your lovers? Was *he* your first?' He spoke lightly, as if he didn't care, but she heard an edge of distaste.

A horrid feeling invaded the pit of her stomach. It writhed as if full of snakes. It was her fault he thought her a bawd, but the suggestion made her feel sullied. She wanted to tell him to leave. But he was knee deep in her midden and he deserved the truth. 'We aren't lovers. Mr Snively is…was employed by my father to watch over me until the terms of my uncle's guardianship ended.' She raised her gaze to meet his. 'It seems my father left a letter that I am to receive on my twenty-fifth birthday. It will reveal his identity. Quite truthfully, I'm not sure I care, but Mr Snively thinks it is important and he also thinks my uncle somehow learned of its existence.'

Robert frowned as he listened to her explanation. 'All this fuss and intrigue over a letter? Where is this letter?'

'A solicitor called Bliss—'

Robert straightened. 'The name Bracewell let slip in Radthorn's presence.'

'Then Mr Snively is right. My uncle has learned of the letter's existence.' Her shoulders drooped, but she forced a smile. 'It is odd of my uncle to go to such lengths to keep me from learning my father's identity, when I'd almost prefer not to know. I would have left as soon as I have my money from the publisher, but Mr

Snively has his heart set on my making an appearance at the solicitor's office in the morning.'

She got up and paced to the window, standing to one side to look out.

'Mr Snively believes that if my uncle catches me before his authority ends, he will do anything to marry me to my cousin,' she said quietly.

Anger surged in his veins. 'Against your will?'

She nodded. 'Uncle Mortimer could have me declared incompetent and locked away until I agree.' Her lips twisted in an unusually bitter line. 'After all, what gently bred woman wants to run off to Italy and p-p-paint when she could m-marry and have children and be happy.'

Robert felt sick hearing almost his own words.

Her eyes darkened, became huge in her face. 'Or they might use my mother's promiscuity against me.' She raised her gaze to meet his. 'Lady Caldwell no doubt guessed about us.'

'Damnation, this is a pretty tangle.' His voice sounded harsh. He wanted to offer aid, but had none to give. As a wanted man, he could barely help himself. 'Where is Snively now?'

'Booking a passage to Italy. He has a friend watching for my uncle outside the solicitor's office.'

The wall-lounger, no doubt. 'Snively should know your uncle is on his way.'

Robert watched her pace around the room, forcing himself to remain where he was instead of taking her in his arms. He was a complication she could not afford.

'I should leave London tonight,' she muttered. 'Forget about the letter. My father never wanted me any more than my mother did. I was an embarrassment when I was born and nothing has changed.'

'And yet you are curious to know who he is.'

'Curiosity killed the cat,' she murmured softly. The tragic set to her mouth made his stomach sink. There was something here he didn't quite understand.

The door slammed back.

Robert leaped to his feet, his hand going for the pistol in his pocket. Too late.

Snively, looking belligerent, had a pistol pointed at Robert's chest.

'To what do we owe this pleasure, Deveril?'

'Is this a private party?' another voice said and John entered with a pistol pointed at Snively. 'Or can anyone join?'

'Oh, r-really,' Frederica said. 'I have never seen anything so r-ridiculous. Come in, Lord R-Radthorn, and close the door before we have the whole inn crowding in here with loaded weapons.'

A rare grin creased the corners of Snively's eyes. He tucked his pistol in his pocket. Robert gave John a nod, and his friend did the same.

'It appears we have a problem,' Frederica said to Snively. 'Robert has been accused of running off from Wynchwood with me and the silver.'

Snively pinched his lower lip between this thumb and forefinger. 'Aye. So I hear at Bow Street. They, too, are watching the solicitor's office for both of you.'

'Wynchwood must have laid information against me,' Robert said. 'He must have reached Town.'

'Could be Lullington,' John said.

Robert wanted to curse. 'We need a plan.'

At almost midnight, the private parlour was stuffy. Frederica looked pale and at the end of her tether. Robert felt as if he hadn't slept for a week.

'All r-right,' Frederica said. 'So we have all agreed

on what we cannot do. Does anyone have any idea of how we should p-proceed?'

The other men, Radthorn and Snively, stopped arguing and looked at her.

'They are watching Bliss's office at all points of the compass,' Snively pointed out. 'There is no way into the building without being seen.'

'Why not a ladder?' Radthorn said. 'Wait until the small hours, climb in through a window. Miss Wynchwood could walk down the stairs from the inside first thing in the morning. *Voilà.*'

'A baby could spot a ladder,' Snively said scornfully. 'What about a disguise?'

'I have an idea,' Robert said. It had been niggling away in his mind all evening. But it was risky. Everyone looked at him expectantly. 'A decoy.'

Snively frowned. 'What sort of decoy?'

'Someone disguised to look like Miss Wynchwood trying to look like someone else,' Robert said.

John gave a soft whistle through his teeth. Snively looked thoroughly mystified.

Swiftly, Robert organised his thoughts. 'We dress another woman to look like Miss Bracewell in disguise. One of us will escort that woman along the street. The watchers will spot the decoy and give pursuit when she runs off, giving the real Miss Bracewell the opportunity to slip inside the office unseen.'

'It might just work,' John mused. 'Lullington will be the hardest to fool.'

Snively perked up. 'I can make a bit of a diversion in the street. Make 'em really confused.'

'We will need someone of Miss Bracewell's height and build,' John said. 'Make her look as if she is wearing a disguise, while Miss Bracewell should look ordinary.'

'Puts Miss Bracewell at terrible risk,' Snively said heavily.

They all stared at Frederica and her face went bright red. 'What about the chambermaid?'

'The lass who let me in earlier?' Robert mused. 'She's about your height and build. Do you think you could charm her into helping us, John?'

John snorted. 'Along with the promise of a guinea or two.'

'We'll need a hat with a veil and a heavy cloak,' Snively added.

'For me?' Frederica asked.

'No,' Robert said. 'You will look like any other woman out shopping. Perhaps a close-brimmed bonnet to hide your face, but that is all. I think this will work.' For weeks he'd felt as if he'd been marking time, going through the motions of living, except for the interludes with Frederica. Now energy coursed through his veins. 'John, find the maid. Snively, your diversion will have to be big enough to distract the men waiting in front of the office.'

'Leave it to me.'

'Then we will plan for mid-afternoon when the streets are crowded. I will go there ahead of time to see if I can spot them and their locations. We will meet back here around midday. Are we agreed?'

Heads nodded.

'Tomorrow, then, gentlemen.'

Despite her cheerful front, Robert worried that all was not well with Frederica. When her blush had subsided, she'd looked paler than before. Her eyes showed strain.

He hung back as the room cleared. 'Are you all right?'

'I'm sorry you got dragged into my troubles.' Her brave smile pierced his heart. 'Whatever happens, you must not take any chances. I could not bear it if you were arrested.'

'A duke's son doesn't get arrested,' he said with a smile and a note of confidence he didn't quite feel. 'Or at least, not for long.' He reached out and took her hand. Her fingers were icy, chilled to the bone, despite the warmth of the room. 'You are freezing.' He drew her nearer the fire and stirred the coals.

She shivered again and stretched her fingers against the heat. 'Robert...' she smiled up at him '...thank you for trying to help me.'

The words held real gratitude. The look of longing in her eyes as she gazed at him weakened his resolve to leave at once and seek lodgings with John. It seemed with this woman, he had no will. 'It is no more than any man would do.' He spoke briskly, matter-of-factly, in case she read his longing to pull her close and kiss away her fears.

After a moment or two, she turned back to the fire, staring into the flames, her shoulders hunched. Drained of all spirit.

He dropped to the seat beside her on the sofa. 'Are you unwell?'

'I'm fine.' She turned to face him. 'I just wish I had left yesterday.'

He put an arm around her shoulder. 'Don't you want to know your father's name? Hear what he has to say?'

She rested her head on his shoulder. God, it felt so right, her looking to him for comfort and support. His chest ached with the pain of knowing he would never see her again after tomorrow.

'I don't know.' She shivered, her teeth chattering until she clenched her jaw.

He pressed the back of his hand against her cheek, felt the chill of her skin. 'You are freezing. You need something to warm you from the inside.'

He rose and rang the bell. A lackey came to the door and Robert told him what he needed. While he waited for the man's return, he pilfered the counterpane off the bed in the adjoining chamber and tucked it around her shoulders. He knelt before her, chafing her hands. From the rigid expression on her face he guessed that this girl, who he thought of as fearless, was deeply distressed.

He ran a finger down her cheek. 'I'm sorry I suspected you of trying to pin the blame on me. I should have known better.'

She smiled, her lips tinged with blue. 'Yes. You should have.'

There was the spirit he sought. The fight. Yet her eyes remained shadowed.

He brought her hands to his mouth, warmed them with his breath, kissed the fragile bones that wrought such magic with charcoal and paper. 'Everything will be fine. I promise.'

She looked away, staring into the fire. Took a deep breath.

A little colour returned to her cheeks. 'I will be glad when it is over, that is all.' She gave him a watery smile.

The sight made his chest feel overly full as if his heart had grown too large to be contained.

A knock of the door heralded the arrival of the wine. Robert took the tray to the hearth, filled the small kettle with madeira, spooned in cinnamon and cloves and added a pinch of mace. He heaped in generous spoonfuls of sugar, then hung the pot on the crane above the fire.

Soon the liquid began to simmer and the room filled with a sweet, heady fragrance as he stirred.

'Now, Miss Bracewell,' he said, pouring the mixture into a glass, 'you will oblige me by drinking this. It will warm you. Then we will tuck you up in bed.'

'I don't feel the slightest bit tired. Will you stay a while? I-I find I don't want to be alone.' The soft pleading in her eyes sent hot fire leaping in his blood. Every nerve ending in his body urged him to accept. He fought desire, tempered it with kindness.

'I'll stay for a while. Until you fall asleep.'

'You may be here all night, then.' She took the glass from his hand and sniffed at the contents.

'Go ahead. Drink. I promise not to poison you.'

She laughed then. 'Silly R-Robert.'

God. He loved the way she laughed and adored the way she said his name with that tiny hesitation. It saddened him to think he might never hear either sound again.

She sipped at the mixture and wrinkled her nose.

'Too hot?' he asked.

'No. I've never tasted anything like it before.'

'Drink it to please me.'

She took another taste and another, sipping delicately, her lips turning the colour of rubies from the wine, her cheeks flushing. 'I like it.'

One glass and she'd be sleeping like a baby. And then he'd leave.

Frederica sipped the rest of the wine in silence, her hands cupped around the glass bowl, her eyes focused deep within. He felt an odd desire to ask her if she'd miss him. Not once in all his years on the town had he wanted a woman to remember him once their affair was over. He preferred to think of them moving on, as he moved on to some new alliance. Just the thought of her sitting like this beside a warm fire in quiet companionship with another man caused his heart to still.

Even if he wasn't the first man in her life, he felt closer to her than he'd felt to anyone, except maybe Charlie. And that had been years ago.

He got up from the floor, and sat beside her on the sofa, tucking her into the hollow of his arm. She leaned back against his shoulder. 'Mmm,' she murmured, taking another sip. 'It really is quite delicious.'

It was no good thinking of the future. He needed to mine what enjoyment he could glean from today in full measure. The knowledge that they could at least be friends. This evening would make for a pleasant memory. For them both.

Her eyelids slid closed and the glass, with only the dregs left in the bottom, tilted. The covering around her shoulders rose and fell with each deepening breath.

The evening was about to end. With a sense of loss, he slowly removed the glass from her grasp and set it on the floor.

She was sleeping. Time to put her to bed and honourably depart.

Chapter Twelve

Carefully, he slid from beneath her and propped her in the corner of the sofa. She looked vulnerable and young. He couldn't leave her here, sitting up, still clothed. He scooped her up in his arms, still bundled in the counterpane, her head lolling on his chest, her breathing wine-laden and heavy. He carried her through to the bedroom and lay her down on her side on the bed. She made no movement as he pulled down the covering and undid the laces down the back of her bodice. Her nape, so elegant, so delicate, so pale in the candlelight, begged his touch. He pressed his lips to the top of her spine and rolled her on her back.

Her eyelids, crescented by dusky lashes, fluttered. Her head lolled on the pillow.

'Hush,' he whispered. 'Sleep. You are safe.'

Held fast by the drugging effect of the wine, her lips parted on a sigh. Her eyes remained closed. The skin of her eyelids was as translucent as the finest porcelain.

Inch by inch, he eased the gown off her softly

rounded shoulders and releasing her arms. He pushed the bodice down to her waist, keeping his mind fixed on the task, not on the rise of pale breasts above her chemise and stays. Practical front fastening stays for the girl who dressed without the help of a maid. It took no time at all to unlace them and pull them free.

The gown he worked carefully over her lovely hips and down her legs. He tossed it aside and went to work on her shoes. How he loved her elegantly arched feet inside the practical woollen stockings, the curve of her calf, the gentle bend of her knee. So pretty. And soft. And lost to him.

Beneath her shift, her veiled body tempted his ardour. The rosy peaked rise of high small breasts. The darker triangle of soft fur between her thighs. Granite hard with desire, he allowed himself no more than a glimpse before he covered her up.

He leaned over and kissed her forehead. 'Sweet dreams, little elf,' he murmured.

Her eyelids flew up. She caught at his sleeve. 'You are leaving?'

Damn it. It was as if she had a sixth sense where he was concerned. 'Sleep. It will be a busy day tomorrow. You will need your strength.'

Eyes wide open, she stared at him. 'You said you would stay.'

'I thought you were asleep.' He sat down on the edge of the bed.

'Lord R-Robert?' she said.

He turned back with a frown. 'What is this lord business?'

'That is your title, is it not?'

'I'm Robert to my friends.'

'Is that what we are?' she asked in a small voice. 'Friends?'

Friends. Lovers. And so much more. 'Yes,' he said firmly, knowing that was all she could be. If he didn't draw back now, he might never be able to let her go.

'Do you have to leave?' she murmured. 'I feel so much better with you here.'

Dear God, she was impossible to resist when she looked at him with such trust.

She trusted him. And needed him. It had been years since he felt needed. He liked it. He stroked a wisp of hair back from her forehead, felt the warmth of her skin. 'If you sleep now, it will all seem much less worrisome in the light of day.'

His gaze fixed on her face, he kissed the inside of her wrist. A shiver ran through her. Imperceptible to anyone else, he felt her desire like a bolt of lightning through his body. He was rock hard and aching.

'Lie beside me until I sleep?' she asked.

Did she have any idea what she was doing to him? Of course she did, the little minx. But she didn't understand that as a practised seducer he had a will of iron honed by years of practice. More experienced women than she had failed to break his control.

He stretched out beside her on the bed, cradled her in one arm. 'Now, close your eyes,' he said.

She snuggled against him. God, it felt good. Never had he experienced anything like this sense of companionship with a woman. Holding her, feeling her warmth, the tickle of her hair against his cheek, the pressure of her elbow against his ribs, the swell of her hip against his thigh filled him with contentment, with the desire to protect. Not in the way a man would protect any woman from harm, but the primal need to shelter and ward.

He would remember her always. Just like this.

Unless he stayed with her.

Something inside him snapped, like a cord pulled too tight, it whipped back at him, flayed at his soul. If he stayed, how would he support them? He could not live on the money she made from painting and keep any shred of himself.

'Come with me to Italy,' she urged sleepily.

Did she read minds? Or only his? The temptation to say yes burned in his throat.

'What would I do?'

'You could carry my bags,' she said, her eyelashes flicking up, a mischievous smile curving her lips. 'Guard me from the *banditti* I hear are rife in the hills, while I earn money painting portraits of rich travellers against the backdrop of famous landmarks.'

He laughed to hide his discomfort as even this vision of himself tempted unbearably. She'd cast her wood-sprite spell, soft, seditious strands of longing, until he lay before her like a willing captive ready to do ought to please her. Had he sunk so low he no longer cared what he became? 'Is that all you want of me?'

'You could bring me my chocolate in bed every morning.' She cast him a knowing little elfin smile that said far too much.

His groin tightened. He caught her and pulled her close. 'Only if I can lie beside you and make wicked love to you as you drink it,' he growled.

She wriggled with pleasure.

Her hands went to the handkerchief at his throat and pulled at the knot.

This was a game he had played many times. But it felt so much more important with her. It wasn't a game. It wasn't casual. Each time he made love to her, it made leaving that much harder. He closed his hands around hers and she stilled.

'Don't deny me our farewell, Robert,' she said quietly. 'Don't deny us our last night together.'

'Sweetheart, it's the wine talking.'

'I need you, Robert. I'm so afraid.'

He stared at her in shock, at the panic in her eyes and the tremble of her full lips.

'My father,' she choked out. 'How do I know he's not some dreadful criminal? A murderer?' A tear rolled down her face.

'Ahh, sweetheart, is this what saps at your courage?'

'It is like some macabre tale,' she whispered. 'You have to know the outcome, but you know it will be terrible.' She dashed the tear away with the heel of her hand. 'I'm such a coward.' Her voice broke and she started to sob.

He cradled her against his chest, held her close and listened to her soft little choking sounds, felt her body shiver and shake and had nothing to say except, 'Hush.' Over and over, he whispered the same sound, rocking her against his chest.

At last her tears stopped and she took a deep breath.

Finally he dared speak. 'No matter who your father is, you are you. A talented and wonderful woman.'

'Nothing good ever comes from bad. What if I'm tainted by two evil parents? My mother and my father?'

'Good God. You are tormenting yourself.'

She shook her head and looked up at him with a smile so sad it sliced right through the wall of his chest to carve a wound in his heart.

What could he say? He dare not give into something she would regret. 'Look at Henry the Eighth. He was a horror. And if I'm remembering correctly, Ann Boleyn was no saint. But their daughter Elizabeth was England's greatest Queen. And besides, shouldn't you give your father a chance to speak for himself?'

A small silence greeted his words, followed by a determined nod. 'Thank you. You are right. If I don't do this, I will always wonder.'

She rolled towards him, then propped herself up on one elbow. She brushed his cheek with the back of her hand. 'I missed you dreadfully, you know.' She said it as if it had been weeks, not a day or two. But he knew what she meant; he'd missed her damnably too. He had filled the empty space with anger.

'Love me, please, R-Robert. One last time.'

He was undone by her tiny smile of hope, her sweet smile. He'd never been a saint. Never been able to resist a woman's plea. Why start now? He melded his lips to hers, felt the quiver of her body against his chest, the heady spiral of desire in his limbs and he took her mouth in greedy thrusts of his tongue while his hand drew her shift up her thighs. He cupped her in his palm and she rotated her hips.

Eager. Giving and damnably sexy. 'Little witch.'

She laughed into his mouth and her hands went to his shirt. She tore it from the waistband of his breeches and wrenched it up.

He lifted his hands from her body and let her pull it over his head. 'Always in a hurry,' he said.

'Oh, yes,' she said, raking her gaze over his chest and down to his breeches.

His body went rock hard at the admiration and lust in her gaze, but it was the soft little smile on her lips that sent him beyond thought. He captured her mouth in his, swept it with his tongue, melded his body to her soft, feminine curves and set reason adrift.

She clung to his neck with her arms as his mouth wooed her lips. He felt as if he could lose himself within her for ever.

He lay her down and sat on the edge of the bed to yank off his boots while she traced circles on his back with so light a touch his muscles quivered and flinched in delight and torture.

'Hussy,' he said.

'I must take after my mother,' she laughed, her fingertips exploring a particularly sensitive spot just below his ribs. He groaned, stood up and divested himself of his breeches and stockings before whipping around and catching her fingers in his hand. A wicked smile curved her lips.

'Think you can play with me, do you?' he growled, lifting her hand to his lips. He nuzzled her forefinger free, then drew it into his mouth with a swift suck.

Her indrawn gasp brought a smile to his lips and a throb of blood to his groin.

He lifted her hands over her head and ran his gaze over her much as she had viewed him a few moments before, taking in the taut perfection of her small breasts, the tightly furled nipples, the tiny waist beneath the upraised ribs, the hollow of her navel. 'Where to start,' he said.

'You look ready to eat me,' she gasped.

'Oh, now there's an idea.' He let his gaze drop to the triangle of curls at the apex of her thighs, her female mystery beneath the fine lawn of her chemise, her lovely pale thighs above the tops of her stockings and the plain garters of brown. He'd seen garters of roses and lace, and none had ever looked so erotic as these.

Her wrists captured in one hand, he lowered his head, swirled each budded nipple with his tongue and watched her hips squirm in delight and longing. He trailed his tongue down between the valley of her breasts and dipped his tongue into her navel. How sweet she smelled, vanilla and roses and aroused woman. A scent to drive a man over the edge before he was ready. How rough the filmy fabric felt against his tongue compared to the silk of her skin beneath.

'R-Robert,' she gasped and there was shock in her voice, and laughter and below all of that wicked seduction.

'What, sweet?' he murmured against her belly. 'Do you want me to stop?'

He blew a warm breath against her skin.

'Oh,' she squeaked. 'No.'

He grazed his jaw against the soft swell of her belly, delighting in her arching spine.

And then he reached his goal. The centre of her femininity. A musky scent filled his nostrils, powerfully erotic. A film of sheer fabric and a nest of pale brown curls hid his prize.

He licked at the shadowed crease, parting her folds with his tongue, rubbing the lawn against her most sensitive spot and felt her writhe and jerk.

With his free hand he raised her chemise, slowly, pausing to run a finger beneath her garter, and all the while he licked and nuzzled and breathed against her feminine flesh.

She moaned, low and guttural. The primitive sound hit him deep in his chest and zinged its way to his pulsing shaft, the blood beating hot and heavy, the demand for entry, the urgings of the feral beast in what was left of his brain.

A master of seduction never let the beast out of its cage, though he had never found it so difficult as now to remain in control, to keep from plunging into her and driving to the hilt.

Letting go of her wrists, he lifted the chemise to her waist and bared her most sensitive place to his tongue, licking and nipping at her clitoris, revelling in her cries of anguished pleasure. Her fingers burrowed into his hair and her hips pressed up to meet his mouth. He placed his hands beneath her buttocks, kneaded the firm, silky flesh, gauged the roundness, the sweet perfection, and raised her higher, opened her for better access and plunged his tongue into her hot, wet depths. She let out a moan of pure joy.

All passion, his Frederica. All womanly desire. God, he wanted to be inside her heat, feel her tight around his aching flesh.

But this was for her. He worshipped at the shrine of her core, flicking her swollen bud with his tongue, grazing it with his teeth when she wriggled, employed every art he knew to keep her on the brink, until her hands fell away from him, her legs lay wide in submission and she whispered, 'Now, R-Robert.'

A demand that went straight to his shaft. He'd never been this hard. But this was for her. He flickered his tongue across her clitoris, then suckled.

Shuddering, trembling, she shattered on a cry.

He raised himself up to watch languid bliss replace the tightness in her face, to watch a rosy glow infuse her pale skin.

Her eyelids fluttered open and she smiled. 'You are wonderful.'

And he felt like a lad again, pure, unsullied and terribly proud. 'I aim to please.'

'But you did not   ' she said.

He kissed her, felt her taste herself on his mouth and eased the head of his shaft into her entrance.

'Oh, my,' she whispered.

Eyes fixed on her face, he concentrated on the blinding sensations of joining her in her pleasure, absorbed the tiny pulses of the aftershock of her orgasm, stroking the walls of her tight sheath fraction by fraction with minute shifts of his hips.

Bringing all of his skill into play as never before, the urge to take her, to drive into her, to lose himself in lust, grew ever stronger. Her body called to him as no woman's had ever done. Her gaze, so full of trust and something he couldn't name, tore at his will. Shook him to the very depths.

Left him primal.

His woman.

The words pounded hot in his veins, setting a rhythm that rode him hard. And still he circled his hips, fighting every instinct with the last atom of his will.

Her eyes widened in shock. Her expression tightened. 'What are you doing to me?' she moaned.

She was almost there. Thank God.

He bared his teeth. 'Bringing you more pleasure,' he panted. Making her his. Binding them together.

The thought sent him over the edge of reason.

He drove into her.

She lifted her hips. He pounded into her body. Her inner walls tightened around his shaft, drawing him deeper. He thrust harder. Faster. Nothing existed but the feral force of their mating.

And then he exploded.

He lost himself in the pure blinding bliss that seemed to go on and on. He shuddered and managed to roll to one side before he collapsed.

Never did he recall such a powerful joining.

Or so much loss of control.

He opened his eyes and looked at her. Had she also reached her climax? God. Why didn't he know?

But the expression on her face was pure satiation. Relieved, he let his eyes close on a groan.

'Thank you,' she murmured. 'That was lovely.'

He heaved himself up on one elbow, kissed her eyelids, her cheekbone, the corner of her mouth. 'You were wonderful. Sleep now.'

He tucked his arm beneath her head and drew her close. She lay still in his arms, her breathing slowing. She snuggled closer.

'R-Robert?'

'Mmm…'

'I love you.'

Blood roared in his head and a pounding shook his chest. It was as if a fissure had cracked in a wall and bricks were crashing down. Those same words hovered on his tongue.

He stiffened against them. Kept them behind his teeth. She was too young, too innocent. And he too unworthy. Cast out by his peers. Even if he believed in love, and he wasn't sure he did, he was not the man for her.

Frederica turned her face away.

Damnation. He'd hesitated too long. Left it too late to say something teasing, the kind of thing he said to all his lovers. *How lucky I am.* Or, *You are the sweetest woman I know.*

'I'm sorry,' he said instead.

'It doesn't matter,' she said.

But there was heartbreak in her voice. He reached out, then let his hand fall away. What she thought of as love was merely the afterglow. When the fire cooled she'd move on. Or he would.

It was the way it worked.

He just wished that the thought of it didn't make him feel physically ill. Or wish he was wrong.

But the glow was still there, bright and enticing. If only he believed it would last. It never did.

But he could stay until it dimmed. Until they tired of each other. He could find work in Italy just as easily as he could find employment in England, could he not? Mother could no doubt be persuaded to use her influence to help him find a position at the consulate in Florence. He could support them both while Frederica painted until her heart was content.

Until the glow faded. It might take a while. Longer than most. They would laze in the heat, travel around the country looking at paintings and ancient monuments. Now the war with the French was over, there were lots of places he longed to see. Perhaps they could even go to Paris. Why not? He had nothing keeping him in England. And until she found someone more worthy of her love, he could keep her safe.

He leant over her and kissed her cheek. 'Let us see what tomorrow brings.'

With a muffler covering the lower half of his face, Robert peered around the corner. Everything was set. While he couldn't see her, he knew Frederica and John were standing in the shadows of an alley a few yards from Bliss's front door. When the hue and cry started, John would whisk her in. Robert was escorting the disguised maid because Lullington would know him despite the drunken stagger he planned to affect.

A fussy-looking lawyer in his wig and gown bustled up the street. A skinny, shabbily dressed clerk with red-and-yellow-striped stockings scurried along behind him, his arms loaded with tomes, his floppy hat falling over his eyes. A trickle of recognition played at the fringes of Robert's memory. He shook his head. Legal types had been coming and going to the various solicitors' offices all morning. He must have seen this pair before. They headed straight for Bliss's door.

'Damn,' Robert said. He hadn't reckoned on strangers being in the office when Frederica entered.

'Oooh,' moaned Betty behind him. 'I think maybe this is a bad idea. What if they arrests me?'

'Ten shillings,' Robert said, doubling her price.

'How much longer does we have to wait?'

Robert turned back and gave her the quick once over. With her rather ridiculous coal-scuttle bonnet and a dress obviously far too big, she looked like a woman in disguise.

The panic in her blue eyes said if they didn't go now, she was going to balk no matter how much money he offered.

Robert put one arm around her waist, and grabbed her hand. 'Remember, follow whatever I do. And when I say run, you run back the way we came.'

They staggered into the street and wove among the lawyers and city gentlemen. A loiterer leaned on Bliss's office wall. He straightened. He'd seen Betty. Another, on the other side of the street, headed for the curb. The traffic would slow him, but it wouldn't take him long to cross to their side.

'Are you ready?' Robert whispered, aware of the

violent tremble of Betty's hand. His heart picked up speed. His muscles tensed, ready to run. 'Keep walking. Just a little bit farther.'

There. Stepping out of the alley, Frederica.

Robert frowned. What the hell was she doing? With a dark cloak and a hood pulled up over her head shielding her face, she looked more suspicious than he and Betty did. She was supposed to be wearing a blonde wig and trotting along as if she was simply out shopping, not looking as if she was a spy for the French.

And where the hell was John?

The man on the other side of the street spotted her.

Robert quickened his pace. Something had gone wrong. He had to get to her before they did. She must have lost her nerve and decided to cover her face.

'Now,' he said to Betty. 'Run.'

With the shriek she'd practised in the inn, she turned and fled with the first man Robert had seen racing after her.

The second man had his gaze fixed on Frederica.

Robert started to run towards her.

A brewer's dray lumbered on to the street. Its driver, with Snively beside him, sped along the street. The diversion.

But was it too late? Robert pushed himself to greater efforts. The gap between him and Frederica closed. Too slowly. The other man would get to her first. He lengthened his stride. Put his head down, bunching his fists, pumping his arms. He dodged an elderly couple with a curse.

A third man appeared between Frederica and Bliss's front door, his arms outstretched ready to catch her.

A barrel bounced off the cart, and then another. Before many seconds passed, beer was running in the gutters and every man, woman and child on the street turned to gape.

Everyone except Robert and Frederica, and the man blocking her path.

Robert hit him at a run. Knocked him to the ground. Robert grabbed Frederica's hand and dragged her along.

'Stop, thief,' someone yelled.

Bastards.

'Run,' he said to Frederica. He looked over his shoulder. Lullington had dodged the fallen man, Wynchwood was puffing along the pavement behind him. Robert smiled grimly. Too late.

He pulled open the door and thrust Frederica inside. A quick glance at the lock. No damn key.

The outer office was empty. Another door led into the inner sanctum where Bliss no doubt hid himself away. The lawyer and his clerk must have gone inside. Damn it all.

He thrust Frederica ahead of him. 'Through there.'

Behind them the outer door opened. 'Robert Deveril,' a voice rang out in stentorian tones, 'I arrest you in the name of the law for theft and kidnapping.'

'Go on,' he urged Frederica and whirled around, pulling his pistol from his pocket.

Frederica stopped short.

'Don't wait for me,' Robert yelled.

He levelled his pistol at the first man through the door and cocked it. Lullington, followed by Wynchwood, pushed their way in.

'Stand back, all of you,' Robert growled. 'This lady has legitimate business with Mr Bliss.'

'The game is up, Deveril,' Lullington said, a triumphant light in his blue eyes.

Robert curled his lip. 'Not yet it isn't.'

'Don't make it any worse for yourself, lad,' the runner said.

'Arrest him at once,' Wynchwood cried, his face red and dripping with sweat, one hand clutching his heaving chest. 'She is my niece. Don't let her get away.'

Out of the corner of his eye, Robert saw Frederica preparing to throw off her hood. Lullington was staring at her in a very odd manner.

'Through that door,' he said. 'I'll hold them off here.'

'Jump him,' the runner said.

'Which one of you *gentlemen* is accusing my son of theft?'

Robert's jaw dropped at the sound of the familiar voice and his head whipped around. He looked into the face of...'*Mother?*'

'May I not visit my lawyer in privacy without all this hullaballoo?' she said. 'I'll have your heads, sirrahs.'

The Bow Street runner faltered in the face of her regal rage.

'Your Grace!' Lullington choked out. He made a leg. 'I beg your pardon. I thought—'

'I know what you thought. I sent for Lady Caldwell after I spoke with Lord Radthorn earlier this morning. While I laud your attempts to help a lady in distress, I do not approve of your methods. Pig's blood indeed.'

Robert gaped at her.

Lullington made a choking sound.

'What is going on here?' Wynchwood said, still game. 'Arrest him, I say.'

Robert closed his eyes briefly. The lawyer and his clerk. They had to be John and Frederica. That's why they'd seemed so damned familiar. They were already inside with Bliss. 'Good God, Mother. If Father caught wind of this—'

Wynchwood pushed the runner forwards. 'That man abducted my niece. I demand—'

'Who is this fat flawn, Robert?' the duchess said in a voice as cold as ice. 'I am certainly no niece of his.' She sniffed. 'Nor would I admit any relationship to such an ill-mannered fellow.'

Lullington's face showed grim amusement. 'Capotted, by Gad. Your Grace, allow me to introduce Lord Wynchwood. Her Grace the Duchess of Stantford. Robert Deveril's mother.'

Wynchwood snatched the wig from his head and threw it down. 'What has the duchess to do with the kidnapping of my niece?'

Lullington curled his lip. 'Where is she, Robert?'

'Actually,' her Grace said, 'I can answer that question, my lord. She is no doubt speaking with Mr Bliss.' She smiled serenely. 'Robert, do tell this gentleman of the law to go away. I find it quite tiresome with so many people crowding this room.'

Robert raised his brows at the gentleman in question, who was mopping his florid brow with a very large handkerchief.

'Beg your pardon, your Grace,' the runner said. He abased himself and backed out of the door in a swirl of chill air from the outside.

'Get back here,' Wynchwood howled. 'Do your duty. Arrest this man.'

Her Grace drew herself up to her full height. 'Are you accusing my son of stealing silver plate, or was it a string of emeralds, Lord Wynchwood?' Her astonishment was palpable.

Wynchwood looked to Lullington for support.

'He didn't,' Lullington said. 'We were simply trying to stop Miss Bracewell from reaching this office. A hue and cry seemed the only way.'

Snively chose that moment to stomp into the office. 'Waste of good beer that. I knew it would never work.'

He stopped short and stared at the duchess. 'Where's Miss Bracewell?'

Her Grace nodded to the closed door. 'In there.'

'Congratulations, your Grace,' Lullington drawled, his lisp no longer in evidence. 'You have us all at *point non plus.*'

'That was certainly my intention.' A gleam of mischief shone in her eyes.

Robert wanted to shake her. 'I'll murder John for involving you in this.'

She cast him a haughty look. 'Your manners have not improved in your absence, my dearest Robert.'

Robert felt like a boy again beneath that searing glance. 'I'm sorry, Mama, but you could have been badly hurt.'

'By this pack of lily-livered fools? I think not.'

'Thank you, your Grace,' Lullington said.

'Oh, do stop it, Lullington. I knew you when you wore short coats.'

Robert grinned as Lullington flushed. His mother was a force to be reckoned with and stronger men than Lullington had been ploughed down by her will.

'As for you, Robert,' her Grace continued, 'you should have been the one to bring Miss Bracewell to me. Not John.'

Dash it. When would she realise he was banished?

A footman in ducal livery entered the office. 'Ah, Frompton,' her Grace said, 'your timing is excellent.

Your arm, if you please. I have had enough adventure for today. It is time I went home. Robert, you will visit me tomorrow afternoon. Without fail.' She swept out.

The men looked at each other, Wynchwood on the verge of apoplexy, Snively wary, Lullington picking at a fleck of lint on his coat and a glint of wry amusement in his usually cold eyes.

The door to the inner office opened. They all turned to watch. Frederica minus her wig, looking decidedly rakish in breeches and striped stockings, sauntered out. Radthorn, now out of his disguise, hovered behind her along with a bewigged and gowned man. The real lawyer. Clutching a rolled document.

Robert looked at Frederica's face. She didn't look too upset. In fact, she looked almost gleeful.

He tucked his pistol in his coat pocket, but kept his hand on the grip.

Wynchwood hobbled forwards. 'There you are, Frederica. You will return home at once.'

'Now see here,' Snively said, bristling.

A half smile curved her lips as she caught Robert's eyes, the elfish little smile that had enchanted him almost from the first. His heart contracted. He kept his face calm, refused to acknowledge the longing to go to her. Instead, he drew back against the wall, ready to act should any of the Wynchwood clan attempt to take her against her will.

'First I must tender my apologies to Miss Bracewell,' Mr Bliss said in a wheezy voice. 'One of my clerks thought to line his pockets by informing Lord Wynchwood of the existence of a very important document held in this office.'

Snively glared. 'Glad to hear you admitting to blabbing and not blaming me.'

Bliss inserted a finger in his cravat and tugged. 'Fortunately, no harm was done, Mr Snively. The terms of the payment to you are not affected by this unfortunate occurrence.'

Snively nodded grimly.

'What does the document say?' Robert asked.

Frederica smiled at him. He grinned back.

'This is all very irregular,' Wynchwood said. His tongue swiped his dry lips. 'This young woman is my ward. I demand she return home with me at once. I have the law on my side.'

'Not any more, Uncle Mortimer. Today is my birthday. Mr Bliss has confirmed that your guardianship ended at midnight.'

Lullington, who had ranged himself beside Robert, nudged him with an elbow. 'Spirited girl.'

'Why the hell are you chasing her?' Robert asked, confused.

'Young Bracewell is a friend.'

'Like hell,' Robert said, ire a burning ember in his chest. 'You saw a way to line your pockets.'

The viscount's cheek muscles flickered. 'You heard your mother, I was doing it for Maggie.'

'Very altruistic. You might fool Maggie and my mother, but I'm no green 'un. You plotted the false kidnapping charges. Why?'

'You deserved it after what you did to Catherine.'

The women they had fought over years before. Robert had won. They'd been idiots to even consider losing their lives over a woman, but Lullington had hated losing and Robert had fuelled his temper by gloating. They'd been enemies ever since. But Robert had never realised how much Lullington's resentment had festered.

'What about your cousin? Are you harbouring ill will about her too?'

The viscount gave a hard laugh. 'When your brother showed her his blunt, she admitted it was all her fault.'

Robert stared at him. 'Charlie?'

'He dragged her before her parents and forced the story out of her. She'd planned it all, hoping to bag a duke. The family married her off with a very nice settlement provided by your brother.'

Righteous Charlie had come through for him. Believed him. What a surprise? 'Glad to hear it.'

'I'd wager you are, since once more you came out of it scot-free.'

Hardly. Robert was about to take issue, when Mr Bliss put his pince-nez on his nose and cleared his throat dramatically.

The room fell silent.

Bliss unrolled the scroll.

A small piece of paper fluttered to the floor. Frederica bent to pick it up. She unfolded it.

'Oh,' she gasped.

Robert couldn't see what it was.

She glanced up at Snively. 'This is one of my drawings.' She touched it with a fingertip. 'Of a pigeon? How did it get here?'

'Your father saw you walking in the village one day, the day he set me to watch over you,' Snively said. 'You dropped it. He kept it with him until the day he passed on. He was also an artist. Some of his pictures of India received acclaim.'

Her eyes filled with tears. 'He came looking for me?' she whispered.

'Ahem,' Bliss said, drawing attention back to him. He glared at the assembled company over his spectacles.

Read the damned document, Robert wanted to yell. He held his tongue and assuaged his impatience by keeping a close eye on Wynchwood.

'I have already relayed the gist of this to Miss Bracewell, but she wanted you all to hear it too.' He looked around. Robert bunched his fists but managed to remain still.

'Her father, Lord Abernathy—'

A ripple of disbelief ran around the room. Wynchwood's jaw dropped.

Abernathy? Her father was a lord? Robert combed his memory. Wasn't he...the richest of all the Indian nabobs? Richer than Croesus of Greek mythology. His name was still mentioned in the clubs with awe and envy.

His throat dried.

Bliss raised a silencing hand. 'The Earl of Abernathy left his entire fortune to his daughter. Miss Frederica Bracewell has proved her identity. Unfortunately, Lord Abernathy was unable to claim his daughter in his lifetime. The circumstances surrounding their relationship are unfortunate and not to be described here.' He glared at Wynchwood. 'But as a younger son with no prospects, he was shipped off to India. Only later did he inherit his title. By the time he received word of his daughter's birth, her mother was dead.'

'Should have let *him* marry the gel,' Lord Wynchwood muttered.

'Should have consulted a fortune teller,' Lullington murmured.

Robert barely restrained himself from strangling the bastard.

Bliss clapped his hands for silence. 'Because of the guardianship arrangements made by her legal father, Abernathy could do nothing until those arrangements ended. He feared when the Bracewells learned of his plans to leave her his fortune they would find a way to spend it.' He glared at Lord Wynchwood, who turned the colour of a beetroot. 'It seems he was right.'

Misty-eyed Frederica placed a hand to her throat. 'I still can't believe my father was a nobleman.'

Robert could see that she was happier about discovering her father was a worthwhile man than about the fortune she'd inherited. She really was a remarkable woman. She deserved a good man.

He felt as if someone had knocked him down and run over his chest with a coach and four.

He was not that man.

Bliss smiled at Frederica kindly and handed her the roll of parchment. 'The details are all in here.'

Wynchwood groaned. 'I should have married you to Simon years ago.'

'Too late, I'm afraid,' Frederica said.

At that moment the outer door opened and young Simon barged in. 'Uncle,' he cried. 'I have brought the special licence. We can marry tomorrow.'

Lullington cracked a laugh. 'Always behind the time, young Bracewell.'

Robert returned a grim smile to this sally. He could not let Lullington know what this meant to him or the viscount would have a field day.

Simon's smile faded as he stared at his uncle. 'I say, what is going on?'

'Ingratitude is going on,' Lord Wynchwood proclaimed, his face drained of colour for once. He looked as if he might collapse. He lurched towards Frederica.

Robert straightened, and imposed his body between Frederica and her uncle.

'All these years,' Wynchwood shouted past Robert, waving his fist. 'I fed you. Clothed you. And this is how I'm repaid?'

'You treated her more like a pariah,' Robert said, shoving him back gently.

'Can I do whatever I want with the money?' Frederica asked.

Bliss nodded and whispered something in her ear. Her eyes widened. Her mouth formed a perfect O. 'My word,' she uttered.

Bliss nodded. 'Do not worry, I will advise you.'

'As will I,' Snively said with a warning note in his voice.

God, they were going to tear at her like dogs over a carcass. He felt sick. Well, he wouldn't be one of those looking for scraps.

Frederica turned a shoulder to the room and murmured something to Bliss. He shook his head. She stiffened. Bliss wrung his hands, then bowed in submission. She cast a considering gaze on the company. 'I thank you for your kind offer of marriage, Simon, but no. Nevertheless, I do owe the Bracewells a great debt. After all, you could have dropped me off at the nearest workhouse and my father might never have found me.'

Robert cursed under his breath. What foolishness was she about? She should have them tossed out on their ears. 'Don't let them sponge on you.'

She gave him a gentle smile. 'They are family. And families must take care of each other, mustn't they, R-Robert?'

'Not always.'

The stubborn set of her jaw told him she wouldn't

listen and she continued in a clear voice. 'I have asked
Mr Bliss to set up a monthly allowance for Simon on
the understanding he is not to use it for gaming.'

Lullington paled. 'I'm done here,' he said in Robert's
ear. 'You win again, it seems.'

If this was winning, he'd hate to lose. Robert
shrugged. Frederica had won. She'd have her freedom.
To paint. To travel. To live life as she pleased. It was
the best possible outcome.

She didn't need him at all.

'What is owed to you will be paid, Viscount Lullington,' Frederica called out.

The viscount swung around with a dumbfounded
expression. 'You honour me, Miss Bracewell.'

She was too soft-hearted by far.

She cast Lullington a saucy smile. 'I suggest you
find a way to relieve Lady Caldwell of her other encum-
brance, for I do believe the two of you would make a
good match of it.'

With a soft laugh, Lullington made her a flourishing
bow. 'Do you recommend poison or a bullet?'

Frederica cast him a mischievous look. 'Ending up
on the gallows will not help your suit.'

Her face changed, lost its happy expression as her
gaze fell on Robert. He started to back away.

'R-Robert—'

'No,' Robert said. He wasn't a man who could be
bought. He went where he willed. He always had. 'I
want nothing.' He would not be a jackal snapping at her
heels. Or a lap dog dancing on hind legs for crumbs.

And yet still his heart pounded, drumming out evil
hope. He headed for the door, feeling as though his feet
were trapped in quicksand and he was slowly sinking.

'Why not?' she asked with a catch in her voice.

He let his expression cool, curled his lip and turned to face her. 'It has been a pleasure knowing you, Miss Bracewell, but I value my freedom.'

Her eyes sparkled. Tears. The sight of them burned acid in his gut, but he kept his gaze steady, his smile cynical and bored.

A crystal drop rolled down her cheek, and yet she bravely smiled. 'Then I must wish you well.'

'This is outrageous,' Wynchwood yelled. 'A woman can't be trusted—'

'Say one more word,' Robert growled in the old man's ear as he passed, 'and you will find yourself on the pavement on your arse with a bloody nose. Be glad she's not visiting upon you the kind of misery she's endured at your hands all these years. She's rich enough to see you ruined.'

The old gentleman shriveled, backing away. 'Preposterous,' he muttered. 'Gave her everything.' He glanced around to see if anyone had heard.

Frederica would have to watch this family of hers, but it wasn't his business. He headed for the door with Lullington and John hard on his heels.

Out in the street the three men stared at each other.

'So, Mountford, once more you land on your feet,' Lullington said, looking sour.

Feeling rather more as if he had holes blown in his chest with a shotgun, Robert glared at the dandy. 'Why the hell are you whining? Your debts will be paid.'

'I'd have got a whole lot more if you hadn't robbed the Wynchwoods of their due. Perhaps I should woo the rich woman you rejected back there.'

Robert cursed vilely. 'Go near her and I'll—' He lunged, fists clenched.

Lullington dodged back and released the catch on his swordstick. 'Fisticuffs? You always were a ruffian.'

John stepped between them. 'Enough. It won't matter who kills who, the other one will end up at the end of a rope. Where's the sense in that?'

'I had hoped to see him carted off to Newgate this morning,' Lullington said. 'Having a duke for a father won't protect you for ever, Mountford. I'll be there the next time you put a foot wrong.'

'With trumped-up evidence, no doubt.' Robert stared down his nose. 'You are lucky charges weren't brought against you. If it weren't for Maggie, I would have.'

'Leave her out of this.'

'And leave Miss Bracewell out of your schemes. She's had enough people taking advantage.' Himself included, damn it. Hopefully she'd find someone a little less jaded. A man with less to regret in his past. He took a deep breath. 'Look, I doubt this will make any difference, but I am sorry about your cousin. She's no less a schemer than you are, and deserved to be put in her place, but I shouldn't have let it go so far. I'm glad she found a husband. And I'm glad Maggie has you looking out for her.'

Lullington's eyes widened, no doubt as surprised as Robert by the apology.

'That doesn't mean I won't do everything in my power to keep you away from Miss Bracewell,' Robert continued. 'Including using my family's power.' A threat if ever he'd made one.

Lullington looked down at the ground, his fingers playing with his quizzing glass, then raised his eyes to Robert's face. 'All right. We'll call it a stalemate. Just stay out of my business in future, or next time I won't fail.' He turned to John and bowed. 'I bid you good day.'

'Bloody bastard,' Robert muttered, watching Lullington twirl his gold-headed cane as he strolled away looking every inch a mincing tulip of fashion.

'Never mind him. What about you?' John said at his shoulder.

'God knows. See Mother tomorrow, I suppose. Look for work.'

'You made her cry.' Robert knew John wasn't referring to his mother.

'She'll recover. They always do.'

But would he? Somehow he felt as if he'd left a piece of himself inside the tawdry little office.

Chapter Thirteen

It was a good few moments before Robert could bring himself to ring the bell at Mountford House. He'd never expected to set foot in the place again. He'd never wanted to. Except for a yearning that would not be denied. Not now, as he stood on the doorstep.

He took a deep breath and pulled the bell, listened to the tolling deep in the servants' quarters.

Grimshaw opened the door. Not a flicker passed across his face at the sight of Robert. The man was imperturbable, as all dukes' servants should be. 'Lord Robert, good to see you again.'

'Thank you, Grimshaw.' He handed over his hat.

'Her Grace is in the blue drawing room.'

'I know the way. No need to announce me. I believe I am expected.'

The butler bowed.

Expected.

How formal it sounded.

But he was the black sheep. Not returning home, but

merely paying a courtesy call. It hadn't taken too many hours of staring into a brandy glass to realise he would not remain in England. Even if Frederica had gone to Italy, her face would haunt him in every field and wood. He might be tempted to follow her.

Early this morning, he'd drafted a note declining his mother's invitation, but in the end he hadn't the heart to send it. So here he was, prepared for tears and admonishments and a final farewell.

He stared at the drawing room door. Did he knock?

Hell. She had called him her son.

He turned the handle and walked in.

As always she looked beautiful for her age. A little pale, a little sad, a little more fragile, but there was a welcome on her lips and in her eyes.

'Mama.' He started forwards.

A movement jerked his gaze from his mother to a figure rising from a chair on the other side of the room.

Father. Bile rose in his throat. He was not even to have this moment alone with his mother.

He bowed and then met his father's gaze. 'Your Grace. Forgive me. I was unaware of your presence.' Heartsick, he turned to leave.

'Robert, wait.' His father's voice.

He stilled. 'My son. Please. I'm sorry.'

Robert turned slowly. Never in his life had he heard his father retract his word or offer an apology. He darted a glance at Mother. Her face showed nothing.

His father strode forwards, hand outstretched. 'Can you forgive what I did?' he asked. 'Your mother cannot.'

His father's brown eyes pleaded. It was as far as

he would go. Far further than Robert would ever have expected.

He grasped the offered hand, felt its strength and its tremble. 'Father.' It was all he could manage without breaking down, without bringing shame on them both.

Somehow he choked down the lump in his throat. 'I'm sorry, Father. I should never have helped Charlie to join the army. It was wrong. I could not have borne it if he had come to any real harm.'

Father's eyes moistened. He raised a hand. 'I know, my boy. I should not have blamed you. Charlie and I had a long talk. Youth believes itself invincible. I had forgotten. I'm glad you finally came home.'

'Come here, Robert,' Mother said. 'Let me look at you.'

He strode to stand in front of her and took both her hands in his and kissed them.

'Oh, my son. I've missed you greatly. Sit down. I want to hear what you have been doing. Radthorn told me a little, but I gather you have been employed in the country?'

He sat beside her on the sofa. She retained hold of his hand as if she feared he might run from the room as he had done so often as a boy.

'Gamekeeping,' he said with a wary look at Father who had taken the chair beside the hearth.

'Learned a lot, did you?' Father asked. He sounded eager.

'Yes.'

'You always did like the land,' Father said in satisfied tones.

He'd noticed? Robert tried to hold his jaw in place.

He wasn't sure he succeeded from the knowing gleam in his father's eye.

'Your mother pointed it out,' Father said, with a fond glance at his wife. 'I should have realised. Lord knows there are enough estates to worry about.'

Robert stiffened. 'They go with the title.' He turned to Mother. 'I want nothing of Charlie's.'

'I know,' she said, her grey eyes sorrowful.

The tension inside him eased. He could almost feel her arms around his shoulders, the way he had as a boy when hurt by his father's lack of interest. 'I'm leaving for America,' he announced, suddenly coming to a decision.

'Why America?' Father said. 'We just lost a war with them. Go to Canada, my boy. I've some contacts there. I'll give you letters of introduction.'

Naturally Father would be glad to see his awkward complication gone. Or was he really trying to help? He swallowed the old bitterness and took the offer at face value. 'Thank you, your Grace.'

The clock in the hall chimed. 'Good lord, is that the time?' the duke said. 'I'll be late for the House.'

Robert rose. 'It was good to see you again, your Grace.'

Father clapped him on the shoulder. 'You've done well, my boy. Surprised me.' He cleared his throat. 'But for your swift action, we might well have lost Charles.'

This was the thanks Robert had wanted all those months ago. The recognition that he would never cause his brother harm and that he was just as important to his family as his brother. The anger clutching at his heart seeped away at the sight of his father's distress.

A hot lump of emotion scoured the back of his throat. He managed a nod.

The duke smiled sadly at his wife. 'Your mother believes Charles will come about now we have found you again.' His grim face said he wasn't quite sure.

Robert glanced at his mother. 'What is wrong with Charlie?'

His mother sighed. 'We have rarely seen him since your departure. And not heard a word from him since he left for Durn after New Years' Day. He'll come to his senses.'

Father closed his eyes briefly. 'I was wrong to try to drive a wedge between my sons. Dem me...' He turned away, but not before Robert saw the moisture in the old man's eyes. So the duke really did have a heart.

His own felt a little less bruised. 'It doesn't matter, Father. You did what you thought was right. For the good of the family.'

'Hmmph,' said Mother.

The duke kissed his wife's hand and straightened his shoulders. 'If you need that recommendation, let me know, but I'd be very happy if you decided to stay.' He strode from the room, not quite as tall as Robert remembered. Not quite as self-assured.

Her grace watched him go with a sad expression. 'Pride is a difficult thing,' she said softly. 'It is so hard to go back.'

'I'm grateful for your help,' Robert said. 'With Father. And Miss Bracewell. Though you should not have put yourself in such danger. If anything had happened to you...'

His mother raised an elegant hand and lightly touched his cheek. 'I haven't had so much excitement in years. Her mother and I were friends, you know. I had a long talk with Miss Bracewell when John brought her here yesterday morning.'

Robert frowned. 'I don't know what John thought he was about.'

'Helping you. You always did command the respect of your peers, even if you never realised it. Poor John, he was devastated when he realised he'd practically cut you outside White's. You have forgiven him, haven't you?'

'Of course.'

'Write to me from Canada, won't you, dear, if you must go. I will miss you.'

His chest tightened. 'I must, but I will miss you, too, Mama. And the others.'

'They will be sorry not to have seen you. Come home to us when you can. You will always be welcome, Robert. Have no doubt.'

He took his mother's hand in his and leaned to kiss her cheek. The familiar lavender scent washed through him followed by the same calm she'd instilled in him as an angry and confused boy.

'Thank you,' he murmured.

'And so Miss Bracewell goes to Italy alone.'

Robert felt a faint prickle of unease at the back of his neck. 'That was her plan.'

'You are not putting her aside because you think her unworthy? Because she was born on the wrong side of the blanket?' Mother asked a little hesitantly.

He stiffened at the faint tone of censure in her voice. 'Good God, no! I—well, to put it bluntly, she is far above my touch, and I won't be a parasite.'

Mother smiled sadly. 'My proud, beautiful boy.'

Robert felt as if he'd missed something. 'Snively will make sure she is safe.'

A crease developed between her fine brows. 'I am surprised at you though, Robert, seducing an innocent and then abandoning her.'

His cheeks stung as if she had slapped him across the face. 'You are wrong, Mother. I was not her first lover.'

'Are you sure?'

'What the hell do you think I am? She told me....' Damn it, what had she said? *I'm not so very innocent.* 'Frederica was not a maid when I met her.' His face fired scarlet. He couldn't believe he was having this conversation with his mother. 'A man knows these things.'

'But Robert, you also know she quite often rides astride, like a boy.'

The truth hit him like a body blow. Shock jarred him off kilter.

His mother looked at him silently, her lips pursed.

Dear God. He'd seduced an innocent. He really was a blackguard. 'I have to go.'

She raised a brow. 'I should think you do. But, Robert, a piece of advice. Pride and love don't make good bedmates.'

And with that incomprehensible admonition ringing in his ears he kissed her and left.

Sitting at the table in her private parlour, Frederica jabbed her fork into the roast beef on her plate, lifted it to her mouth, and then put it down again. She just didn't feel hungry.

She left the table and moved to the sofa by the hearth. The sofa where she'd sat just the other night in Robert's arms. She'd been so contented, secure. Without him, she would never have been brave enough to face the lawyer. So why did she now feel so uneasy? The worst was over.

Wealthy beyond her wildest imaginings, she could do anything she wanted. Snively had hired a maid for her and a lady's companion to accompany them on their journey. The old man had beamed when she asked him to go with her as her major domo. Everything was perfect.

Or it would be if Robert hadn't walked way.

Because he wanted his freedom.

Maggie had kindly told her a little bit about his past. The parade of women through his life. She was just one of many. He was a rake.

The piper must be paid. Or was it *no good crying over spilt milk*? He didn't want her. He'd said so in front of everyone.

She sighed and gazed at the trunks standing in the middle of the parlour floor all packed and ready to go at any moment.

A knock came at the door.

The man for the trunks.

She went to the door and unlocked it.

'R-Robert?'

He looked so handsome in his gentleman's clothing, dark blue coat and cream waistcoat and newly shaved.

'May I come in? We need to talk,' he said grimly. He inhaled a quick breath as if he had something unpleasant to say. 'I just left my mother.'

She backed away cautiously. 'W-what is it?'

'There is something I have to ask you. I want the truth.'

She perched on the sofa's edge, wary, uncomfortable. 'What did you want to know?'

He kept her hand clasped in his. 'Were you indeed a virgin before we met?'

His mother had betrayed her confidence. A confidence the formidable lady had extracted with a cleverness that had left Frederica in awe. But her Grace had promised to say nothing to her son.

'She had no right to tell you.'

He drew in a sharp breath. He looked appalled. 'We must be married right away.'

Married. Her heart gave a happy little lurch. Her gaze took in the tightness of his mouth, the darkness in his eyes, and she knew it would be a mistake.

She attempted a laugh. It sounded brittle instead of light and carefree. 'La, this is sudden, my lord. Such a declaration.'

He glowered. 'On my honour, I must make this right.'

'Must?' She'd spoken to him of love and he spoke of honour. She pulled her hand from his grasp. 'Why must you?'

'It is obvious. I took your innocence. I can do nothing else.'

'I was never an innocent, Robert. I have eyes in my head. I saw the beasts in the fields. I can read. I knew what men looked like and what happens between a man and woman.'

'Good God, woman, it doesn't matter what you knew. I debauched you. It is my duty.'

'Duty?' The word was a shriek in her head. It hurt worse than years of hearing her family's horrid slights. She lifted her chin and put chill in her voice. 'Why is it your duty to marry the daughter of the Wynchwood Whore?'

'That has nothing to do with it.'

'Did the thought of the money make you change your mind?' she said cruelly, knowing it would hurt him as much as he was hurting her.

'I don't want a penny of your damned money.'

'To hell with duty, then. I don't need your name to make me respectable.' She clenched her fists in the folds of her skirt and turned her face away. 'My wealth will do that. I will never marry. I'll take my pleasure where I want and with whom I want. The way my mother did.'

He flinched. 'You can't mean that.'

Drawing in a breath to garner every ounce of her strength, she turned to look at him. 'Yes, R-Robert. I do. Think back. I wanted you. I seduced *you*. Now, I don't want you any more. Surely you of all people can understand?'

A muscle in his jaw flickered. There was anger in his eyes and something else. Anguish? Surely not. The pain in her chest grew so bad she thought she might fall to her knees, but she must not, for then he would know what it cost her to send him away. He'd know and he'd try to change her mind.

To tie the man she loved to her in wedlock against his will, knowing he didn't love her… It didn't bear thinking about.

Frederica got up and went to the door of her adjoining bedroom, unable to look at his beautiful face in case she weakened. Hand on the doorknob, she spoke quietly, calmly. 'I must ask you to leave. Please, do not come here again. I will not see you.'

She went inside and shut the door.

She stood rigid and shaking on the other side. No tears. No sobbing. He mustn't guess how much she was wounded.

After a moment or two, she heard the outside door close.

He'd be glad she refused him. Later.

He'd be thankful for his escape.

She sank down on to the bed and buried her face in the pillow and sobbed.

She didn't want him.

Furious, Robert slammed out of the parlour. He'd offered her his name and she'd given him his *congé*.

Now he knew how all those women in his life had felt.

God damn, it hurt.

He tore down the stairs in fury.

Why wouldn't she let him put things right? She'd talked of wanting other men and thrown him out. His body shook. His heart raged. His fists opened and closed. Wanting to strangle her. To make her listen to reason.

He needed a drink. Something to take away the turmoil in his head.

On his way to the taproom, he collided with Snively. He glared at him and pushed by.

Snively grabbed his sleeve. 'You been up there upsetting her again?'

'Hardly,' Robert said. 'She doesn't give a tinker's cuss for me.'

'Hoity-toity bugger. Up in the boughs, are we?'

Robert brushed him off. 'You've no idea what you are talking about.'

'I know she looks like she lost half a crown and found a penny.'

Robert paused.

'She ain't eating much either.'

'What are you saying?'

'She's miserable when she should be as happy as a grig.'

'What has that to do with me?'

Snively shrugged. 'I wouldn't know. You're the man who understands women.'

'Understand them? No one understands them.'

'Maybe not. Can I buy you a drink?' Snively walked to the bar, pulled out a pipe and shoved it between his teeth. 'I'd have a little think before you acts with haste.'

'Think about what? I asked her to marry me. She turned me down.'

'Happen you're right. Though I never saw her look so down as when you left the lawyer's office. Went down on your knees did you? Begged for forgiveness after what you said?' The older man looked at him sideways and sighed. 'Too high in the instep for that, I reckon. You a duke's son and all and her nothing but a base-born child.'

Robert slammed his fist on the bar. Tankards jumped and rattled. 'That has nothing to do with anything. I offered her my name.'

'Not good enough, my lord.' Snively shook his grey head.

'Drink, sir?' asked the barman, wiping at the bar in front of Robert with a rag.

'Brandy,' Robert said. 'For two.'

The barman poured and moved away. Robert downed his drink in one gulp. It didn't make him feel one iota better. 'What do you suggest, then?'

Snively's eyes twinkled. 'If you don't know, I'm sure I don't.'

Robert's fingers curled around his glass. He wished

the slender stem was Snively's neck. 'Fat lot of help you are.'

'All right. Why do you want to marry her?'

'Because it's the right thing to do.'

'Empty words.' The old man turned away. 'You don't deserve her. Bugger off.'

He picked up his glass and wandered to the settle by the hearth where he picked up a discarded newspaper and proceeded to immerse himself in its pages.

Robert signalled for another brandy and when it came he stared into its depths. Why else would he want to marry her? He liked her. He felt good when he was with her. Hell, he felt terrible when she wasn't around.

It was as if they were joined by an invisible thread attached to his heart and the further it was stretched, the more painfully tight it became. Was that what people called love?

He raised the glass to his lips. Then put it down.

Love was romantic nonsense.

Wasn't it?

What had Mother said—pride and love make bad bedfellows? Was that his problem? Was he too proud?

Or did he fear she'd reject his love, the way Father had?

Which meant taking a terrible risk.

What if he couldn't have her any other way? What if she met some handsome Italian count and fell into bed with him? Or worse, married him?

She had said she loved him.

How could he offer her anything less?

And if she turned him down again?

At least he'd be able to look at his face in the mirror and not be disgusted by his cowardice.

He glanced over at Snively, who had finished his

drink and was now dozing with the newspaper over his face. No help there.

He climbed back up the stairs and let himself in quietly.

The remains of her supper still lay on the table beside the window. She hadn't eaten more than a mouthful or two. The sight gave him heart. Perhaps Snively was right. She wasn't happy.

Silently, he tried her bedroom door. Locked. He knocked.

'I'm finished with the supper dishes,' she called out. 'You can take them away.'

Her voice sounded thick and damp as if she'd been crying. A good sign? The tightness in his chest said not.

'I've not come for the dishes,' he said. 'I've come to make a confession.'

Silence.

'Frederica, there is one more thing I need to say.'

Frederica stared at the door. When would he stop torturing her? 'G-go away.'

'Please, sweetling. It won't take more than a minute or two.'

Ah, how could she resist the plea in his voice? She wasn't going to change her mind, though. Whatever he said. Not even if he tied her up and stood her in front of the altar. All she had to do was remain calm. Strong. In control.

She ran to the mirror. Her eyes were red, her cheeks blotchy. She dipped a cloth in the ewer and dabbed at her tear-streaked face.

He tapped on the door. 'Frederica.'

'A moment if you please.'

A quick smooth of her gown, an extra pin in her hair. She looked in the mirror and shook her head. He'd know she'd been crying. She fixed a cool smile on her face and opened the door.

He stood a little back from the door, dark, aloof, his face grim. Much as she'd seen him that first day by the river, except in his fine clothes he looked every inch the duke's second son. Generations of knights lived in his bearing.

Inside, she began to shake.

Did he now hope to force his will on her? The way her uncle had intended with her cousin?

She kept her face calm, politely interested. 'Lord Robert, back so soon? I really cannot think of anything else that needs to be said.'

'There is one thing.' His voice was deep and dark and her insides quivered at the sound; her wicked body yearned for his touch.

'I'll hear no more talk of duty and honour. I have neither. Please close the door on the way out.'

She went to the sofa and gazed into the fire's depths, waiting for the slam of the door.

Instead, she heard his step across the floor as he drew near. She held herself rigid, ready to resist a seduction if necessary, primed herself to be deaf to his words.

A faint rustle and a small thud sounded behind her.

She couldn't stop herself—she turned to look.

He was on one knee, his head bowed, so that all she could see of him was dark waves of hair and the breadth of his shoulders.

She started to rise.

'Lady, grant me one boon,' he said softly. 'Hear me out.'

She sank back on the seat, too amazed to do more than stare at his lowered head.

'I am sorry,' he said quietly. 'I came to you in pride. Now I come to you in humility.'

'R-Robert, no,' she whispered. Never had she wanted this proud man to abase himself before her. 'P-please, get up.'

He didn't move, didn't raise his head, didn't look at her, but knelt before her like some knight of old before his liege, humbled, penitent.

She couldn't breathe the sight pained her so much.

'You said my offer wasn't enough. I thought you meant I wasn't good enough. It hurt. My pride was hurt. But far worse was the sense of loss deep in my soul. Only when I realised that I stood to lose you forever did I realise my greatest wrong. I offered so little of myself in return for the priceless gift you bring to my heart.'

'Oh, R-Robert,' she breathed, unable to believe what she was hearing.

He looked up then and the humility and love shining in his eyes almost sent her to pieces.

She reached out.

He took her hand, kissed the back of it with gentle reverence. 'It was family pride that kept your parents apart and pride that set me adrift from my family's love.'

He looked up and gazed into her face. He looked beautiful and sad. 'Today I walked away too proud to beg for what I needed. I let pride speak instead of saying what was in my heart. Can you forgive me, Frederica, for being such an arrogant fool? If you can, I beg that I may spend the rest of my life trying to win your love. I will abide by your wishes. If you send me away, I will never trouble you more. But I want you to know, I love you with all my heart.'

These were the words she had longed to hear. And the truth shone in his eyes and rang in his voice.

Her heart swelled with joy. And yet how could she let him make such a sacrifice? By marrying her he would be giving up his place in society, possibly in his family, if what she knew of the duke was half true.

She had turned him away because he spoke only of duty; now he spoke of love, but she still wasn't convinced it was right. She loved him too well to ruin his life.

She was a bastard. Illegitimate. Unwanted. He was the son of a duke.

She would bring him nothing but shame.

Frederica slid off the seat onto her knees and cupped his cheeks in her hands, felt the warmth of his skin and the faint haze of stubble, inhaled the scent of his cologne. 'Don't do this.'

'Ah, sweetheart,' he said. 'If you won't have me as your husband, I'll come as your servant. You can pay me to carry your bags, arrange for your carriage, keep the damned *banditti* at bay.'

'You would do that for me?'

'I would do that and more to remain at your side. To protect you when asked. To serve when needed.'

Tears blocked her throat and burned the backs of her eyes. 'And will you bring me chocolate in bed in the morning?' she whispered huskily.

'I will.' He smiled. 'As long as I get to lie beside you as you drink it.'

'Oh, R-Robert, are you sure this is what you want? I will never be entirely respectable, you know.'

'As sure as I am of needing my next breath to live. I

love you, elf. Without you, I'm a shell. An empty husk. It took a while to get it through my thick skull, but without you, I might as well not breathe. You are my life.'

She pressed her lips to his, and his arms came around her. 'Marry me,' he whispered against her mouth. 'Please.'

'Yes, R-Robert. I will.'

He cradled her nape and she dissolved against his lips and his hard body.

'Here? Or in Italy?' she asked.

'Wherever your heart desires, my love,' he answered and then couldn't help a soft chuckle, 'though I am sure my mother will never forgive me if I don't let her welcome her new daughter-in-law properly. And I would like you to meet my twin.'

'Then England it is. I find I like your mother very much. I'll let Snively know.'

'Later.'

Then there was no more talking because his lips devoured hers and ecstasy carried all thought away.

Three days later, Robert stood on the steps of St George's in Hanover Square with his wife of five minutes and gazed at the crowds madly cheering him and his bride. It was a cold January day, but inside he felt warm.

When he'd told his parents of his wedding plans, he hadn't expected such an elaborate affair, but ducal pride required they celebrate in grand style.

It was right. Frederica deserved the homage.

He raised her small hand to his lips. 'Happy?' he asked, smiling down at her glowing face.

'Never more so,' she answered.

A figure pushed through the crowds and up the steps.

Two days' growth of beard shadowed his jaw, his coat was rumpled, his neckcloth limp. He had his gazed fixed on Robert's face.

Charlie. Late. Which really wasn't like him. Their mother had been frantic.

When Charlie reached the top step, he hesitated, then thrust out his hand. 'Congratulations.' His expression said he wasn't sure Robert would take it.

The idiot. He grabbed the large hand and pulled his brother close, slapping him on the back. 'Glad you made it.' His voice sounded thick and husky.

His brother pulled away and cleared his throat. 'I would have been here sooner, but my horse threw a shoe. Had to walk miles for a replacement.'

'A fine tale,' Father said, coming up behind them.

Charlie shook his hand. 'It is true.'

'Better late than never,' Robert said with a sympathetic grin at his brother.

Charlie glanced towards Frederica.

'Let me introduce my wife. Darling, this is my brother Charles.'

Frederica's eyes widened. Her gaze ran over Charlie and she smiled. 'You are even more alike than your p-portrait suggests. I would like to paint you some time. You'd make a wonderful Zeus.'

A growl rose in Robert's throat.

She laughed. 'Draped in a sheet, R-Robert.'

He grinned and pressed a kiss to her wrist. 'Fully clothed.'

Charlie's eyes goggled.

'Family joke,' Robert said.

'Who would have thought *you* would ever marry?' Charlie said. His cheeks turned red.

'I did,' Mother said. 'Welcome, my son.'

Charlie enfolded her in a bear hug. In the next moment they were surrounded by the rest of the Mountford clan. His chattering sisters, who'd been bridesmaids, his youngest brother, whose voice gave no sign of breaking for all that he already topped Robert's chin in height.

It was a good feeling. And Frederica looked thoroughly at home and happy. As she deserved.

The bridal carriage rolled up to the steps.

'I'll see you back at Mountford House,' Charlie said.

''Fraid not. We've a ship to catch.'

'To Italy,' Frederica said.

Charlie looked worried. 'I need to ask your opinion.'

'Whatever it is, Charlie,' Robert said, 'you'll have to deal with it yourself.'

Charlie looked stunned. And just a bit terrified. Robert looked at him. 'It's a woman.'

Charlie nodded.

'Then I definitely can't help you. I don't understand them at all.'

He snatched his wife from the bosom of his family and escorted her into the waiting carriage. They waved from the windows until they turned the corner at the end of the street.

Robert pulled her on to his lap and kissed her soundly. After a long while, he let her go.

She snuggled against his shoulder. 'Your brother really would make a wonderful Zeus.'

'No.'

She grinned up at him. 'Then I suppose I must make do with you. Probably better,' she added hastily at his glare.

He would do. He would do his best to make her believe that for the rest of her life.

'I love you, sweet wife.'

'I love you, dear R-Robert.' She kissed his cheek and wriggled on his lap.

He groaned. 'How long before we board ship?'

'An hour, I think.'

It was going to be the longest hour of his life unless he found a way to fill up the time.

He untied the ribbons of her bonnet and tossed the confection aside. 'That's better. Now I can see your face.'

She laughed up at him, her pretty lips inviting his kisses.

He cradled her nape and plundered her delicious mouth, and many minutes passed before the need for breath forced him to raise his head. He rested his chin on the top of her head. 'You are sure this is what you want?' he asked. It wasn't so much that he doubted it, he just liked the warmth her confirmation gave him.

'I can't quite believe it,' she said softly. 'It is as if every dream I ever had has come true. But, R-Robert, are you sure you won't be bored?'

'Not a chance. I'll be too busy keeping you entertained. And naked.'

A laugh bubbled up from her throat. A warm, encouraging sound. 'I can't wait.'

Nor could he. He let his hand slide up one slim calf beneath her skirts.

She sighed. 'But you do realise I will be occupied with classes during the day,' she said softly.

'I do.' He nuzzled her neck. 'I'll be busy too. Father has asked me to look at some properties he is thinking of buying. And I've some other commissions to undertake for him.' Robert had been delighted at the request. He could finally play a part in his family's endeavours.

'R-Robert,' she said hesitantly, 'when we come back, do you think we could buy a house in the country? A place good for raising children?'

His wandering hand stilled. A bubble of hope he never knew resided there tightened his chest. 'I didn't think you wanted children?'

'I didn't. Before. But now I think I do. We'd be a real f-family. I like the countryside. I could have a studio. You could farm, breed horses, if you'd like to, that is.' She sounded worried, as if she feared he might not be pleased.

'Lady Robert,' he said, laughing, but with his heart full of tenderness, 'you never cease to amaze me. That is *exactly* what I would like.' He tipped her chin. 'But right now I have the overwhelming desire to kiss you again.'

Looking pleased, she placed her palm against his jaw. 'R-Robert, did I tell you I love you?'

'Not in the last five minutes.'

'Well, I do.'

'And I love you, elf.'

He kissed her delicious mouth, promising her a future of love and happiness the best way he knew.

HISTORICAL

Regency

CHIVALROUS CAPTAIN, REBEL MISTRESS
by Diane Gaston

Amid the chaos of Waterloo, Captain Allan Landon stumbles upon a young boy who turns out to be beautiful Miss Marian Pallant. He vows to protect her, but, back in London, though the battle may be won, Allan and Marian are now on opposing sides of a different war...

Regency

COURTING MISS VALLOIS
by Gail Whitiker

Miss Sophie Vallois' looks and grace make her an instant hit with London Society. No one would know that the French beauty is a mere farmer's daughter...except Robert Silverton. Sophie's spirit and compassion intrigue him, but he has reason to stay well away from her...

Regency

REPROBATE LORD, RUNAWAY LADY
by Isabelle Goddard

Coming across runaway Amelie Silverdale, reprobate Gareth Denville recognises a kindred spirit wanting to break free and offers to help. While they are on the run together the attraction builds, but what will happen when their old lives catch up with them?

On sale from 7th January 2011
Don't miss out!

Available at WHSmith, Tesco, ASDA, Eason and all good bookshops

www.millsandboon.co.uk

1210/04a

HISTORICAL

THE BRIDE WORE SCANDAL
by Helen Dickson

When Christina Atherton first saw notorious Lord Rockley she could not hold out for long against his dark and seductive ways. Now she's pregnant and the only way for Rockley to restore her virtue is to marry her...before the scandal ruins them both!

THE GUNSLINGER'S UNTAMED BRIDE
by Stacey Kayne

Lily Carrington wants revenge for the murder of her father. She's finally tracked down the killer. Only Juniper Barns is now a hard-working sheriff and she's in danger of losing her heart to the one man she's forbidden from loving...

KNAVE'S HONOUR
by Margaret Moore

Lady Elizabeth of Averette comes face to face with Finn—an outlaw with more honour than most knights—when he rescues her from a brutal abductor. In return Lizette agrees to help him find his brother by posing as Finn's wife!

On sale from 7th January 2010
Don't miss out!

Available at WHSmith, Tesco, ASDA, Eason and all good bookshops

www.millsandboon.co.uk

Regency

HIGH-SOCIETY AFFAIRS

Rakes and rogues in the ballrooms – and the bedrooms – of Regency England!

Volume 8 – 2nd October 2009
Sparhawk's Angel by Miranda Jarrett
The Proper Wife by Julia Justiss

Volume 9 – 6th November 2009
The Disgraced Marchioness by Anne O'Brien
The Reluctant Escort by Mary Nichols

Volume 10 – 4th December 2009
The Outrageous Débutante by Anne O'Brien
A Damnable Rogue by Anne Herries

Volume 11 – 1st January 2010
The Enigmatic Rake by Anne O'Brien
The Lord and the Mystery Lady by Georgina Devon

Volume 12 – 5th February 2010
The Wagering Widow by Diane Gaston
An Unconventional Widow by Georgina Devon

Volume 13 – 5th March 2010
A Reputable Rake by Diane Gaston
The Heart's Wager by Gayle Wilson

Volume 14 – 2nd April 2010
The Venetian's Mistress by Ann Elizabeth Cree
The Gambler's Heart by Gayle Wilson

NOW 14 VOLUMES IN ALL TO COLLECT!

England's Forgotten Queen

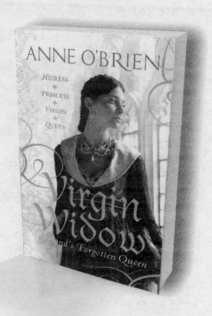

Anne Neville is the heiress and daughter of the greatest powerbroker in the land, Warwick the Kingmaker. She is a pawn, trapped in an uncertain political game.

When the Earl of Warwick commits treason, his family is forced into exile. Humiliated and powerless in a foreign land, Anne must find the courage and the wit to survive in a man's world.

Available 21st May 2010

www.mirabooks.co.uk

2 FREE BOOKS
AND A SURPRISE GIFT

We would like to take this opportunity to thank you for reading this Mills & Boon® book by offering you the chance to take TWO more specially selected books from the Historical series absolutely FREE! We're also making this offer to introduce you to the benefits of the Mills & Boon® Book Club™—

- **FREE home delivery**
- **FREE gifts and competitions**
- **FREE monthly Newsletter**
- **Exclusive Mills & Boon Book Club offers**
- **Books available before they're in the shops**

Accepting these FREE books and gift places you under no obligation to buy, you may cancel at any time, even after receiving your free books. Simply complete your details below and return the entire page to the address below. You don't even need a stamp!

YES Please send me 2 free Historical books and a surprise gift. I understand that unless you hear from me, I will receive 4 superb new books every month for just £3.99 each, postage and packing free. I am under no obligation to purchase any books and may cancel my subscription at any time. The free books and gift will be mine to keep in any case.

Ms/Mrs/Miss/Mr ———————— Initials ————————

———————————————————————————————

Surname ——————————————————————————

Address ——————————————————————————

———————————————————————————————

———————————————————— Postcode ————————

E-mail ——————————————————————————

Send this whole page to: Mills & Boon Book Club, Free Book Offer, FREEPOST NAT 10298, Richmond, TW9 1BR